City of Bridges

City of Bridges

(or Clemency)

DAVID MICHAEL BELCZYK

RESOURCE *Publications* · Eugene, Oregon

Resource Publications
An Imprint of Wipf and Stock Publishers
199 W. 8th Ave., Suite 3
Eugene, OR 97401

www.wipfandstock.com
www.davidbelczyk.com

PAPERBACK ISBN: 978-1-5326-8786-0
HARDCOVER ISBN: 978-1-5326-8787-7
EBOOK ISBN: 978-1-5326-8788-4

Manufactured in the U.S.A.   11/26/19

To C

Father of Heaven and Earth!
Deliver us from darkness.
Part the clouds and give us day—and since
thy sovereign will is such, destruction with it.
But give us day!

THE RIVER WAS SWOLLEN with stories the night the Courier died at the crown of the bridge. His life spilled into the river, and whatever he carried spilled into oblivion. It happened on the evening of the spring equinox, when our city was bursting with life.

The season had been long with rain that shook early petals from the city's budding trees. Petals blanketed the streets, tumbling over dirty cobbles. A brief afternoon storm struck. Its heavy shed wended to the river bank in a misted flow teeming sashes of color. These innumerable paths arrived at the lumbering power of the river shimmering with dusklight. People came into the temperate evening to fill up its shimmering. A march of leaping bridges flung their arches across the silver spill.

It was the Courier's Bridge, as we call it now, that the Courier crossed carrying something secret and precious. Then this springtide promise shattered with the cry of the Lamplighter, who discovered blood upon the bridge. But no one discovered how the Courier died, or what happened to the secret he carried.

†

TO UNDERSTAND THE COURIER, you must understand our ancient city— where we have come from, how we have survived.

Our city is older than memory, but we preserve many stories about its early history. In the most common version, our city began with a nomad who had passed between wars and lived off the wild fruits of the land. He was looking for a place to settle with his pregnant wife. The two discovered our gentle hills and soft-hued vistas, vast forests for fuel and shelter, and nearby, an ancient virgin cave with deep channels into the riches of the earth.

They chose to settle in the cave, not knowing that it was the home of an enormous serpent. The serpent had grown for millennia. Making a circle with its tail in its mouth, it would enclose a city or small island—wending round the entire world that the encircled knew. The valley where the river runs now, through our city center, is supposed to be the depression where the giant snake often lay. When the snake returned to find its cave inhabited, our founder had to fight for his family's lives. Because this place was destined for them, the hero slew the serpent by climbing on its back and plunging his sword deep into its head.

Some claim that this was the same serpent who had conned the first people into forbidden wants to be like gods. Some claim it was the liar serpent, who said we were not like gods already. Still others claim our city's founders were themselves the first people, wandering in the exile of their power over the world and confronted with an ancient foe.

But then, there are two sides to every story. And there are those who claim that there was no serpent. The serpent slain was only the river itself, when our founder built the first bridge, and the river returns on itself like a snake, end to end, so that its flow continues replenished forever. And finally, they claim that the bridge itself was the first disobedience, and the wild river was the serpent's wrath striking at the precarious and precocious bridge, the earth's fury at nature unexpectedly yoked.

The hero surveyed the liberated landscape, in need of laborers to build a city. He wrenched free the serpent's teeth and sowed them in the ground. As he watched, the earth churned with growth, and from the teeth sprouted legions of men and women, naked and battle-hungry, their eyes coiled with serpents. New to life, they wanted life for themselves and did not want to share it with their brood. They fought, and destroyed one another, until only the strongest survived. These champions were satisfied with their preeminence, and were beholden to the hero for giving them life. So they helped him to build our city. Some of these people, too, became our ancestors.

As you might guess by now, our city's religion is a religion of stories. But the old gods themselves, and myths and heroes, those that have come down from the immemorial: those are gone. We tell their stories; we speak their names, but as you would speak a name to a tomb. Their fires have not burned for many generations. Though we live among their ruins, no one worships them. But no one forgets them.

Standing with my friend Clement in an empty temple, a vacant dais loomed above us, where once stood a divine statue long ago looted or destroyed. Clement's eyes were coiled with serpents. He said to me, "We need what he carried. We need to find it."

"No one will find it," I said.

"No one wants it. They want what is associated with it. I want to carry it."

"I don't think he carried anything valuable. He died with the secrets of another, who did not die."

Clement exhaled disapprovingly. "It's the carrying," he resolved.

In our city, all things are married. As our founding hero knew love, he also knew suffering. And the wedding of love and tragedy is in the blood of all his children, then, in the fabric of our city itself. It is in our past. It is in our modern selves and in our mysteries. The hero's pregnant wife gave birth to a daughter, who grew to adolescence in the protection of the cave her father won.

Clement reminded me of the old story, gesturing to the cold altar, "Beautiful and innocent. An adoring daughter, a perfect victim." She spent day after day tending her garden. Colors leapt from the earth and lifted wanting to the touch of her gentle hands. Her roses grew so heartily that they strangled their lattices and splintered the wood. The weight of the tremendous blossoms collapsed even trellises made of heavy timber. Yet they never pricked her. Once the roses escaped her yard, collapsed the fence, and got hold of the nearby stone house, reducing it to rubble.

This precious daughter died young and unexpectedly, and her father claimed that Death, who was still young himself, stole her away in his lust to have the most beautiful bride.

She was in the garden and had filled her apron with new blooms, which she liked to lay in the sheets of her bed, to sleep infused with their soft fragrance. Death came so suddenly that she fell in the midst of her work, spilling mountains of petals that wept in flurries for three days, scenting everything with their sweet melancholy.

On the night of the Courier's death, when the storm had stripped all the tender blooms of spring, it was as though she had just spilled her tumult of petals over the whole city.

"It's the carrying," Clement said again.

"Is it?" I challenged. "Or is it the one who carries?"

Our ancestors have taught that it is a great privilege to remember how our city began, in a world where very few can remember their own beginning or the beginning of the things around them. Our city has been spared the ravage of this awful forgetting.

According to the story, a goddess protects and preserves our city and its memory, but takes from us a ransom for her protection. This patroness is the bride of Time itself. Time, who swallows all its children, because Time eventually destroys all things that come into it.

I reminded Clement, "Time was given a poison by its bride," who loves our city and wished to save us from destruction. The poison forced Time to disgorge the memory of our beginning. Time gave to her the redeemed prize that she has made the love of our city's men, who in her godlike appetites she seduces with knowledge of herself. And so our strong and young and beautiful men die, to go to her in the place of our city. She adorns herself with the life of the city she saves.

So we say our city is a mural crown worn by the wife of Time, where prowl the lions of her unthieving lovers. She takes these brave loves because she wants a passion that is not temporal. She is intemperate because each brazen love is indiscriminately destroyed, like Time's other memories. Often on the tops of our buildings, at the heights of our bridges and towers, there is an architectural crown, wreathed in carved stone of lions and roses, the courage and the blood of love.

Like our city's first love and suffering, this marriage between love and death, between death and the salvation of memory, has become the type for all our city's kings, descended from our founding hero. In our city, as in other first cities, we believed that our protector goddess was enshrined in the very entity of our city's togetherness.

"She preserved us. But she expected the love of the king, and that meant that she finally required his life. The undying goddess went down to the dead, cyclically, to remember the differences between death and life. She spent three days in the underworld, then exchanged her life for the king's, to return to us. It was the king, only the king, who lived this bridge between the human and the divine. Amid festivals, he would go alone into the goddess's temple, at the highest point in the city, and submit himself to the stab of her desires. And when the king died, he went not to a paradisal afterlife promised the mortal; he went to her, he went in her place to death, and she returned to sustain us. He went in the stead of our city and the lives of its people. His death was in our place. Only the death of the king could ransom so many."

This practice, and the monarchy, endured for millennia.

"But now the kings have been deposed," answered Clement. Replaced first by various mobs, then governments and what we call civilization. Their lineage lives, and persists through wealth and poverty, with blood and memory and no authority. At first, their lives seem much inferior to the noble stories of old.

Clement and I stepped out of the temple into the sunlight and the sweep of our city's bridges. "We should be the ones to find it," he said again.

Beneath the Courier's Bridge, where he died, and our other bridges, the river rolled endlessly onward. It has many moods. On the night the

Courier died, it slipped like silk beneath a veil of delicate mist, a still bride on the verge of tears and lost in contemplation. Through the white spring haze the water twinkled with the lights of buildings, adorned in the reflected splendor of the city. Upriver, the gas lamps came on in time, passing on their fire from one side of the river to the other. The Lamplighter had not yet reached the Courier's Bridge. The sky above clung to grey and powder blue. The sun was still setting early.

Other bridges near the Courier's also reflected on the mild water. They arched networks of iron. Big shoulders expanding their musculature in the purpling night. Rather than leaping the river, they seemed to grip the earthen banks and hold them fast from fleeing the river's knife. So the water would not widen until it covered the earth, and the bridges would not crumble.

Upriver from the Courier's Bridge, an arch of iron, paired with its reflection, transformed the single arch into the oval of a mouth. The bridge half of the mouth is our own creation, but the mouth is made one-half from our river of stories. And it seems to create as it speaks—the river issues forth, murmuring the secrets of the Courier's death in an unintelligible and forgotten tongue. Downriver from the Courier's Bridge, another iron-truss paired its twin arches with their reflection to make two ever-open eyes, the only witness to his death. One-half our creation and one-half our river that pours on and on into their unblinking architecture. Between these two works of fierce metal and the supple water that transmits them, the mammoth cables of the Courier's Bridge trace the swing of time's pendulum that ticks out the river's flow.

†

THE COURIER'S STEPS TICKED on the pavement in a fast and regular rhythm, as he hurried to catch the evening train—his immigrant face lush with life, flushed red against the damp night. His early manhood radiated youth. The Courier was his own spring; his final youth was its own season, fragrant as the petals littering the ground at his feet. The clarity of his eyes shone ancient and idyllic. In them I watch turning a parade of precious history, that is, identity, a mural crown turning and telling my own repeating story.

I see in the Courier's face, that final night, a silent depth and still an effortless awe, as though all answers would be given him in patience. Cropped hair swept up from his brow in a lively arc, wind-tussled and sandy with light. He looked like the unreal man who labors tirelessly, gives generously, and despite both has none of his freedom lost. He was beautiful with carelessness, wore a confidence that out-mastered appearances. I see him in simple clothes, some of the few he had, and yet they looked like the best in all the world, made for him.

This is how the Courier looks to me on the last night of his life. And so he looks to all because I am the one telling about him? It is how I wish I looked, or maybe how I looked once. And so it is how he looks to me. But then, I know that he is going to his death—a death to distinguish him from the others who lived and died around him, those I do not know. It is the unsolvable mystery of the Courier's death that makes him beautiful. There need be nothing attractive about him.

He may be thin, or pale. He may be tired. Physically, he may be weak. He may even be hungry himself. After all, he is a victim. He may have shivered in the spring wind damp with inky night and cutting his poor clothes like knives. He may have worn his shabby best for deliveries from downtown, where the customers were professionals, and he may have looked disappointedly at his reflection in a street window. He may have polished his thin shoes to a fine shine despite the wet streets, anxious that shoes are said to tell the story of a man. He may have had the look of an unmarried lover, who waits and waits in agony, as he went to carry another careful parcel, dreaming that something precious was within his unknowing care.

There are no pictures of him. It was a long time ago, and no one takes pictures of a poor and immigrant Courier with no family in our city. There is no one alive who knew him. And with his body unfound, who could sketch the face of tragedy but to tell the story? Sometimes, when I look into the faces of the poor upon the streets, I feel that every drawn and tired gaze might have been his. The deep lines of long suffering. Uplifted eyes, his surging life across the bridge. The hopelessness of the blade in his heart.

On the night of his death, the Courier met a well-dressed man downtown. The Courier wound through the towering shadows in our city's heart, past rough-hewn stone campaniles and marble-clad temples, old temples to dead gods and modern temples of finance. The street-sides bristled with tobacconists, optometrists, advocates, offices of city government, cafés, soup kitchens, and gifts from philanthropists. The daytime down-river wind had shifted round with the dusk, and up the throat of the city came back a steam of progress. Acidic grey lingered in the noses of the onrushing crowds.

The Courier hurried through sidewalks dense with shoulders, plowing against the muscular river of flesh and bone and breath. Everyone hurried away from their labor and to their homes—whether it be children and hot meals, young loves, old mothers, mistresses, corner bars, or backroom tables; they had eyes like bulls, and the singleness of an arrow speeding.

The Courier found his destination, a little square with an old fountain, where he was to meet his client. The fountain was one of many scattered through tiny squares about our city, part of an ancient effort to make clean water available. We still drink the water today, where it streams in cardinal directions from raised stone pillars into basins below. It comes from an aquifer deep under the city and is sweet with sand and limestone. Cold and clear, its minerals smooth the skin. It wells up from absolute darkness to emerge once in daylight, sparkling in its single fall, and the basins carry it away to the river. While flowing to the pool below, that is when you catch it on a long tongue, and the cool snakes run down your neck in summer's swelter. Once, the square might have been strung with laundry lathered in the fountain's basin, while a line of children waited with wooden buckets in both hands to carry the flow back to their parents' mouths. Homeless bathe in the basins in the middle of the night, and in the morning, rich women collect the flowing water in elaborate vessels to wash their faces. Travelers discover our fountains like they are fountains of youth. And then there's me: I visit the same square because the Courier was there. I drench my hair with the sweet water in the humid nights of my soul, and its cold races over my flesh in waves like ecstasy.

And so the Courier's journey that night began at the fountain, where life wells up like an unstaunched wound. He circled, making it plain that he was looking for someone.

"You are looking for me?" said an elderly man wearing an impeccable suit, an ebullient handkerchief spilling from his breast pocket in a premonition of red, and thick glasses splashing wide his sentient eyes. His hands crossed at his waist, cradling a mahogany case. It seemed to pull his whole frame forward with its weight, rounding his shoulders like a penitent's.

The case was the size of a large book. The Courier compared it to the tome of myths moldering on a sideboard in his home far away. He was to carry the ornate package by evening train for delivery in another city tomorrow morning. When he took it from the elderly man, the Courier's ample hands enclosed the wood tightly. He held it with an excess of strength and energy.

"You will return to me, young man, once I have word that you have done your job well. I know your employer pays you, but I will show you my own gratitude. This parcel is important to me."

The old man did not say the package was valuable. Carrying things for other people, the Courier learned quickly that many precious items have no value. And some will pay dearly to protect what they cannot buy. Sometimes the Courier was asked to carry people's wealth, other times to carry the wrecks and remnants of their most private selves, the secrets of their hearts. And any poor heart knows the opportunity of escape—dreams of being in

open spaces in a stranger's hands. That is why the mind lords suspicion over
the heart's freedom, and uses its locks and its currency, for fear of betrayal.
It is a cagey business, asking strangers to deliver your life, and yet it is all we
ever do.

"You're carrying my future," added the elderly man; "mine and no one
else's."

The Courier nodded somberly.

"This box cannot bring a future to anyone else, but to me alone it is
irreplaceable. I would carry it myself, but look at me," and the man looked
down to survey the well-fashioned shamble of his age. The two shook hands
heartily.

"I must go," said the Courier as he turned exuberantly. His feet began
ticking again upon the cobbles, counting down the numbered seconds to the
evening departure. And all about him yet crashed and plodded the endless
permutations of our city life and its people. He passed the work-weary, kick-
ing dirt from their shoes on stone stoops and turning over the hollow bolts
in their narrow doors. He watched the frame of a man filling the transept,
outlined in spilling light and uplooking long black-marble stairs flanked by
a filigree of iron, leading to his home on the upper floors. At his feet a blind
beggar looked to the ground at nothing, muttering aimlessly that in another
life he had killed his father because he did not know his mother.

Around the Courier and above him, the ornate building faces and broken rooftops began to twinkle with soft light behind the gems of window
panes. Ahead, the emptying street terminated at the river, so that the canyon
of stone and glass opened to a darkening sky that bloomed with stars. The
Courier wound his way out of the labyrinth of city life toward the simple
and direct artery of water.

Our river has its story as well. The river was once a young woman pursued relentlessly by an undesirable suitor. She rebuffed him, and at last the
suitor lost himself to rage. He tried to overpower her by force and mingle
himself with her purity. She ran from him with all her might, praying, leaping wildly through the forests and fields as twigs broke against her soft skin,
marring it red, as surprised birds scattered from rushes. But he was catching
up to her. He would have caught her, but she cried out, baring all her heart,
begging her unknown god that she would be saved and keep her innocence.

She was transformed into the river, which leapt underground where
the man could not follow. Her river emerged on the other side of the hills,
taking a course through the valley where the giant serpent once lay, where
our city lies. She retained her beauty and inaccessibility. She can run forever, can outrun any man, and yet never leave the repose of her shimmering
banks. Her river runs unmingled until it pours into the oblivion of the sea.

Those who believe the river and the serpent are the same say that the woman was allowed to join to the river and be made one, in pure opposition to her pursuer. As he wished to put his hunger in her beauty, subjugating her, so she takes her beauty to the serpent and overpowers him. And the result always is life. That is the divine genius of creation, whether it be the child or the nourishing river in which he plays. And this life is always a marriage, between love and suffering transformed. Hunger, too, is suffering.

It is said that, while underground, the river encountered Death and his bride, the founding hero's stolen daughter. Life and beauty, in a spill of swirling petals, betrothed to the dead. Now, of course, we have traced the river from its start to its end, and have seen the deep crag where it wells from the earth. But we have discovered no corresponding river that dives down into the earth at its end.

The trip through our city, then, is the river's venture underground. As though underground, it flees the peaceful, verdant wilderness to find this hard city. And it finds, as I find every day, hunger that hides in recesses and shadows, toil and exile, and familiar dreams of escape. Drunkenness upon the river banks, drinking oblivion of former lives. A city where, despite our gifts of life and love and thought and freedom, we feel as abandoned children, and wail starving for a mother's love. I have seen a man mingle his streaming tears with the great emigration of the river, begging the river to carry his sadness to the finality of the sea. Meanwhile, all around us swirl colored petals of creation, the play of children, art and architecture, music and song, actors, sculptors, painters, scientists, explorers. A great pageant of beauty collects in us and spills into the world. And all of it betrothed to the dead. As our strong men consort with the wife of Time. As our vernal women go to the serpent. All of us and all of our creation plunging recklessly in arcs and rapids toward its ending. As the Courier was just a young man full of promise when someone took his life away.

At the railing of the walk along the river's edge, the Courier looked up to the penetrating points of light in their unending and impenetrable dark. Below them resided the powerful, ancient hills that framed the river valley. The stars seemed to rest upon the shoulders of the mighty hills, as though a great strong hero upheld the sky. Or perhaps a doomed god. The Courier's eye fell past the jagged rooflines to human lights making their own stand in falling night. Before him, a stretch of muddy turf and rocks extended to the placid water. The breeze now was ever so gentle; it had come fully around, upriver for the night. It was just faint enough to bring the smells of progress from the bend a few miles down, where sweating men churned out glowing snakes of steel that made the bridges of the world.

The tender-looking water waiting before the Courier was littered with light, decanting windows and stars. Across the river a fast sash of flame where a person struck a match and held it to a cigarette that bobbed in his mouth. He was headed the same way as the Courier. Two bridges upriver, the Lamplighter was making his way across, lighting the gas lamps each in turn, each sparking to life their unreal soul that doubled on the sparkling water, aflame but unquenched. When the breeze rippled the implacable water, all the lights and shapes and stars ran together in a shimmering and brilliant puzzle, so that the Courier could not tell which lights were human and which were the gods.

One bridge upriver, the Courier eyed his future namesake, spanning the reflective flood with a deep and powerful reach. It was the reach a captive would make to a savior, a dying man to his lover, the hungry to a provider. It was mighty and brilliant with desperation. With all its being, its long, curved tendons ached for the other side of the divide. Heavy with stone and steel. And yet. The steel seemed to dance and wheel across the open space, suspended like a held breath, waiting. It seemed, for all its might, heartbreakingly delicate, like the hand of the wind might shake the suspension cables and twist the thin deck. Mired between the ever-flowing river and the boundless sky, flung between the stretch and climb of progress, the hills of the river valley, the Courier felt like he could blow it over with a puff from his lips light as a kiss.

"I must go." He was reminded by the sight of the bridge that the evening train would be departing soon on its far side, and he set out again. The afternoon storm that stripped petals from the blooming trees had collected them here, along the river wreathed like a victory garland, where the air was clearer and the traffic less. The abundance of flowers rained upon the streets like ancient stories, fallen myths and memories, transfiguring before the Courier's eyes.

Across the street, a young woman looked after the horizon, watching the receding glow where the sun had sunk below the hills, filled with longing for the lost day, urged to fly with the sun out of the city and over the expanse of the world. She was the young girl long ago, the sun's lover filled once with the holy fire, who could not live without the god. She pined after him, fixed upon his golden train and sobbing to herself, unmoving. Her long tresses flowed over her little frame and spilt upon the earth. She remained in contemplation, growing into a flower that turns to face the sun's daily path. And there, the Courier saw the petals of the famed and real flower dancing about the scuff of his feet.

Up ahead, a group of mourners departed the restaurant they had rented for a wake. A middle-aged couple lamented the death of their firstborn son, lost in the prime of early manhood. Their sobbing words flew upward to the silent gods, and the Courier perceived sobs of love returned by heaven: a goddess who once loved a beautiful young man and feared for his mortality. She warned him not to hunt, not to put himself in danger, so she would not be so alone and so undying. But swathed in his beauty and the courage of youth, he did not listen. Gored by a wild bull, he died. And the goddess, in memory, made a flower grow from his blood, with petals the color of pomegranate. The flower is short-lived. Its bud waits to be animated by a breath of wind; the wind enchants the petals open and then blows them away. These flowers are common in our city. The Courier counted the flecks of deep red tumbling in the streets with the others.

The Courier also saw the buds of human love. A thin little girl moved among the buildings that lined the river walk, traipsing between shadows with hollow laughter, echoing what others said around her. She tried to play with a boy her age who squatted at the river's edge fawning at his reflection. The boy rejected her for himself and pushed her away. She fled back into her shadows to tease more passers-by. The old story goes that a boy who loved himself above his admirers was lured by his reflection to sit rapt until he rooted forever, turned into a flower. Those drooping, gazing flowers, too, dot our river's edge. Their petals also churned beneath the Courier's feet.

It was the season—when all new life that is the story of life past comes up out of the fertile loam and reaches skyward. The wind freshened and flung a new rain of petals into the air. It was the season—after the petals had fallen from the trees, fruit would grow, and bitten bleed summer's nectar. Remember, our story of the man in love with the young woman who spent her life tending her orchard. The suitor dressed like an old woman, to counsel the girl from his disguise that refusing love was turning to stone, and afterward the violent wind would scatter the precious fruit blossoms. Is that what the wind was saying—that it was time to leave the orchard, and its fragrance, and its sunlit dew, that it was time to leave beauty for the sake of love? The wind bit at the Courier.

Moving through traffic in the street, avoiding lovers leaning along the rail over the river, the Courier continued toward the bridge when he saw his friend, Percy, at a table in a corner café. Percy was sipping a grappa to brace for his walk home.

Percy came to our city as an infant, when he and his mother were expelled from his grandfather's house for reasons Percy did not understand. Set adrift, and without money to travel, they emigrated down the river in a makeshift and treacherous boat, him clutching his mother all the while with his frail and tiny arms. Percy hailed the Courier loudly, swallowed his drink in one proud throw, dropped a handful of coins upon the table and bustled across the street. As he approached the Courier, a few rolling coins trickled from the tabletop.

"I'm on my way across the bridge. You'll have to follow me."

"I'll walk with you a ways," Percy said, lighting a cigarette as he kept pace. "You're going across the bridge to the train station?" Smoke meandered around his sharp jaw like a silk scarf.

"Yes." The Courier could see the glisten of the rails across the river, their network enclosing a stout, baroque building on the river bank below the opposite side of the bridge, his bridge.

"That café I've come from—"

"Yes?"

"There was a sculptor there with some students. He lives above. They were joking that he has fallen in love with his own work. A statue of a woman, lying on a sumptuous bed of white marble flowers. They say he sleeps with it. He was incensed." Percy sighed. "Everyone was laughing and everyone was misunderstood."

The Courier was silent at Percy's prattle, thinking on the caress of smooth stone, the touch of stone in hunger, weeping at grave stones, bleeding against our city walls, the dream of a stone of woman, the dream of a stone of bread, and he thought finally on the love of idols. The stone and not the woman. The stone and not the bread. And the weight of them that we carry, to lift them to our shrines, the weight like stories of warriors carrying ships over land to the next sea. Except no, that was an act of love—the ship would carry them in return. And what love awaited him, the Courier, what idol, but he was betrothed to death. And all these many scenes played through his silent heart as Percy pressed on with stories.

"Have you heard about the girl in the river?" continued Percy, brimming with gossip. "In the river," shouted the thin girl the Courier had seen earlier. She scurried about nearby and threw her echoes from a narrow silhouette behind a lamppost.

"What?"

"Have you heard about it?"

"No," he said, so that Percy would continue talking.

"It's an unbelievable thing—I just heard it at the café. You know the people that live in the tenements? You know them?" he repeated before going on.

"I am one of them, they would say."

"Well you know they haven't anywhere to wash clothes, except the corner sinks in a room of twenty?"

"Yes."

"Well they wash their clothes in the river."

"I've seen them." They dodged another lamppost that slipped between them like an anxious passerby.

"Well a young mother went down to the river to wash clothes with her twin boys. She had the boys on each hip, they're infants, and the laundry in a bag over her shoulder. There were men swimming in the water nearby. They don't want her to wash clothes, you can imagine. They wanted her to join them for a swim, never mind the babies. So they taunt her, and she ignores them. But then they mix up the mud from the river bed, all around her, so she can't wash. She tells them—at least let me draw clean water for my sons to drink—but they don't listen. The muddy water stained the hem of her dress, and they told her—that dress needs cleaned, too! Do you know what happened?"

"Tell me."

"The river took them. It sounds impossible but it's true. They lost their footing, or the current strengthened unexpectedly, or something, and the men were pulled beneath the river! Swallowed them like a serpent. Three of them. A crowd pulled one from the bank about twenty blocks away. He had hold of a tree limb that stretched into the water. He's the only one yet recovered, though the others may have got out further downriver. You know what he said? He said the men were bathing and didn't want to be seen naked and that's why they stirred up the mud. He said they were ashamed, that she should see them."

"And the woman?"

"Beautiful! But also, she's fine now. I know who she is. I saw her in the street with her twins. The line of mud was still on the hem of her dress white as a swan. Like the high-water mark—that's the most the river will stand."

"I think the water can rise higher than a woman's dress hem."

"You're waiting for it to sweep everything clean? Rise up and wash the dirt from our streets, anxieties, needless possessions, and all that. It's muddy water, my friend. Muddy. I saw it on her hem. That man they pulled from the tree branch was gasping for breath. They said his cheeks were full up with mud from the water that filled his mouth. Mud all over his gums and filling the gaps between his teeth."

"That came from his mouth, Percy, not the river."

"Well, it's scandal."

"It's every day, Percy, but at least she is safe."

"It's like the story of the soldiers years ago. You remember? They were put up in town and welcomed to a wedding in the square, and they got drunk and threatened the bride, and a brawl broke out, and they were slain."

"What about what happens in people's hearts all day long?"

"You don't think it matters? I think the river was like a justice."

"A muddy justice? I think it matters, but not as you do. You want justice. But do you think those three men, while at the mercy of the current, do you think they learned what it was like to be the woman? We all go our rocky ways to the same patient end."

Though it lay in the impenetrable future for Percy and the Courier, I know that the woman's twins grew to become soldiers themselves who rescued their kidnapped sister from captivity, as they and their mother had been rescued. And that is because in our history, in our city, all things are married.

By now, the two had arrived at the Courier's Bridge. The Courier had come a distance from his meeting at the fountain, and the heavier crowds of workers had subsided. Slowly, they changed tide with the roving bands that loved the revelry of night. But here, in the flux, the Courier moved through a temporary lull, between the works of the day and the night. He looked across the bridge and nodded in the direction of the train and its waiting power at the platform across the way.

"I must go," he said.

The Courier's Bridge is only one of many bridges that stretch across our city's mighty river. It is called the Courier's Bridge now, because the Courier's death upon it is the great unsolved mystery of our city. It was originally called the Wayfair Bridge, when it was associated with direction, that is, direction in the place of death. It has its own very old story as well.

In the early days of our burgeoning city, two young lovers lived next door to one another; they were forbidden to be together. Their rooms, however, adjoined among the close-built tangle of structures and ramparts that people made into homes. Their parents did not know this. A single wall of stone and plaster separated them. And a long crack rolled down the center of the wall like a rivulet. They could not see through the crack, but they could whisper. All night long, they would pour hot words and breath through the rift, riding on the crest of one another's promises. The boy could smell her perfume and the taste of her lips, and he kissed and caressed the opening like it was her purity itself.

Sometimes the girl wept, overwhelmed with passion and injustice. Her father heard, and he began to listen through the slit beneath her door, prostrate on the cold and dirty floor because he thought he could understand why daughters weep. In the end, he learned only that they planned to be married in secret, beneath a mulberry tree by a spring, near a famous tomb outside of the town. To thwart the secret marriage, her parents moved houses and took their daughter to the opposite side of the river. Now the river separated the two itself, instead of its image pouring down the wall.

At the time, there was no bridge, and people crossed the river in boats. The boy had no boat, but he could swim. When her family was asleep, the girl put a torch in her window at the river's opposite edge. The boy crept from his house and swam the river, using the torch for his direction. From beneath her window, he whispered to her, and they resumed their plans of escape and marriage. But one day, at dawn, the girl's torch had burnt down to nothing, and no sonorous whisper had called her from her delicate and impatient sleep. The next night was the same. And the next. She thought herself unloved.

The boy had drowned in a fast current. His parents were destroyed and ashamed when his innocent body was found broken upon the peaceful banks. News of the funeral came across on the boats. The girl, feeling life was now meaningless, threw herself from the dock into the frenzied river during the next storm and drowned. For the rest of his life, her father slept at the threshold to her empty room, hoping to hear across his own divide her voice in the whisper of his dreams.

Moved with pity, the city decided to build its first permanent bridge. The families of the lost children laid the first stones on their respective sides. Since that day, a bridge has always stood on that exact spot, where the boy was found and the girl was lost. The Courier's Bridge is the most recent incarnation.

It is a suspension bridge, one of the earliest of its kind, spanning the river that opens the center of our city. Its two powerful stone pylons lift from the banks of the murky river to the deck. Above each pylon, a heavy stone arch thrusts into the sky. Immense eyebar-chain cables sling through the solid stone arches and bend down to carry the weight of the deck. The deck arcs to meet the strength of the cables. Atop the arched towers, above the saddles where the cables pass through, a high mural crown lifts the bridge to its full majesty. Despite the power of its elements, the bridge spans the river with lithe grace and clarity. Its arched deck, light as a rainbow, is like a promise between the separated halves of the city. A promise between past and future, like a rainbow, both physical and non-physical, made of water and light, knowledge and nourishment—to drink life and to ponder the untouchable color. The builders engraved across the tower stones: *Yield not to disasters but press on more bravely.*

"I'm sorry," said Percy. "I've kept you. When you return, we'll share a drink." Behind Percy's wan smile, a distance lifted his eyes. Behind Percy rose several low blocks of row houses and stores that are city fixtures. But behind those rose taller the city's Exposition, with majestic galleries and fair grounds for celebrations of art and science—its eventual destruction was one of our most painful architectural losses. Aspiring buildings glowing with light and triumphant with elegance surrounded Percy's silhouette. Steel and glass multi-floored atriums, chateau-like palaces with broad porches: they were once the heart of the city's future, bedecked with banners and welcoming travelers with concert halls, theaters, and exhibit promenades for the arts and artisans, inventors, and manufacturing tycoons. Parents visited their futures there, while halcyon youth who would own those futures frolicked in obviousness.

A band played the strain of a happy past near laughing children that whirled on a carousel, the air alive with intercepting birds of conversation. Percy looked at the Courier with love, but also as the bygone Exposition looked toward the future, with fascination, with hunger, and knowing it would not last forever.

The Courier smiled. "See you then." He turned on the curt goodbye that friends understand. A goodbye that need not linger because of the promise of friendship. Following him as he started over the bridge, one would have seen his friend sighing at his back, the Exposition and its sensational color bubbling toward him and painting his figure iridescent, and the bridge cables like lulling fronds bowing to shroud his stark shoulders.

Across the river, the Conductor looked at his watch. The station was informed that the Courier was coming. His company had called to say he would be on the train with an important parcel and may be a moment behind schedule. It was near the eight o'clock departure.

"I'll give him almost five after," announced the Conductor, squinting again at the walkway across the bridge. "We can make up five minutes in route. But they must understand that the trains don't wait for one man; we serve the public. We serve the time."

On the other side of the bridge, Percy had nowhere to go. His head was mellow with drink, the damp night feeling fresh and mysterious in his hot lungs, and the lights dancing on the river, and the dancing water mark on the hem of a beautiful girl. He watched he Courier, imagined him opening the night with the rush and thunder of the rails. Percy never asked him what he carried. He felt it somehow wrong to ask. His friend had his secret—or another's—he would carry it through the darkness, in the embrace of his arms, plunging forward on unraveling and fiery breath. Percy imagined the Courier, holding the case tightly while he watched his reflection in the portent of the blackened glass, spreading over racing shadows beyond.

"I will watch you, friend; take your secret on into the starry sleep and waiting arms."

The Courier's shrinking form strode deliberately across the bridge. No one else came or went. The river lay placated below. Smooth and soft as a lover that waits. The Courier's shadow passed the first tower, the tall stone arch that carried the cables; he traced the arc where the weightless cable extended down to meet him. Percy saw the Courier's form fading into night as he crested the center of the bridge, at the climax of the deck, where he could have reached out and touched the mighty cable.

The Courier went west with the setting sun. The cable turned upward away from him. His shadow began to descend, down the curve of the deck that eclipsed him. Percy imagined a ship going out to sea and disappearing behind the curve of the earth.

†

I WAS WALKING IN the opposite direction on the Courier's Bridge, and paused to look up the long slope that leads past the tower to the apex of the arched deck.

As I started across the bridge, I watched my shadow. To my left, over the railing, I could see it keeping pace below me on its own shadow bridge. My shadow lay askance on trees and rooftops, at an angle to intercept my path ahead. As I ascended higher over the ground, approaching the bridge tower at the river's edge, my shadow closed on me, scuttling over the railway lines, up walls and across roofs, leaping over chimneys, feathering through rustling tree leaves. Ahead I saw a shadow arch, prostrate at the foot of the stone arch bridge tower, where my shadow's path met mine. My shadow rose higher, treading upward its oblique dais, hurrying to me. Up the higher branches now. Even with the bridge deck. It leapt the rail. Stretched for my feet. Then all was eclipsed in the shadow of the stone arch—the Western bridge tower. I passed out of the light into its cold secret—my untouchable companion, made of more than flesh, of both flesh and light surrounding, and yet composed of nothing. He vanished. We met and dissolved, to go over the river together.

When I emerged from the tower's shadow into the light, the new spring sun dazzled my eyes. It was the equinox. And I was approaching the center of the bridge, strung between the city's halves. It was the centennial of the Courier's death, and I was standing just near the place where his blood had stained the deck. No one knows any more the exact place. And the stain is washed with one hundred years of storms. I may have passed it by the time I reached the apex, because everyone remembers that Percy said he saw the Courier's form receding over the curve of the bridge.

I stood upon the crown. The railing was wet with dew, they say the tears of the dawn that weeps for a lost son. I had awoken that morning from a flow of feverish dreams and stood, still bedraggled, on the floating light-ness of the bridge. The wind that rolls down the belly of the river tossed my hair and shook clinging stories from my locks, pulled wisps of bed heat from my limbs. They say that in the old days the wind rolled with the river, from the bridge like a mouth to the bridge like eyes, from creation to vision. But these days it rolls against the current, from vision to creation.

I love the wind's fingers in my long morning hair—combing the past out of me and making me free. The pull on my scalp like the unraveling of bandages. Our city has fought wars over its uncountable years, but it was conquered only once: long ago when the city was under siege for months and the daughter of the ruling family fell in love from a distance with the captain of the attacking army. She watched him day after day from the towers of our city's old walls. Her father kept the key to the city's gate tied in his long hair. While the father slept, the daughter cut the lock that tied the key, and offered our city to the conqueror if he would have her as his wife and only love.

I looked east, where Percy watched for his friend that night, until he heard the train mount up steam and rumble away from the station. He presumed that it carried the Courier, and strolled off in the contented night. He saw no one else on the bridge. He heard no splash in the placid water. The Courier went quiet as a lamb into the silence. The Killer did not yell for fear of his own death.

†

ON THE OTHER SIDE of the river, the Conductor kept his word and waited until five minutes past eight. When he did not see the Courier board the train, he said, "I suppose that Courier will have to answer to someone, but his employer doesn't pay my wage."

"All aboard!" the Conductor cried. The porters hustled along the platform, pulling up the wooden steps below the train doors. They swung on gracefully as the cars began to creak and edge forward. They saw no one running along the platform to catch them. No one racing off the bridge begging they wait. All was silent but the shrill notes of the train's departing, metal wheels squealing on metal rails, heaviness clacking over seams in the track. They wondered, after, if the sound masked a scream.

The Lamplighter met Percy just as Percy was leaving the Courier's Bridge. "Just going up to light this one," he said with a smile.

"Fine night," answered Percy.

"Fine indeed," the Lamplighter replied. The heat of his flame eddied the thick air between them. The scent of fire uncurled the luxuriously humid night. The stirring city murmured around the tongue of light.

"Well, chase off this black coat with your flame, my friend."

"Always." And the Lamplighter started across the Courier's Bridge.

The Lamplighter carried his flame in a glass globe at the end of a long brass taper with a wooden handle. Inside the taper was a thin beeswax candle, which the Lamplighter made himself by dipping bare wicks into a hot vat of wax. His wife wove the hefty wicks. A knob in a track running the length of the taper allowed him to control the flame. When the Lamplighter needed more flame, he slid the knob upward to expose the candle. Between lamps, he retracted the candle for a slower burn. The glass globe with a tall chimney allowed him to carry his flame in all weather. His chapped hands closed on the wood handle, worn and black because the Lamplighter had carried his flame through rain and snow and gales for many years.

Every night, he protected his fire throughout his circuit of the city, spreading light. A flame divided but undimmed. The single small spark, kindled in his own hearth and sheltered between his rough hands, illuminated bridges in the city and made paths of light for many thousands of eyes.

He began to raise the Courier's Bridge from out its hiding in darkness, one lamp at a time, moving east to west. The lamps burned like torches plunging into the labyrinth of a tomb. They cast pools of yellow on the stone arch, on the intricately forged railing, spilling over the lip of the cables and down onto the roadway beyond. The cast of light made even the cold stone and steel glow with the warming tempt of a body. The globes of light brought their boundaries close, closed the world, and made it intimate: this stone is every stone, this path every path, and all are in the reach of a hand.

One by one, the gas lamps formed the spine of the bridge, animating the bones of a beast that would rise.

The Lamplighter did not hear himself, and he was never able to say for certain whether he screamed from the depths of his surprise. Some people by the river's edge heard a cry of fear, but they did not remember if it was before or after the train that they heard it. They were not paying attention. They did not know if it was the Courier's last breath or the Lamplighter's life calling out in the night.

What he found was a great impersonal expanse of blood slick on the walkway, the devastating enormity of what is finite. The lifeless blood had the texture of motion in the sulking shadows of the flickering gaslights. It looked like someone had opened a large red silk brocade, warm and smothering, it would wrap him in the mad heat of fleeting life. And he thought, a slight steam still wove into the mist.

The gaping red was a great wide mouth. A great wound in the side of the bridge itself, pouring its life into the river that drained it greedily away. The Lamplighter never dreamed that his light would uncover this desolation. The blood gave back the flame of the light, flame for a flame, red from red, light from light, divided and undimmed. The spill crept toward the precipice of the bridge's edge. The Lamplighter gazed over the railing to see the thick strings pulling long over into the void, drawing out in ribbons as the pleas of furious violins. The wind beneath the deck ripped the viscous strands free, where they tumbled end over end into the ever-waiting.

In his shock, the Lamplighter dropped his light. In the freedom of the fall the flames engulfed it. It shone like the fiery sword that they say in the story closed the gates of paradise. But the fiery sword was extinguished in the river.

When he recovered his senses, "Help!" he yelled, as though he were the victim. He did not know what to yell. "Help! Help me!" He felt distinctly like a child in the grip of an absurd and inexplicable power. A power yet undeniable. He did not think to move. He knew nothing but to cry for help. To cry for other life out from the red sepulcher.

His song carried up the long betraying serpent of the river, and life came running. Percy's satisfied pace kept him within earshot. A crowd gathered, Percy among them—half lit, half shadowed, standing at the break where the Lamplighter doused his flame. Half the bridge lights remained cold, suspended over the river's flow. There was no body. There was no locked mahogany case. No one knew who had been killed. They turned about to the swirling stars in wonder.

†

THE CHAPPED WIND CURLED around the fresh skin of my face. On the morning of the centennial, I had followed one of my rituals: a slow and deliberate shave with a fine straight razor. I do it to mark important days, and I do it as much as I can. I believe in transforming into art the ordinary, especially the routine or mundane. To create beauty where there would otherwise be cold boredom—then life becomes gratitude. Introduce danger, and routine becomes beautiful. And I savor it.

It is nothing to rush through a shave. When there are convenient ways, they are all fundamentally inconvenient. They make of me a burden to be relieved. It is toil and task, and I want it over. But, now, to have the rosewood in my palm. To run my fingers over the filigree and swing open the glimmering blade. To strop it, correctly, honing it to its finest edge. To shave artfully, sanguinely, having paid admission to the privilege with a history of nascent pain. That is not task, but transformation.

And most of all—to have that blade at my neck in the early morning— I tell myself to make the day a good one. I am at the razor's edge. I know what my blood looks like on metal: tiny firefly rubies, precious and pulsing with vigor. I work carefully over the sharp angles of my jaw and think of the wounded Courier.

I was walking over his bridge on the centennial because the city was going to tear open the walls of my home. I wanted to visit the man who was the cause, and to visit his bridge, his only memorial. I live in the room where the Courier lived, on the top floor of a quaint five-story mid-rise that had been generously built with ornamented stone but had become a tenement in the Courier's day. For the centennial of the unsolved mystery, the city was buzzing with a new effort to unravel the old crime. By the time it was over, they opened the walls of three houses and a grave. They started with the Courier's room, now my home. The city wished to learn whether the Courier might have hidden within my walls the parcel that disappeared one hundred years ago.

It was a futile search from the outset, and hopelessly limited—to look only in the few places that remain, in the few places that are known, when the world is so vast and unconquerable, and the answers could be anywhere. But then again, a search depends upon the answer sought. After one hundred years, no one cared much to solve the mystery of who killed whom. What they cared about was their own gain—what could be got with the item he carried.

And so there were two mysteries at one time in our city, like the two sides of a bridge: the ancient mystery of the Courier, and the new mystery of what he carried. The first was a mystery of life and identity: who died, and why. The new was a mystery of liberation: the dream of means, and the cost of freedom. And, depending upon the seeker, one was a selfless mystery, and the other a selfish one.

One hundred years ago, however, when the detectives arrived on the scene, the bloom of red cried to them for justice. They were led by a man named Glaucus, who carried the name of one of our city's long-remembered stories.

The ancient Glaucus was a fisherman in the river. He loved his trade, and the river was good to him, providing him with many fish and a comfortable life. But after years of security, he discovered that the money he earned did not bring him peace. What he loved most in life was to be on the water, where he did not need the money he made from fishing. He was a powerful swimmer, and one day he leapt into the water with a vow that he would live in it. He was seen thereafter swimming powerfully about the river and fishing for food as he needed. He made his home upon a tiny island in the river, one that time has since washed away. When he was not fishing or swimming, or caring for his island, he received visitors who were brave enough, and taught children how to swim.

But, as the story goes, ancient Glaucus came to love the water so much that it changed him. He became like a fish in appearance, and spent more time in the water than on land. Swimming one morning, he saw a beautiful young woman bathing in a small cove where a fresh stream joined the river. He watched her in secret; he adored her. He swam close enough to call to her gently. But she feared him because he was strange, and she ran. He searched the river, looking for her, and when he found her bathing again, he begged her to let him speak with her. She ran again in a flash of pale skin, wet hair clinging to her soft back. After that, she would not bathe, and because she would not bathe, she had no other suitors. Her unwashed skin, once beautiful, developed sores. She lay ill, mired in bed, a shoal in the water and full of a monstrous anger, until she died.

When the ancient Glaucus took to the water, he became it. To his beloved, he became all of it. And his coveting was her death. And Detective Glaucus, in the Courier's time, was true to his name. He became his mystery, to the suffering of love, as I will tell. And the same goes for anyone who enters mystery. Enter, and you become it. Covet the secret carried, and the result is jealousy and death.

The night of the crime, Glaucus surveyed the scene. The gawking crowd stood barred at either end of the bridge by police with rifles athwart their hips. Glaucus directed young men on the force to ask the swarm of faces floating in the dark if they knew anything. If they saw anything. While they went hurriedly about the task, Glaucus stood over the stain.

"So here is a life destroyed at an impasse. Here at the neck of a bridge, where there is nowhere to escape. A bridge has two faces. You can run back where you came from. You can run toward where you are going. It is linear. From this blood, we surmise someone is dead. The Killer, he does not want his victim in the expanse of life. He does not want him in the city, in the twists and turns of the closes. He does not want him on the winding river's edge. He wants to intercept his victim on a known straight line. Would the Killer want his victim in a closed space, instead of on a line? Maybe, again the victim cannot escape. Maybe this Killer had no knowledge of, or access to, the victim's closed spaces: his bed, his room. He could have killed him in a dead-end alley. Ah, but here—a dead end, a closed room, has one face. It is an aperture. There is one way in, there is one way out. The victim is there, the Killer is not. The moment is frozen. But a bridge has two faces. It has the aspect of confinement, while it has the free flow of a river. Did the victim go toward the sunset? The sunrise?"

Glaucus turned, saluting the opposing hills beyond each riverbank. "Does our Killer go the same way? Does he go the opposite way? Does he come from behind, a bustling traveler about to pass, hurrying toward the departing train? Maybe he says, 'I am making the train,' to keep the victim calm until he opens the body, spills the blood. But maybe the Killer comes the other way, so there is no suspicion of a person hovering behind the victim's back. The Killer is a passing pedestrian. The victim casts eyes downward, so to show trust and not challenge, and then comes the unexpected blow."

He peered into the opaque water, asking as one might ask a mirror, "The victim, a man or a woman? The Killer, a man or a woman? Force or guile to get close enough for a blade? A woman could push a man over this low rail. And yes—we have no body. The Killer wishes to destroy even the identity of the slain. That is important. Or the Killer wishes to conceal a motive, for as long as it takes to discover the dead. But why, then, show us there was a crime; why spill blood? The Killer should throw the victim over the rail as the train wails—then the murder is unknown until someone is found missing, or a body is discovered, and he has bought himself more time. Maybe the victim could not be forced over the rail unless he or she was injured first; maybe the Killer could not wait for the sound of the train; maybe the Killer was unsure a fall alone would kill."

Glaucus stooped down to the blood at last, so its iron smell was in his nose. "The victim must be cut. A gun is too loud. It would have been heard. And why so much blood only in a pool on the ground. There is no splatter on the rail, on the cable, flanking the walkway."

"Maybe. . ." began a young officer who was taking notes.

"I'm not finished," said Glaucus definitively. "The Killer opens the body with a knife, in a way that causes much bleeding and leaves no resistance. Unless—could the victim have lain on the ground, allowing the blood to collect? Then the wound might be smaller, but there is the increased danger of delay, discovery. Most likely, the Killer passes on the bridge, quickly turns, covers the victim's mouth with a rag while opening the throat. The victim bleeds. There is no fight; the Killer knows the victim is dead; the body goes over the side. . . Maybe. . . Maybe. . ."

Glaucus turned his closed eyes to heaven and drew a deep breath of the cool night air, a long frown on his expressive mouth.

"Maybe. . ." began the young officer again.

"There are two faces to this crime like there are two sides to a bridge, like the bridge is made to seem confining but in actuality it is utter freedom. There is the face of the victim. Who is it? Where does the victim go, and why? Does the Killer want to hide the crime with the body? Why the blood and no body—was that necessity only? Does he know the blood is on the deck—mind that the gas lamps were yet unlit. Or perhaps he wants his crime to be known? He wants it writ in blood. That creates the face of a killer, and it creates a face that may not be the Killer's real face. Where does he go? The Lamplighter comes from the east, shedding light that is sure to uncover the crime. Thus the Killer goes west, past the departing train, where he knows there will be people? Light or eyes?"

Glaucus glanced all over the bridge, his eyes playing over the treacherous wet cables, the high, sheer stone arches. "If he's up there, he can come down and give us the proof. Or else he can die up there." But from either end of the bridge, one could see there was no silhouette. Officers walked the length of the bridge, peering upward for a hiding form. They climbed the bridge cables to ensure the Killer was not crouched in shadow where the cables passed through the stone arches on the cable saddles. "There was nowhere else to go. He melted into the city. Into one half of it or the other. Maybe into the Exposition, into its laughter and surfeit and chaos. He becomes one of infinite faces. . ."

"Maybe the Killer is on the train?" suggested the anxious young officer, finally able to express his treasured thought. He acted as Glaucus's assistant and secretary, admiring the detective through heavy glasses. His name was Melic.

"That is a direct train, it need only be stopped and secured. That would be an easy way to be discovered, since the Killer would have joined the passengers only at the last moment."

"Maybe the Killer is not so smart."

Glaucus looked long at the young man, with a penetrating expression that revealed nothing of what he thought. "This Killer is a genius of bridges," Glaucus said deliberately, smearing the stubble on his face with a fleshy palm. He looked the young man over again. Through the fingers gripping his chin Glaucus added, "I already ordered that we stop and search the train, but the Killer is not on the train."

"Sir," approached another officer, "we have teams combing the streets and searching buildings near the bridge, looking for anyone suspicious, asking if any witnesses noticed a hurrying person or a person splashed with blood. They're searching the river's edge for someone hiding in the brush."

"Good," said Glaucus. "Like the train it will be a futile task, supposing the Killer's work has gone according to plan. There are innumerable places, immediately accessible, where he could be sheltered by now. We don't know who the Killer is, so we don't know who would shelter him. And we don't know who the Killer is, because we don't know the victim. But, on the small chance that his plans were somehow thwarted, perhaps if he did not account for the Lamplighter, maybe he will be trapped somewhere unprepared. Then again, perhaps he was depending upon the Lamplighter."

"What makes you believe the Killer had such a scheme?" asked Melic. "Could this not have been a random robbery, a random meeting?"

"The Killer had to know the victim was on the bridge." Glaucus took his time articulating the words. "The Killer had to know that *this* victim was on the bridge. A victim worth killing. At a time when the Killer could remain unseen."

In silence, Glaucus turned to look over the river flowing away from him, toward the two reflected arches of the next bridge. They stared back at him in patience. "We must dredge the river," he ordered. "Start far down so there is no chance the current could carry away the body. Find the face of the victim—a victim who should be killed but should be hidden. Then you will have the face of the Killer."

A few officers peeled away from the group, muttering about Glaucus as they hurried to execute their orders. Another who had been interviewing the crowd nearby approached briskly.

"Sir, we've little in the way of witnesses. Many of the people were nearby when they heard the Lamplighter call for help, but none were on the bridge and none heard a cry or a struggle or a splash. They were all about their own business. But there is one man who says he had watched his friend, a courier, cross the bridge to catch the train. He claims he waited, watching the bridge until the train sounded. He saw the Lamplighter go across as he turned away."

"What side was he on?"

"The east side."

Glaucus's eyebrows were high arches. "Bring him to me. And bring me the Lamplighter." One officer hurried off as Melic approached again, opening a stenography notebook. A pencil waited behind his ear.

Glaucus whispered to him, "So we have a bridge with two faces, with two sides, with two stories: one of confinement for the victim, one of freedom for the Killer. If we have a reliable witness at one side, we take away one face of the bridge, right? But if we have an unreliable witness, then we only have more faces. Look now," he swept his hand toward the barred crowds, "these people are here because they are curious about suffering, their own is not enough for them. They want this raw life that is opened like a body. They want to look at death. The Killer should not be not among them. Why would the Killer stay here at the bridge to give a name and address and be no one? The Killer does not need to learn anything about the aftermath of the crime, already we are in the Killer's maze. But this witness—why would he stay so long, watching the Courier leave? He may be here to make an alibi, otherwise he would have said goodbye and gone his own way." And his arch face was higher yet, peaked as his mind bridged questions.

Percy and the Lamplighter told their stories, the same stories I have already told. Percy described the mahogany case. They were interviewed a dozen paces from the bloodstain, and Percy peeked queasily around Glaucus to try and see it, wondering if it was the last of his friend's cooling life that he would see. The Lamplighter looked down only, as he had already seen all and was frightened of authority. Glaucus noticed the difference between the two and was intent on several points with Percy.

"You do not know what your friend, the Courier, carried?"

"No."

"Did he know what he carried?"

"I don't know."

"You are certain that, from the time your friend crossed the bridge going west until you heard and saw the train pull away, you stood here and no one else came on or off the bridge? You are absolutely certain?"

"Yes. Until the Lamplighter."

"Yes," said Glaucus. "And you heard nothing of a struggle."

"Nothing whatever."

"You saw or heard no splash in the water."

"The river was dark."

"You heard no splash?" The question agitated Glaucus's shadowed frame like fleeting ripples.

"None." An answer like a small drop into the dark expanse.

"And you were drinking?"

"Just one drink, for the walk home," said Percy, surprised the scent still hung on his breath. Glaucus glowered down at him from inches away.

"Wait over there."

When Percy left, Melic offered another idea. "That's an easily-recognizable parcel that Percy described, the mahogany one the Courier carried. If that parcel is on the train, then we have our Killer."

"If the parcel is with the Killer, it is not on the train," snapped Glaucus, "for exactly the reason you describe."

"Find the parcel then, wherever it is. . ." the young man volunteered.

Glaucus continued as though nothing had been said. "You assume it is the Courier who is dead. I agree, this parcel may well have been the Killer's quarry. If that is so, then its distinctiveness should have gone over the rail of the bridge with the body. But also, the Courier may have his parcel upon the train, none the wiser for what happened in his wake. This Percy," he continued, "makes his alibi too well. It is as though the Killer must vanish; the body must split the water so silently, like a perfect descent."

"But we must remember," he continued, roused with fresh excitement, "we have not only Percy but also the Lamplighter, who also came from the east. Now we must have the western face. We must know what the staff at the train station saw. The passengers and staff on the eight o'clock train especially. We must know who came and went from the other side of the bridge. This Killer is no ghost. If he is made to look like one, then we can be sure he has flesh. The flesh of one who would wish him a ghost."

"We've already begun, sir," replied the officers. "The train will be held at its destination, no one to board or leave."

"We are faced with possibilities . . ." said Glaucus, and the remaining officers huddled around him.

"It is possible that this blood," he upturned a rigid, open palm, "belongs to the Courier—that Percy watched him start across the bridge to catch the train, but he did not make it to the other side. He could have been killed by a stranger, unknown, who would be forced to escape the bridge on the west side where the train station is. He could have been killed by an acquaintance, perhaps one who could approach him easily to make the fatal blow; this acquaintance also would have escaped on the west side. It is also possible that an even better acquaintance is at work. Percy could have walked across the bridge with the Courier to catch the train, killed him as they went, and returned going east. The Lamplighter encountered him contemplating the kill, not pining after his friend. Percy then remains to play the role of troubled friend and wash off suspicion, but he tells a story that, if the west end is no escape, must implicate himself. Himself or one other . . . But either way, if the Courier is dead, it would seem to be by the hands of one that knew what he carried."

"It seems risky," offered one of the officers. "What if the Lamplighter had caught up to Percy on the bridge, or what if anyone had run into the Killer as he was fleeing the murder?"

"Again, the genius of bridges—they only seem confining. From the crest, the Killer can see if anyone is near on either side, or silhouetted against the lights of the shore. Meanwhile, a passerby in the darkness must cross half the bridge to discover the crime. Until then, one suspects nothing. Someone passing the other way is irrelevant until there is a crime. You might not even look at his face. You might not even notice him. Then, it is too late. He has vanished. The direction of the bridge creates time. And, as it is, the Lamplighter did not see Percy on the bridge; their stories are consistent."

After a silence, he continued, "Of course, the Lamplighter could be the Killer. He creates the crime in his withheld light, then plays the role of its discovery. But if the Courier is the victim, then something must have gone amiss with his plan. Percy waited until the train left. Therefore, the Courier would have missed the train and been coming back across the bridge. This seems wrong, because the Lamplighter would have to plan on the Courier missing his train. That is, unless the Lamplighter knew the Courier would miss his train. If he arranged for it. This seems fantastic—it would require that he disclose his involvement to others who could betray him. Unless, of course," he gave a short, cynical laugh, "Percy is the one who ensured the Courier would be late. Percy and the Lamplighter could protect one another and share what the Courier carried. But if they are in collusion, we need believe nothing we have heard about time."

He resigned a helpless exhale, raising his face again with his eyes closed. Stroking his throat with his fingers; flexing his demonstrative mouth. With devastating alacrity, he added, "And we must remember: the Courier may have caught his train; a stranger entered from the west; met a killer who walked along or laid in wait; who killed the stranger victim and left again by the west. And we are nowhere. We know nothing."

He let the resignation pass. "And finally . . . Finally . . .," his left hand wandered over his jaw, "the Courier. He carried something. He wanted it. But no, he does not steal it. Instead, he dies for it. He could have arranged for someone to meet him at the center of the bridge; he could have lain in wait for a stranger. The body is gone, but the blood tells the tale—a faceless fact of murder. And he offers us his face as the victim. By the time we discover the victim is not him, he is far gone. He does not even need his friend to see him off. It is a chance benefit. He and his parcel would have been found missing regardless, and the connection would be made. If we find that the Courier is not on the train, it does not mean he is dead. Perhaps he hopes we will never find the body, and he will be forever the necessary victim."

Glaucus motioned to one of the river barges making its way against the current, churning its deep and heavy props, approaching the bridge where they stood. His face was grave.

"I am reminded," he scrawled in a gravelly voice, "of the story of the man who carried his own death warrant. Do you know it? He was said to be a hero in his own city. He was sent here by his king with secret letters, on the auspices that only he could best guard his king's most private words. The letters contained, however, a request for the man's death, because of the king's jealousy."

"Did he die?" asked one of the young officers.

"Not just then," said Glaucus with determination. "We must find someone who saw the events at the west side of the bridge. We must find the body in the water before it is destroyed. And we must know what this man carried!"

†

REGARDING GLAUCUS'S FINAL HYPOTHESIS, I want to tell the complete story, but I also feel compelled to add, here at the beginning, that the Courier was trustworthy and would not steal. He certainly would not have killed an unknown victim, especially for no reason but to masquerade as his own death. Shortly after the crime, the police visited the company where he worked, to investigate the parcel he carried that night, among other topics. While they were there, the police learned the following story.

When the Courier appeared, looking for work, the company gave him a test it had devised for new applicants from abroad with no references. The company gave him money to hold in trust, secretly marked, so that the company could identify the specific bills it had given him. If an applicant returned all the bills after ten days, he was considered for a position. If an applicant spent some of the money because of dire need but admitted it honestly, he might still be employed. But if an applicant used the money and tried to replace it, to conceal what he had done, then the applicant was dismissed. According to his employer, the Courier was more concerned about the desperation of others than he was of his own temptation. He carried the money with him throughout the ten days, in case someone should force the simple lock on his tenement room. He slept with it beneath his pillow. He earned for himself the trust of his position.

Additionally, the parcel the Courier carried came from a man who stressed that its contents were important to him alone, and he promised the Courier a reward after delivery. The Courier would have wanted to deliver the parcel, thinking it was something of personal and not market value, and also because of the reward.

Living in the same room as the man, I understand intuitively, perhaps as others cannot, that the Courier was the victim. I am in the peaceful room now. There are children that play in the alley below my window, near a little alley garden. I watch them from my desk as I write this, as I think the Courier watched others. I walk over to lean my head against the window frame. It is an old, single-pane window, certainly from the Courier's day, and I see how the wood is worn at the place where I lay my head while I think. The window is good for thinking. And I know the Courier's breath fogged the glass pane the same as mine, as the reckless and innocent children frolic in their holy and stolen joy.

And so convinced on the morning of the centennial, I completed my transit of the Courier's Bridge, passing on the east side the place where Percy watched his friend disappear. As I said, the city was planning to open my walls, and I was walking to meet my friend, Clement, to share the event. As I lived in the Courier's room, I believe Clement lived in the room of the man that killed him. He was on the opposite side of the river from me. I wanted Clement to see the circus of the search, and what I assumed would be deserved disappointment.

"You should have opened the walls yourself," said Clement. "Looked under the floorboards. It's your home; they can't stop you."

"The landlord could stop me."

"If you patched the holes no one would catch you."

"I like to imagine something is hidden there. I like the idea of being hungry and sitting upon a hidden treasure. First I imagine it is there, then I imagine it is not. It gives me kinship."

"That's your pride."

"I see you recognize a long-time friend."

Clement scowled. "You could have had it. All that money. Then these fools come and find nothing, and you say: I'm sorry, I wish you success, and give them your sympathy. You put some aside, buy a boat, go right out the river to the sea, with a curse to the city, and live as you please. You could write every day like you want. You could write your thieving black heart out."

"And how would I explain the repairs? Clement," I said, resting a hand on his shoulder, "nothing's there anyway."

"Well what are they going to do if they find something?" His tone indicted the unjust possibility.

"I don't know. Return it to the descendants of the rightful owner."

He scoffed enormously. "Whoever finds them is the rightful owner."

"I don't know who had the fantastic idea that people wall up valuables anyway; it's something out of a bad novel."

"Owners don't. Thieves do. Killers do. You bury evidence."

"We're not talking about evidence—we're talking about the reason for the crime, the desired object itself."

"The desire is the evidence."

I sighed. I loved Clement, but he often made me sigh. "The Courier vanished from history—if he didn't die on the bridge, he certainly didn't wall up the precious fruits of a soul-killing crime before he ran off, never to return."

Now he put his hand on my shoulder. "They are opening your walls because they are like me, not like you. They do not care to revel in a dead man's life. They open your walls because the walls are the last thing left."

When the Courier disappeared, and the rain washed the bridge clean, and all the old unfortunate suspects all died after an old and tired life of suspicion, and all their rooms were cleaned out to be as bare as their bones are now—nothing came of it. Life and time and patience produced nothing.

All the keeps are pillaged, and they are all barren. But we cling tenaciously to what remains, wanting marrow in the brittle bones of the walls.

"They are the last part of a receding past that we can get our fingernails into before it slides entirely away," said Clement. "And see, I have these strong hands, a tenacious grip. And an empty belly." He was flexing the knobby fingers of his large and empty hands.

†

THE MORNING AFTER THE murder, as the sun rose, the evening train from our city pulled into its destination: another city different from our own. The train was direct; it had no intervening stops. Local police had been contacted ahead of the train's arrival, as our own city's officers were well behind. In cooperation, the local police held the train at its stop and methodically searched the passengers. They did not find the Courier's parcel. They did not find the Courier. Our officers arrived hours after the search was concluded, to question the irate passengers. As they went compartment to compartment, they asked each passenger in turn: had he or she seen anyone on the west side of the bridge before the train set off? Unsurprisingly, the passengers had been about their own business and remembered nothing specific. I often wonder whether an impatient soul held his or her tongue and changed history. After the passengers were released, one at a time, from questioning, the officers interviewed the train staff.

When the evening train disembarked from our city, as the Conductor gave the order and Percy listened across the river and the Lamplighter approached the bridge and the train staff swung up onto the rolling cars, neither the Courier nor what he carried were aboard. He did not go where he was expected to go. He did not carry that former hope through the streets sparkling with morning and dew, to a recipient that waited joyfully for the present in his hands. He did not keep his secret to its end. He did not transmit what he carried. And things began to happen.

At the start of business the morning after the murder, a man in the destination city began to pace back and forth in his store. He was dressed as immaculately as the other who had given the Courier his parcel. He waited to receive it. He watched the time, then paced again. He shined the display of his little store—he displayed very little, as all he sold was of great value. He adjusted his suit in the reflection of the glass. He fidgeted with his watch. He caressed his hair, his face, as he waited in stillness, his breath so shallow as to be imperceptible. He had the patience of a desert. He sweated in his shirt collar.

At lunch, when he could not eat, when the train had long since arrived at dawn, he sent word to his counterpart.

"Your man did not arrive."

By now, our city was alive with the news of a death upon the bridge. A connection seemed instantaneously apparent. Glaucus was surprised to see the Jeweler burst into his offices like a rolling storm, dapper appearance askance with desperation.

"You must find the Courier's parcel!" he shouted. "Please, sir. Please, you must. If you do not, I am ruined." His eyes pleaded ferociously.

"Why? What is in the case?" asked Glaucus deliberately.

"Jewels! Many precious ones. My entire stock. I am selling my business that I have built with my lifetime. I was transporting them to my buyer. But he will not pay now. I have been robbed blind!"

"And you sent these jewels with a courier last night?"

"Yes, a courier, to travel by the eight o'clock train overnight and deliver them this morning. When I heard about a killing so near the station, just when the train was to depart, and now the jewels have not arrived . . . They killed him and have stolen my life!"

"Where did you exchange the case?"

"I walked a short way from my store, maybe five or six blocks, so as not to be in the immediate vicinity. There is a small square there, with a fountain. It is a place that is busy, but also where the crowd changes frequently. I arrived early, to see if someone was waiting, watching me."

"You are a cautious man. Did you notice anything?"

"I did not. I felt safe. When the Courier arrived, we spoke privately. We did not exchange money. We did not linger. I saw no one interested in us. I saw no one follow the Courier."

Glaucus studied the man's exactitude at length. "So you doubt that someone could have learned the value of the case by chance at the exchange?"

"I doubt it very much."

"Then who would have known about the sale of your business?"

"Other than my family . . . no one."

"Why did you send something so precious by courier?"

"The danger!" he cried. "You can understand the danger of carrying something so valuable. It is a danger that has come to pass. People know I am a jeweler. Should they know I am to sell my business, they might expect such a transaction. If they were to see me carrying a case, they may want my life for their wealth. And look at me: I am old. I cannot defend myself like a young man. The safest way to transport things of value is in hiding. An ordinary courier, a nondescript man with an unremarkable case. Something that is palatable, something that does not overwhelm a hungry person with intrinsic value, or make the person think they can destroy their hunger."

"I see," mused Glaucus. "But the case you sent was not so unremarkable."

"Of course the danger!" the Jeweler resumed, speaking over the last of Glaucus's words. "That is why anyone hires a courier. But—I'll die anyway. That was all my livelihood. You have to find it," he begged. "You have to find it." No longer shouting, he moaned with defeat.

A few officers took the sulking man into the adjacent room to give him a drink. They shut the door, eying Glaucus inquisitively through the closing gap. When the Jeweler was out of hearing, Glaucus spoke to several officers who had gathered at the commotion.

"We must expand our search. We need not only the enemies of the Courier, but also we need the enemies of the Jeweler. And we have a new motive for anyone who knew what was in that parcel." He raised a finger to indicate silence. He went to the door, deftly turned the handle, then slowly, quietly cracked it open again. Glaucus studied the Jeweler, who sat coddling a brandy in his shaking hands, two unsympathetic officers standing over him or alternately slouching about the room. "He seems nervous," added Glaucus discreetly. "I wonder if he owns the jewels in his store or merely sells them. He may have them on loans or consignment. Look at him," he said, peering intently, "a rude man with a fine suit, but a rude man. The gems may be more valuable than the price he negotiated for their sale. Should they disappear—and he is absolved—maybe he has broken his business but gained enormous secret wealth. Maybe he finally possesses what was never his. Maybe he hides in poverty, until his debtors are satisfied there is nothing, then flees with the patient treasure."

"Why not flee now?" asked Melic.

"He wants not only wealth but freedom."

The distraught Jeweler turned, startled to find Glaucus leering through the narrow opening. The Jeweler almost dropped his glass. Glaucus revealed himself at the door and crept into the room, positioned over the Jeweler's shoulder in an impending shadow.

"Just another question—sorry to startle you," Glaucus said without a strain of sympathy. "Where did you go, after your delivery to the Courier?"

"I went to my shop."

"An empty shop?"

"There are things to do. I have to keep my books and records. I have to collect my personal things; I'm to sell the building. I wanted also to remember the years there. I worked hard there. The business was my whole life."

"And you were reflecting alone?"

"I was alone."

"How long did you stay?"

"I went to a café after maybe an hour. Like a fool, I had a drink to celebrate, and I watch the young people in the evening, flitting through the streets."

"Meet anyone?"

"No."

"How long did you stay?"

"Another hour or two, I can't be sure."

"Where did you go?"

"Home. I was tired."

"And did you meet anyone there?"

"No." The Jeweler looked into Glauacus's unbending gaze and added in a tone of sudden offense, "I see you do not spare victims your suspicion."

I have thought, myself, that Glaucus could have been gentler with the Jeweler. He was a remarkable man. His name was Melager. Because of his age when Glaucus met him, much of his ample fame had dissipated. Melager was, in fact, much older than anyone would have guessed from looking at him—so old that a mere few of his friends were still alive, so old that a dozen, perhaps, remembered his story. Glaucus was not among them.

Melager had been a jeweler for a very long time, a trade he and his two brothers inherited from earlier generations in his family. Each of the brothers established his own store, and they were the three best and most respected jewelers in our city.

When Melager was full of youth and vigor, a pack of wild boars came frenzied from the country into the city streets. They overturned fruit carts, they broke down the doors of grocers for the food within, they gored people in the street, people who turned a corner to discover a pack of charging beasts. The police of the city did not have authority like they did in the days of Glaucus. They were a relatively new and disorganized force—many people alive then still believed in the old militias and justice in the public square. It was a time of self-sufficiency, when victims were expected to cope, when vengeance was clean. Moreover, the uncertain officers could get no orders, because their chief was in the midst of an affair with a poor singer in a tiny flat in the shadow of a city temple—a place where no one expected to find the chief of the burgeoning police. The officers could not organize.

A group of shop owners, led by Melager and his two brothers, took to the streets to corner the animals. Butchers brought their knives. Restaurateurs brought chairs and pans. Grocers brought food to lure and distract the beasts. Milliners brought fabric to throw over their faces and blind them.

Some of the shopkeepers were injured by the thrashing tusks, and some were lamed. But Melager kept everyone together, shouting encouragements during the midst of the fray. He helped them to cooperate: a grocer lured one of the boars with apples, then two men caught it in a fine floral silk, and Melager delivered a fatal stroke to the neck of the writhing beast with a jeweled dagger he brought from his store. His stabbing blows were swift and fatal. Melager was the reason the others stood their ground and did not suffer more injuries.

Afterward, when ladies went to Melager to consider an ornate broach or a fragile necklace, and he brought it delicately from the case and held it, in their minds they saw only the jeweled hilt in those large, sinewy hands, the fire of the gems quenched in hot blood.

Melager knew how to kill. But that is only half of his story. His heroism made him beloved in our city, so that men wanted to buy for their lovers only jewels imbued with his courage. Women wanted to see the hands that slew the foe and yet could handle beauty tenderly. When examining a proffered piece, ladies pulled his powerful hands close, to study their knits and scars alongside intricate metalwork. He became a successful man, so much so that his brothers were forced out of business. He offered that they join with his shop, but out of pride they refused. Instead they moved away, to other cities, to make their lives. They forgot they were brothers.

Meanwhile, in our city, the myth outgrew the aging man. It was said that Melager was blessed by the gods with wealth and strength, that he was invincible. This invincibility became linked to the beauty of his jewels. At last it was said: so long as he protected the fire of his gems, his life, too, would burn unquenchably.

Decades passed, and generations were lifted from superstition. But Melager kept his boyish laugh, his energetic—if blemished—skin, his pure fierceness. He aged, it seemed, at half pace, and so his myth echoed. The city gossiped, too, about his mother, who had been tortured by his success, caught between lauding her son the champion or blaming him for the destruction of his brothers. She had considered taking back the inheritance of Melager's father that allowed him to start his business. She lived and died with her heart full of sadness, because a mother never wants to see her family torn apart, no matter the reason. Some people claimed this sadness killed his mother; some people laid that death also upon Melager's still-powerful hands.

When the Courier was killed and Melager's jewels disappeared, the few who were still alive and remembered Melager's youth wondered what would happen. And a few elderly widows went into the sanctums of their bedrooms to withdraw from hiding gems they had long stopped wearing, gems they had already willed to a younger generation to preserve the memory of grandmothers. They held fire in their decimated hands and remembered a man they had once desired. They pricked their fingers with the pin of a brooch, to see ever-so-small a gem of red, and mingle the fire of life with the fire of brave promise. Or they brought out their antiquated clothes, like them, stunning in handiwork and ragged with age, so they could wear once more their bouquets of frozen fire on the changing city streets. They wondered now whether Melager would live or die.

†

CLEMENT WAS MY BEST friend, but he lived with chronic hollowness. His apartment felt hollow as he did. His place was part of an especially old building, one of dozens scattered about the city center that dated from some unknown time in the distant past. It rose with walls thick as a fortress and had been annexed to other buildings, whose walls scabbed upon the ancient ones. Clement's room was carved out of the labyrinthine interior. It was small, but so sparse that it echoed. The flat white paint and lacquered stone floors filled with abundant light from tall windows set deep into the outer walls.

The room contained two unmatched chairs he had collected from a dumpster. An industrial spool, four feet in diameter and once used for dock line, served as a table. Clement had found it at the wharfs for the river barges. A small sink and tiny stove stood against the wall—bread, rice, soup cans, a red apple on a wooden shelf above. A mattress lay on the floor, swimming in mismatched blankets. His few clothes were folded in a nook in the stone wall. Pages from his favorite books of poetry, which he tore from volumes at the library, hung from nails and sewing needles. An aluminum coffee pot perked on the stove as he expounded on why I should have found the lost jewels and kept them for myself.

His feelings did not surprise me. For Clement, money could solve many problems. His father was an alcoholic. His mother alone could not afford to live, so Clement gave her almost all of what he made from his loading job at a nearby warehouse. Often that money was not enough, and Clement developed a good reputation as a thief. He did no violence—ever. But every couple of months, he passed himself off as a worker in stores receiving inventory shipments, or else as a deliveryman picking up shipments from suppliers, wearing uniforms provided by someone he did not know. He delivered the goods to empty buildings, as instructed, and left them there.

He could get away with it because he was charismatic. He could talk to anybody naturally. He walked away calmly with hundreds of diverse items plucked from their streams of transit, items that never reached their owners. Usually these were things with immediate street value, but occasionally not. Once, he stole several cases of expensive women's perfume and kept some for himself. He wore it daily, and walked like an art form in the stale rainwater streets. Linen and patchouli on his dirty skin, sweaty from hoisting boxes at work—it was the passing scent of baked and gnarled trees on a saltwater beach, pebbled sand mixed with anise and lime, and the ocean's breath.

I believe Clement felt that his work daily robbed him of his youth, despite his tremendous love for his father. So he drank as well. Though he lived like a pauper, and frequently skipped meals, he would have his fêtes at the finest establishments: to inflame the contrite room with loud conversations advocating his atheism, glorifying human endeavor, then reciting memorized poetry until ousted into the rainy streets, yelling until he was hoarse and ill, and executing a whole mess of contradictions in love until someone sweet would come to see his sparse life out of pity and tuck him in. His drink was his cure for the cure of his father's ill. If he did not drink, he probably would not have had to steal. But he said that both made him feel full and real and embraced of the world. They gave him an image of himself that he could love. And though I know that he felt trapped and wronged, I admired what I saw as selfless freedom. He was like the fresh air itself. I always thought he lied about his atheism. To me, he seemed a new myth daily.

"Youth!" He would cry, "Youth is what one wants. You think of all those fools in the old stories that cursed themselves forever because they asked for eternal life and, idiots, not for eternal youth to match. And they wasted away like shadows. And you know the stories of the ancient mystic women with their potions of youth—and you remember how they worked, too. She had to kill you. You had to die for the potion to work, and then the body went on in some animated unreality of eternal you. But are you dead or are you young? See, I am both. Drink," he roared, and he would toast. He would toast so hard that he would shatter the glasses in our hands, and he would not care that they cut him, and he would laugh uncontrollably, like a maniac. The next day he grimaced as he hoisted boxes at work with the same old rust-stained handkerchiefs wrapped around his hands.

"You see," he would insist, jabbing at me with pointed fingers and fists, "This is what I am. I am the mystery. I am the labyrinth. I am following back out the lost maze of myself on a fragile string millennia old; it may break at any moment. And see—look on this marvel. I am the monster in the labyrinth, hunting the man who trails the string. It is my father's labyrinth, that he made to trap me, to search empty corridors forever with no escape.

To die in here. But I'll go high. High out of the maze, out of the maze of these city streets. I'll go high on my father's wings. You see. And that's how I'll have the lavish death of my youth."

These were the nights when he was really brilliant, when an untamable life seized him and he seemed a fountain of language and creation. And he was triumphant. He would leap walls and sing in the streets and wink at you and clasp his arms around you. And he could meet anybody and carry on as though they had been friends for years. And exhausted at last, he would watch the sunrise silently and talk in gravelly whispers, playing like a child with all the ideas we ever had concerning things greater than ourselves. He made me feel at those times that he was ill, and gods and angels were ministering to him on his sickbed, and he was talking to them and not to me. That I was like a disheartened family member who could only watch helpless from the corner of the room.

Clement was not like the Courier. Clement was a free and electrified and overflowing man with vigorous limbs who traveled unencumbered and needed carry nothing. And he retained nothing. He could walk away from his apartment never to return and miss nothing. Even at work, he acted as though he might leave any time he chose and find a different job. His freedom was glamorous to me. Pure freedom, however, includes the freedom to carry. I watched curiously to see whether Clement was so free.

Clement was in love with a girl named Catherine, whom he affectionately called Cat. His love was an untroubled, extravagant kind of love that invited Cat to come along and jump in all the world's mud puddles with him, wearing a wild grin and rolled-up pant legs. But he was devoted to her. He lured a remarkable number of women to him and, so far as I know, stayed faithful to Cat. And even if he hadn't, Clement, a man of indefatigable words and zeal, must truly love if he is to keep a silence of himself. If he is to feel shame enough to keep silence.

Catherine lived next door to Clement, in the rooms where Percy once lived. On the centennial, her walls were the next to be opened after mine. She and Clement met as neighbors, but not in the hallway, as ordinary people. There is a crack in the ancient, heavy stone and plaster dividing their rooms. It pours down the wall in a rivulet, a deep portend, and through its curtained flux the other side of life awaits. Woman and hope. I could see three shaded pools where Clement leaned his head and hands to inhale upon his knees a perfume blooming through the wall. He could not see through the opening, but he could smell her deliciousness. And the two of them could whisper, which they did, even though they could walk next door.

One day, as Clement tells it, he was naked and sprawled across the sun-hot floor, bathed in light, reading. He paid little attention to the cleft in the wall before he knew Cat, because he had only worthless neighbors and did not care if someone could see through it. But on that day, he heard singing. A voice he loved for its clarity, true to tone and unornamented, "like a vast field gently rolling, with no flowers but tall sweet grass, fresh and honest," as Clement said to me. I thought Cat's voice so plain as to be uninspired, but this is how Clement loved her—that she was inspired in spite of her lacking talent, that she would sing anyway. In Clement's world, being afraid to sing was a terrible flaw, especially for one who could not sing well. When you cannot sing, enthusiasm for life and expression become the melody. If you are unafraid, then the song is good.

Clement sprung to his feet and began complimenting and wooing her through the rivulet. But he stayed hidden, coming and going at odd times to avoid meeting her in the hall and to preserve her wonder at an unusual and fluent neighbor. After a night of drinks, when jumbled streets and ornate stone seemed lit with diamonds, Clement would beg me, "Let's have a coffee now." And when I protested, he demanded, "No. We must stay out and stay awake and have a coffee. Just one. We've been watching a blurred and milky rainbow of light and faces, and we must get sober to remember what we've seen. Besides, if she was out, she will be in the hall, coming back. She might be lying in wait to discover me. Also, I told her I would be out, so that she could look at men throughout the night and wonder if they were my voice. She might be watching. We should sit below her windows."

"What does she look like?"

"I don't want to know yet!"

The cleft in their shared wall is another reason why I think Clement stayed faithful. He would have to go somewhere else. He does not like to be separated from the backdrop where he sets himself as a hero.

On the morning of the centennial, Clement finished hating me for letting them open my walls right about when the coffee finished perking. Juggling the cups in one hand, he swung past the crack in his wall as the sun glinted from the burnished pot and blinded me.

"Come on, Cat, we're going to see the tragedy," he yelled into empty space.

"I'm dressing," came through the wall, faint and cute.

"I know. I can hear the sun upon my favorite curve of your bared back."

She gave a hopeless giggle. He winked at me as he returned with the steaming cups. "Listen, don't look surprised," he said, "when she comes over."

I hadn't seen Cat in a week or two. "Why?" I asked.

A few nights before, Clement had taken Cat to see Percy's grave. Percy lived only several years after the Courier's death, himself a young victim of illness. He is buried in a cemetery atop one of the hills bordering the river valley. The cemetery runs right to the edge where the land plummets into the valley, opening on a vista of buildings and river and bridges. It is especially beautiful at night.

Cat had never seen the cemetery. Clement thought she should because she lived in Percy's rooms, and the timing was right with the centennial. They walked across the city and up the crooked mess of cobbled and brick streets that clung to the side of the steep hill. Ramshackle homes abutted the streets and seemed to hang from the hillside like a picture hangs from a nail. Near the top, thick trees closed over alleys and lots, so that the sheltered and unused streets have turned almost to dirt. No one has been buried in the cemetery for a long time. The gravestones, writ in many languages, are overgrown. Their caretakers are themselves interred, or else closed up in thin knives of light that penetrate locked shutters, surrounded by all the evidence that the world has stopped turning. People like Clement are the only visitors up there anymore.

Though it is an old immigrant cemetery, it is new in the history of our city. The headstones come from the last millennia, one marked by the desire to live through death, rather than because of death. In the truly old cemeteries, there are no stones. The graves are only small sunken vaults with stairways, filled to ground level with dirt. The stairs are for the soul to walk easily out of the grave. The dead mouths are stuffed with jade, for the ever-green and undying. But Clement preferred a monument.

Clement was hot; the stones were cool. The ground was damp and mossy. He stretched himself upon Percy's stone to look sidelong over the city like a prodigal king, to open his shirt and make steam rise up as proof in the dead night. Cat came to him. She was his hopeless devotee, stark and pitiable beauty. She caressed him with her soft face and lips; she laid her forehead against the heat of his chest. She played her fingers over his pensive face like bouquets, to honor how he made an irreverent bed of dying. He let his head ebb backward until his mouth opened to the heavy air, exposing the long, taut muscles of his neck: tense and coarse like burnt leather, hard like marble, curling, washing against the cinquefoil of his Adam's apple.

She bent low to kiss him. To homage him with tender body. To drape with her unselfish love the flesh that drapes the monuments of death.

The wet, uneven moss gave way beneath her foot. Her legs splayed. Her face crashed against the tombstone. Blood was all over her hands as she tried to see if she had lost any teeth. She had not, and Clement wrapped her face in his shirt. He showed the shirt to me as proof when he told the story. It was full of blood. He said he would not wash it but would wear it like that, on special occasions when he wanted to be sure about life. Meanwhile, her split lip was healing; she was icing it and had an ointment from the doctor. But one of her front teeth had died from the impact. It turned dark in her mouth.

"They're going to have to pull it," Clement said. "She won't smile, but you can see it when she talks, if you look hard. Don't stare—I promised I wouldn't tell you."

Even so, Cat was in good spirits when she came over. "Did Clement tell you about my accident?" she asked coyly, as she entered the room. She knew him so well that she was willing to risk the secret on the chance that it was told. It was easy to understand why Clement was with her—she understood him, and there was something energetic and increasing about her that was like the spring outside.

She bounded toward Clement. Proud of her outfit, she showed off smartly to him. But I was looking at something else as I watched them. Her skin possessed a melting coolness like subsiding snow. Strawberry gold ringlets of hair and green eyes shone like sweet fields in the country where sun piles on rolled hay, bastions of certainty and fertile earth. Her freckles, her mouth, bloomed, early blooms and innocent like crocuses in frost diamonds. Her wound did not mar her but seemed more proof of her life. She crossed the room in a breeze, fresh but humid. Her eyes to me seemed like leaping fountains, like the fountain of buried water leaping skyward, where the Courier received his final charge to carry.

"He said you tripped somewhere," I answered, feigning disinterest in their affairs. Her healing lips twisted toward a smile, but she would not let them open.

Cat was a mystery that enamored me, because of Clement. It was all the jealousy a lover endures for a beloved's past. A new love feels entitled to every moment, even those moments and choices made in ignorance of future love. And desire, denied, feels the same, or else denies the past. But for me, there was no denying what I saw of those two day after day. There was only the question of why it was Clement and not me, a terrible question for a friend you love. A nagging unknown and unknowable intimacy haunted me, a strange desire to know everything. And jealousy can keep you warm. It can become a habit. You can grow hungry for it, if you develop a taste.

Together, we three friends set off to my apartment, to watch the city desecrate its memories. I crossed the Courier's Bridge again that morning, first heading east and now west, approaching the rail lines. First alone, now together. The early sun still glinted off the water, innumerable lucid gems. Unspoiled gems. But a cool morning wind persisted in the abundant light.

Clement mused about the coming revelations as we crossed, "You have to sleep to dream. My friends, we dream so that we torture ourselves to sleep. But gorged on sleep, more sleep will not come. And waking up is cold."

†

"So you were waiting for the Courier?" the officers asked, surprised.

The Conductor of the eight o'clock outbound train stood at attention before the officers. He had a young face—certainly he seemed too young to have risen to such a position as conductor. His uniform was immaculate. A stiff field of fitted navy. A double row of brass buttons lined his chest, looking like a pilgrim path of gold to a cherub's face in the rock of a far-off mountain. He looked at nothing over the shoulders of the officers, with an official air that said he was doing them a favor by keeping the interview formal. His father was the General of the Railways. His name was Faton. He was even younger than he appeared.

"Yes," answered Faton. "We had word from his employer that he should be on the train with a recent parcel. They hadn't known about the delivery earlier, so their courier had rushed off to collect the package and was hurrying to catch the train. They asked, as a professional courtesy, to spare him time."

"How long did you wait?"

"Not long. I can't. The train must be on time. I can't wait for individuals no matter what they may be carrying. That's their affair." Seeing the officers unsatisfied with his answer, he continued, "Five minutes. That is what I waited, because we can make that up en route. We left at eight-o-five, and there was no sign of the man. Even had he appeared on the bridge just then, we would have left anyway—the wheels were already turning. It would have been ten after by the time he boarded, and I'll not be responsible for a late train. Passengers already aboard have connections." He said this last sentence deliberately, evoking the consternation caused the passengers by the police searches and interviews.

"What do you mean there was no sign of the man?" pressed the officers.

"When the train was in order and ready, I took a position on the platform where I could see the west side of the bridge. The Courier was not yet aboard, or at least, no one spoke up and said 'I am the Courier arrived.' And I understand now, from your efforts, that he was not aboard. So, I wanted to see whether he was nearby before I gave the order to pull away. There is a set of steps from the west side of the bridge that leads down to the station below. That's the way anyone in a hurry would have come. I could see those steps as well."

"And what did you see?"

"Nothing. No one."

"What do you mean?"

"No one coming or going. The west end of the bridge was empty."

"How long did you watch?"

"Until I gave the order to depart and swung up on the train as it began to move."

"When did you begin to watch for the Courier?"

"Before eight. I know, because I hoped that we would leave on time."

"Did you leave your post at any point?"

After reflecting a moment, Faton answered, "No."

"So once you began to watch the west end of the bridge before eight, you never took your eyes away from it until the train pulled off."

"That's correct," he said confidently.

"Could you see anything in the middle of the bridge?"

"The lights were not yet lit."

"So you looked?"

"Casually, to see if someone was running across. But I saw nothing."

"Did you hear a splash, or see one in the river? Did you hear a yell for help?"

"The night was calm and still until we pulled away, but I heard neither. I saw no splash."

"If you don't mind," ventured one of the officers, "you've merited your position at a young age."

"I was appointed, same as any conductor."

"By your father?" asked another.

"By my father, same as any other conductor," Faton answered dryly.

When the officers later returned to our own city, they shared with Glaucus what they had learned from the train passengers and staff: there was no case, no jewels, and no Courier; the passengers had little to offer; and Faton had watched the empty west end of the bridge.

Glaucus stopped them, "But it does not preclude that some killer entered upon the bridge before the conductor began his watch. We know the Courier had ample time to make that train; assuming he wanted to, he would have been aboard before it left. That means the Courier was already dead by the time the train pulled away."

"Dead but not in the river," added Melic, striving always for Glaucus's approval. "No one yet has seen or heard a splash in the still water before the train pulled away."

Glaucus grunted assent. "Perhaps. But the body was in the water before the Lamplighter arrived, if we believe him."

"The departing train would be the perfect time to conceal the sound."

"Let us say this much: if the Courier wanted to make the train, then he was dead before the train left. Faton is a useless nepotist." Glaucus threw up his hands. "He tells us only that the Killer was on the bridge before his short watch, and we already know the Killer was on the bridge before the train left. We already know he was alone with the Courier, because no one saw the murder. Naturally, the Killer would want to wait for the train to leave before passing that way—and we see that, despite the risk of discovery, he had time to wait. And though the wait of those few minutes would be agonizing, the train did not hold long. The Killer could have escaped over the west end after the train and before the Lamplighter was the first to discover the blood. Faton's story does not seal the west end of the bridge—he did not watch long enough. Now, assuming instead that the Courier did not want to make the train, there is still no surprise that Faton saw nothing. He is still useless, except he tells us the Killer is not an idiot, which I knew from the moment the Killer chose the bridge. This is discouraging. I had hoped—I had hoped this Faton would have made a liar of someone."

"There is more, Sir. Faton told us something important by what he did not say. You recall, we interviewed the entire staff of the train. Most of them were about their work, but the kitchen staff was at rest. From a porthole, one of the cooks saw Faton leave the train and walk down to the river bank. Faton may have seen more or less of the bridge than he claims."

Glaucus knit his brows. He gave a deep and unhurried sigh.

As he stood at the crown of the bridge the next day, a light fresh wind ruffled Glaucus's hair, and his eyes squinted in the sun. The bright, buoyant day made murder seem impossible.

"We must know where he went, so that we may know if and why he lied. If we know why he lied, we shall know the rest about the Conductor." Glaucus scanned the horizon alongside an obedient Melic. He took only one officer with him, he said, so that he would not be distracted and could think clearly.

"He could not have gone very far, and yet he himself recognized the quick path to the west end of the bridge from the stairs to the train station. So he knew the stairs, and he knew they were fast. He could make himself busy when the train arrived and disappear until five to eight, when he makes a show of holding the train for a man he knew would not come. In between, he goes along the river bank, out of view he believes, and up the steps fast to meet the Courier as he crossed the bridge. Not only does he know there is a fast route to accomplish his task; he also knows that the lights on the bridge were not yet lit. He sees opportunity."

"But would he have set those facts before us if you are right?" asked Melic.

"I do not say I am right, only that it is possible. Moreover, we asked the questions; he did not volunteer the information. And he likely felt compelled to tell most of the truth. Had we caught him lying in a trivial matter, then he would be in greater danger of discovery. He may have told the only lie he had to tell—the one that protects him. He did not expect to have been seen."

Glaucus continued, "Even if he does not lie to conceal murder, he lies for a reason, and we must find it out. If he saw less of the bridge than he says, then we remain where we began: the bridge is sealed on the east end but not the west. But consider if he saw more of the bridge, for a longer time, and he is telling the truth that no one passed the west end. Everyone cannot be right! If Percy is truthful and the Lamplighter is truthful and Faton is truthful, then is the Courier alone on the bridge? Who is the Killer? And if the Courier is not dead, can it be that some unknown victim has not yet come to light? Surely someone, someone must miss a lost person!"

Glaucus scanned the river bank as he grew calm again. "We must also remember," he added, "Faton had information that the Courier came with a parcel, presumably a valuable one if the train is asked to wait. Is this not the first person to know, admittedly, that something of value was upon the bridge at the moment of the murder?" Glaucus thought a moment. "If Faton did not visit this bridge, where else could he go? What else would he need to conceal that is worth lying to officers investigating a murder? The cook looks out a porthole on the river side of the train and sees Faton. Between the river and the rail is only a thin strip of rough earth. If he had meant to reach the city streets behind the train station, he would not fool around on the river side of the train."

"Perhaps Faton was already returned from the bridge and was seeking a place to hide the stolen parcel," suggested Melic. "We searched the train thoroughly, and all its passengers and staff. There was nothing on the train."

"Buried treasure seems a bit romantic for Faton, no?"

"What else then?"

"Yesterday, after the interviews and search of the train, Faton conducted a return train to the city?"

"Yes."

"So he was back last night," observed Glaucus. "He would not wait to obtain anything he had hidden, unless he was afraid of being seen from the bridge. He may yet return. Or there may be a sign, upturned earth perhaps, or something . . ."

The jagged water skipped and wheeled along the lucid flow, wagging millions of speechless silver tongues in the ageless and peaceful light. The land was paper torn in two, an unjoined story, broken like a life at its height.

And the rolling blast of cleansing light poured through the tear. Glaucus felt he was looking at his own eyes in the reflective side of a knife.

The river banks were a mess of mud and reeds, the clotted edge of a story or a wound. Behind that, a thin rim of trees firmed the soil. Then the train rails curved in long, luminescent arcs in tandem with the river. Birds cawed and chirped in the scrub and thorns. They perched on a dilapidated bridge pier of crumbling stone that protruded from the clay lips of the shore. Their calls lulled over the water as in the amphitheater of an ancient, deserted city. Bits of scrap or trash dotted the reeds, where they slowly sank into the soft mud, splinters that would not be extracted until someone tore up the bank generations later.

Almost to the next bridge, right about where the eight o'clock train would have ended while it purred at the station, lay the carcass of an old rusting river barge that had broken loose years ago in a flood. The river rose and snapped its mooring cables like thread—as no weight of the barge could ever have done. It was nothing to the river, a shallow inhale only. The barge drifted free to its resting place, where its bow plowed into the shore. As the river receded, the barge was hard aground, fixed until the next flood. It was not large, but it sunk deep into the earth and sloped down into the river that submerged about half of its deck. It was one with the river bank. Its bow rested in the trees that lined the shore. The trees had gotten root in the mud below the barge and began to entwine it. Trees grew up out of the metal husk. Vines crept across their branches and wrapped the hull, so that it was strangled with fleshy brown and broad green.

"Are those grapes?" asked Glaucus.

"I don't know, sir."

Glaucus returned to his earlier thoughts, "The eight o'clock train will be through here again tonight. Wait here."

"Wait, sir?"

"Yes. Wait and watch." They were standing on the wooden bridge planks that drank in the stain of the Courier's death.

"Stay right here, and let us see if this stain speaks to you."

†

I CROSSED THE COURIER'S Bridge for the second time on his centennial: first to meet Clement and Cat, and then to return with them. It was still early. A full day of hunting lay ahead: my apartment, then Cat's, and finally the grave. The hunters had just unwound themselves well-fed from a garish breakfast, with speeches and history. I was invited but did not attend. I did not need them to tell me the past of my own city.

Spectators attended all the openings. The news was there, malnourished journalists, vain academics, stout city detectives who auspiciously reopened the case with pride and showmanship, artists asked to capture the event and looking for anyone to speak their name, a meager work crew for the demolition and repairs who cursed among themselves, public officials brimming with toothy smiles, a frail but impudent lawyer monitoring the events, my complacent landlord, spouses with casual infidelities among the lot, me, Clement, and Cat. The whole sated group looked like they had died their thousand incremental deaths to stay full.

Despite her split lip, Cat shone gorgeous before the other women wearing their lines of worry. She, so slender and full of curls and spirals, looked like a long pour of hearty cream. The three of us kept to ourselves and challenged their inquiring stares. Even entering my own home, the home of the Courier's own life, we looked like we were sneaking in without tickets. And this was the assembly present at the opening of the Courier's inviolable.

I was thinking, why did I do this? Why did I betray him? If the jewels are there, it will destroy him. But then, if not me, the next one—the next buoyant and momentary youth who took this apartment, or the next unknowing one, after I gave up the Courier's ghost or died myself, or fell in love and fled this solitary room. This room that, like the Courier, dies with its killers only, like we are rooting through the pockets of its corpse. But should the Courier be destroyed, I thought, it should be me to do it, because I love him. Better to be destroyed by the one who loves you. It was, in a way, my duty to labor at this task and deliver it to fruition, so that it could be carried out with honor. I was like a priest that makes a sacrifice holy. I unlocked my door and ushered the crowd inside.

"Why did you do this?" whispered Clement as we were the last to cross the threshold.

"It will exonerate him," I said.

"If the gems are there I'm going to kill you." He was never serious, but he was good at sounding desperate.

My room is meager. A single bed, a wooden dresser with books, my simple desk, a sofa, and a chest that holds my manuscripts and doubles as a table. I couldn't fit much more. There are still communal sinks in the hallway corners from the building's tenement days, where I get a glass of water at midnight. A hundred years ago, when this section of the city was tightly crowded, a single room like mine might have had an extended family living in it. The Courier, however, made a little more money because he was paid for the trust required of him. I know from the building records that he had this room to himself.

One of the city officials prepared to make a speech, and the reporters collected to take down its salient points. The cramped room felt half its size. I cleared my throat loudly and eyed a man who picked up a poem that lay on my desk. "Nice desk," he said—made of straight lines of pine and varnished a cherry brown. He did not seem ashamed.

"This is an exciting day," began the official. "Everyone knows that today is the one-hundredth anniversary of our city's great unsolved mystery: the disappearance of a huge cache of jewels on the Wayfair Bridge. We are here in the room once let by the Courier who carried those jewels. As we've been told by our parents and grandparents, and as our centennial re-opening of the investigation has confirmed from old police records, the Courier started across the bridge with the parcel containing the jewels. He was never seen again, nor were the jewels. A death was reported on the Wayfair Bridge because of a large blood stain, but a body was never found. Was it a hoax? If it was the Courier who died, where is his body? If another was killed, how was the victim not missed? If the Courier was killed and robbed, how is it that every suspect lived out the rest of their lives before the eyes of our city? They did not flee. They were not rich. In fact, some died as paupers. If the Courier took the jewels, how did he live the rest of his life without discovery, without seeing any of his family or loved ones again, as they claimed? Why did he never appear again as a rich man? Why did no one report a suspicious attempt to trade in a large quantity of jewels without the proper papers?"

He paused for effect, his eyebrows high as mountains and his lips pursed like he had a giant jewel hidden in his mouth. I could tell he felt like he was making history, whereas I thought history was making him. And I deeply wished for him to be made a fool. I know it was my selfishness. I called out in my heart to the Killer himself: kill him, kill him, spill the Courier's blood and take the jewels, take them fast and run, so they will not be in this room. I wished the Courier's death in his own defense, I admit. And when you stop his breath, Killer, stop also this theft—this thieving speech that agrees upon a new lie of history. Kill him, I thought, and teach this poor fool a centennial lesson that I am the one to write the Courier, to give him life beyond the ceasing of his breath. The Courier who lives in the hidden truth, in the unanswered question. He is mystery. But this foolish man was a pane of glass, a barrier only, seen through and easily shattered, and better to let in the wind and scents of flowers.

"Some have proposed—some of our city's respected academics and police officials who have examined the case—they have proposed that the Courier took the gems. Perhaps he killed an unknown or immigrant witness who could have testified that he was out-waiting the train on the bridge. Perhaps he killed no one but left a token of a death that did not occur."

I hated how they robbed him of his death. Even Glaucus, with all his scrutiny, would never have done such a thing so brazenly.

"Fleeing with the jewels, the Courier had enough time to hide them. No one knew he was missing until the train was searched the next morning. But perhaps, after hiding the jewels, he did not have the opportunity to retrieve them or enjoy them. Maybe an accident happened, maybe he became scared and fled without them, maybe he was killed by someone else who knew he had the jewels, a jealous accomplice. Maybe he was killed by someone for whom he stole the jewels, to protect them. Maybe the ones who hired him to steal chose to kill rather than pay him, but they could not find where the Courier hid the quarry. Maybe the Courier lied to his killers, so that he might die with his hidden secret. No matter how his end came, the Courier had few possessions and no place of his own to hide anything outside this room. In a cavity of these walls, beneath these floorboards, the cache could be waiting. Waiting through a hundred years of ordinary people walking right above them, sitting just a foot away from them." He indicated me. "We are on the hunt for our city's greatest treasure!"

As the official concluded his speech with a flourish, the demolition crew had already fanned out and begun tapping the walls and listening for hollowness. Apparently, they felt the official was too longwinded. Everyone waited restlessly as the men tapped and listened all over the walls, their trained ears waiting for the past to speak. My few pieces of furniture were pushed into the center of the room, and the workmen moved around the puzzle in carousel.

"These outside walls are plaster on solid masonry—no seams, no breaks," murmured the team leader as he listened intently. "These inside walls are plaster and lathe. Contiguous. I don't hear any changes. No anomalies." Silence continued as the men came round to the last wall. I watched Cat smiling close-lipped where she stood in a ray of sunshine.

"Ah!" started the leader of the demolition team, still probing. "We have something here. A space. A foot wide. A foot high, roughly. There's plaster here, but not on lathe. Boundaries seem irregular." A thrill rippled through the tightly-gathered crowd.

"Open it," ordered the official impatiently.

"I give the orders in my home," I yelled at him without thinking. Everyone turned, shocked, and embarrassment blazed on my face. Clement looked suddenly hopeful.

"You gave us permission; you signed—" began the attorney, like an insolent man who believes in laws made of words.

"I don't care about your rights," I said, as I approached the wall. "I mean—you've waited a hundred years . . ." I laid my palms flat against the coolness, then my cheek against the place they said was hollow. I closed my eyes and held my breath.

"He is listening for a heartbeat," said Clement with all seriousness.

I imagined the Courier in the solemnity of his home, his life in this temple we were about to defile. I imagined him returning in the early morning after carrying his secrets. Did he come home to silence? Did love wait sleeping in his bed? I imagined his heavy task writ in his face, obscured by long and luxuriant strawberry-gold curls that bathed him in green sleep. I imagined them together in the morning light that streaks my floorboards, these unbroken walls looking down upon their vibrant undefeated youth. But no—that is my own forlorn wanting. I have transposed myself again.

I imagined him alone in the long afternoons, drunk with the luxury of boredom, laid out on the cooling wood like Clement does, watching clouds travel the sapphire sky, shouts of children in the playground below playing in his ears as they played in mine when I wrote at my desk. No.

I felt his oneness. I felt he loved me as I loved him. That he was forever frozen in the transfiguration of his task, alive and endless and vital. Against the wall, I laid my head upon his chest that dared to fill with light and breath and to exhale this room. This figment. This little tabernacle enclosing the jewel of life, borne upon the river of time, carried upon the skyline. This lost and dying kingdom, mystery, which is nothing without him, without me.

"Open it," I ordered, and separated myself from the unbroken secret. "It's empty."

The demolition team approached. A workman positioned himself before the wall with a sledge in his hand. The leader nodded at him. He nodded back and raised the sledge above his head, where it hung. He had me in the corner of his vision. I closed my life like the first pain of love, welling up and overflowing with names and will and unfamiliar hopes and unrequitedness. The workman seemed emboldened as I stood firm for the blow, as though it were me waiting to receive my pain.

"I hate you," whispered Clement as the sledge fell, so his words were part of the impact and intractable. I looked at him, and he gave me a puzzled face, motioning with his head that there were better things to watch.

The sledge cracked and depressed the plaster. A second blow broke through. The ribs of my apartment shook as though commending their sanctity. A wraith of dust oozed from the opened hole and fanned out at our feet. The man slowly lifted the heavy sledge out of the debris.

†

THE RIVER WAS GREEN as Cat's eyes beneath the deep sapphire of the morning sky. At a distance, dredges searched diligently for a victim. "Yes?" asked Glaucus, who stood on the bridge deck in the dawn of another new day.

Melic had stood his post upon the bridge throughout the previous day and night, his friends bringing him coffee and flour-dusted bread with dried, salty meats, and later in the night some unleavened bread and wine. "No one has come, sir, to retrieve anything from the river's edge. But there was a strange thing last night. There's a light inside the barge. It came on after dark. I could see it through the sunken portals, not in the ones above the water. It flickered like a fire."

"And no one came or went?"

"No."

"So someone has been in there all along."

"It seems."

"Did you see Faton with the train last evening?"

"No, Sir."

"No?"

"No. But I heard murmurs from the staff on the train. I moved to the part of the bridge above the track to see and hear all I could. Faintly, I heard talk about Faton being advanced to another post, and they were glad to see him go. There was also a girl, one of the maids aboard, who listened from a distance but said nothing. I'm not sure, but I thought I saw her wiping away tears."

Glaucus thought for a long moment, palming the stubble on his early morning face. "Well, I think we know what's next. Come on." And he hurried toward the west end of the bridge, down the steps to the empty train platform. Glaucus bounded over the rails gilt with morning, while Melic tottered to catch up, legs stiff from standing through the night. They pushed through the brush at the shore until they came to the barge. Nettles and pollen stuck to their trousers.

The barge had lain beached so long that dirt filled its hold. The trees rooted in its body grew enormous, larger than they appeared from a distance. Their network of shade spread over the barge and kept it cool beneath the dazzling sun. The hull was rusted but solid. Grape vines wrapped it tightly and entwined the arbor of the trees. Their broad leaves cloaked the long flanks of the hull, and hushed in the light wind that lulled along the water. Near one of the portals, the earth was clear and hard, the way a trail in the woods takes definition. Unabashed, Glaucus rapped heavily on the portal and rapped again, invoking his authority.

A slow beating began, a heart within the felled giant. Footsteps. The steps were unhurried. The officers waited with breathless anticipation.

"If it is the Courier, he'll be armed," said Melic. Glaucus, though defenseless, did not stir. He faced the portal unflinchingly. A scrape of metal sounded as the old latch twisted within. The hull resonated with the creaking of stiff, rusted hinges. The portal swung open.

A tiny elderly man with long white hair looked out from the darkness of the hull.

"Inspector Glaucus," he said, his worn voice as raspy as the hinges. "I thought you might visit me."

"Who are you?" demanded Glaucus.

"Because you have come, I will tell you everything I know. Come in." He stepped back from the portal so they could enter. Glaucus did not hesitate; he had already in his long career found himself in every type of squalor. But Melic was slow in following. The portal was small and hard to manage. Beyond it, the interior of the hull ran alongside the open cargo hold. It was narrow and long. The young officer had the intense feeling that there was no easy way of escape, and he kept his hand on his weapon. At the end of the long extent of the hold, the interior opened to a large area that once would have been beneath the bridge, at the rear of the barge. The room sloped in two directions and lay beneath the water line. A line of condensation ringed the askance room and showed where the cooler water licked the metal. A glass portal looked out at streaks of light piercing the azure water.

In the center of the room, a clean-burning lantern flickered on a table. The table was bolted to the slanted floor, but its stem was bent so that the table-top was roughly level. Four bolted chairs that surrounded it remained on angle. Another lantern hung from the ceiling at the lowest corner of the room, above a cot with a deep pile of blankets. On the high side of the room, a broken door led to a stall where the man kept a bedpan. A portal in the stall looked out just above the water's level. It was open and let in waves of cool air. Near the door was a wash basin mounted to the wall on ornate swirls of iron. A pitcher of water stood balanced inside the lopsided basin.

The space was not dirty. It did not smell. It was bright and neat and bare. The man, destitute as he was, seemed proud. The place was his home.

"You like my suite," he asked. When they did not answer, he added, "You are just like it. You came the way they bring me food. A kind young girl brings it to me every Sunday. It is hard now, for me to get out of the small portal." But Glaucus was surprised by the way the man moved gingerly about the awkward room.

"You saw my lantern?" the man asked.

"Yes."

"I kept my lanterns lit so you would come. I did not cover the portals at night. I usually do." Like the Lamplighter, he spread his undefiled light into the darkness of death.

He dipped his hands in the wash basin and dried them on a towel that hung from it. From beneath his cot he produced a small folding stove, the kind hikers might carry. From some netting that hung from the roof, he gathered a fresh egg. He lit the gas stove with a match, then broke and fried the egg in his one cast iron pan, a single-serving size, deep black with age. He spent his time preciously. Waves of inquiry and excitement overspread his face as he tested the roundness of the egg, listened to it crack, inhaled its fresh warm scent. The two others watched in amazement.

"Why did you want us to come?" asked Glaucus at last.

"My name is Bacca. You know, I have lived here a very long time, and people have not noticed. This barge is anchored in tree roots, but once—" he rapped upon the hull, "it traveled far up the river, as far as is navigable and you can go no further. And it has gone down the river, mingled with other water, seen the great and final sea. Believe the old myth: the river does go down into the earth. It's just that the world below is a great mimicry of the true, and one has to look very keenly, like you might look for a hair fracture in a mirror."

"You know about the Courier," said Glaucus.

"That," Bacca said with a flourish, "is your crime." He loosened the little pad of cooked egg with his fingertips, salted it, rolled it, and forced it into his mouth in a single bite. His grizzled jowls worked vigorously as he contemplated the empty space with awed eyes. "Delicious," he said when his mouth was again vacant. Every word he spoke rolled with a slow wry savor. "I'll tell you a story. This barge was beached by a very young boy, not by this gentle river."

Melic shifted uneasily. He had already been awake all night. His new, young wife waited for him. But Glaucus listened patiently. This story was all he had to do.

"A crew of young and sterling men worked this barge, with arms and grips like steel. And they were full of valiant and poisonous vigor. They were near the river's head, deep in a yawning and arcane forest, hauling long raw trees, for the saw mills. In a remote town where they passed, there was a boy. A fair boy with long, blond hair. He played and ran wild about the forest like a nymph, but he was a frightened boy. On warm days, the men would strip as they worked the heavy saws in twos. And the boy would watch sadly at a distance, not for the tall trees, but for the men." Drawing out elongated words, Bacca seemed to look them through.

"Well, the men knew where they were going, a long way down the river, to places where a boy like that was worth a lot of money. They could keep him on the ship and use him, or sell him outright. And he would be theirs for the journey at any rate. One of the men showed the boy the sharpness of the saws out among the trees on the day they left. He let the curious boy feel the pointed edge, then grabbed the child up, tucked the boy under his monstrous arm, and carried him struggling helpless to the barge. The boy cut his finger on the sharpness he fondled as he was snatched away. The saw, it was left behind. When the men came back the next year it had rusted and never cut again."

Bacca nodded ominously, drawing one fingertip slowly across his lips. "The men came down the river. The boy cowered among the felled trees, and they let him hide. They threw him food, and he ate among the rough bark. He had nowhere to go; they could wait.

"The men came to this city, and the siren city intoxicated them and made them thirsty and made them hungry and made them impatient. The boy fled to the bow, where he stood tall, charged between the lights flanking the river. The city lights were as spectral galaxies, feathered spangles resting on his frail shoulders. He looked like the power of death itself was in his becalmed splendor. As they reached for him, the bow shifted violently, toppling the logs and the men upon them. Some were trapped. In the following chaos, the barge ran hard aground. And the boy was gone."

Hauntingly, Bacca stared as though he saw the fierce and frail boy god winged with galaxies. "The grape vines grew immediately from the ground and entwined the hull, so it would be captive until it rotted to nothing. I came back after many years. After seeing all the world, I came back, to fill this empty shell and live the moment of my liberation. When the grapes grow, their juice inside is already fermented. I eat them all day and stay drunk on their sweetness."

"Why," said Glaucus deliberately, "did you want us to come here?"

Old Bacca looked at him, lingering. Haltingly he said, "So you could ask me what happened upon the bridge."

"What happened upon the bridge?"

"A woman wept."

"Upon the bridge!"

"The bridge was shrouded in darkness before the Lamplighter came. But she wept just the same."

"Who?"

"This was not the first time the Courier would take the train, no? And I am out here, watching through the portholes, while those in the train think there is only a silent river. And, you see, I am fixed while they are moving on the river of the rails. And now a woman is weeping."

"What did you see upon the bridge?" demanded Glaucus abruptly.

"Only that her heart was pierced."

"You saw the murder."

"The bridge was shrouded in darkness."

"So you did not."

"The bridge was shrouded in darkness," repeated Bacca, who spoke at less than half the speed of Glaucus.

"Did you see a body fall into the river? Did you hear a splash?"

"I heard the woman weeping, and the deafening train."

"Why did Faton come here," demanded Glaucus, taking a guess that Faton had been on his way to see Bacca when a cook spied him from the train.

"Faton did not come here. I have nothing I can offer Faton."

"But you know him."

"Of course I know him, but he did not come to me."

"Who then?"

"Ask him."

"Did he go upon the bridge?"

"No."

"How do you know that—if the bridge was dark? Why are you aware of his movements?"

"Because the west side of the bridge is above the train platform, bathed in the lights of the platform, and I can see it. And I can see the stairs. And there was no one on the stairs, and there was no one that came or went on the west end."

"When?"

"From before the train left until the crowd gathered at its crown."

"Then why did you tell us the bridge was dark?"

"The only the place that matters was dark."

"And you did not see Faton."

"Faton did not come here."

"Then you saw him. Where did he go?"

"You will have to ask him."

"Why did you want us to come here? You don't say much, for someone who wanted to be asked about a murder."

"You are a wise and captivating man. And I am an old man. And I wanted you to know. There was no one who came or went on the west end of the bridge. Not until I saw the tiny light of the Lamplighter's torch fall and extinguish. And then the people came. And now a woman weeps."

"Was there a splash then?"

"The Lamplighter's torch bounced on the deck then fell into the river, as I listened to his frightened cries."

"You heard it."

"I heard his cries."

"Then you saw it?"

"It was very dark."

"Then how do you know!"

"There was a splash. There must have been because his torch fell from his hand. What else would seek the water but the flame that wants to be quenched? I realize that I know quite little, but these small and disparate things are all I have."

Melic came forward, maddened with Bacca's tortuousness, "You won't mind, then, if we look around?"

"Leave him his dignity," said Glaucus.

†

WE PEERED INTO THE gaping cavity—into the catacomb of things destroyed. Plaster wisps unwound round our ankles. Cold history oozed from the long unlit space, and the bridge of my nose tingled with coolness as I leaned in with the crowd. At first, the depths were shrouded in darkness, but then the man with the sledgehammer exhaled into the opening and stirred away the remainder of the churning dust. Light penetrated the hollow.

On a bed of brick, beneath the fleeing shadows was, not the mahogany box, but a small leather journal. I reached first, dipping into the cool liquid of the long-unbreathed air, and retrieved the journal. It was covered with a fine dust but otherwise pristine, preserved in the dark and cool dryness. It had been waiting how long, I wondered, for this moment. What face, what era was the last to look at these pages. I gently unworked a leather strap that twisted round to bind the journal closed. Free, the supple leather dangled like untied fetters, and I opened the pages.

There was, first, a little map made in a child's script, and with a child's exaggeration of the size and proximity of its landmarks. It showed, not continents and famous cities, but intimate places: a swimming hole, a pasture with a scalloped wood fence, a cabin, a flowering tree. And a river. A river that sprang from the ground at the high left corner of the page, as at some exotic and mystical distance. It wound down through a city, apart from the important features of the map.

The following pages showed sketch after sketch of the little cabin, all in the same child's hand, with talent improving over time. The cabin surrounded by reaching flowers, then crowded by the thick, full summer. Then the trees were shedding leaves, and the porch was full of baskets brimming with harvest. Then the snow banked high against the cabin walls, and the stripped trees held their ragged spines to the blow. Page after page covered every detail of this little sanctuary: fallen leaves collected in the corner of a window, tulips around a little stone well, fruit littering the ground beneath a laden tree, and high grass where, far off, two bodies lay free in the sun and the sweetness of the rustling stalks.

There was no name in the journal. Who the boy or girl was, where the child went, what life the child lived, and in what strange far corner of the world the child finally lay down: all are unknown. A number of the last journal pages were blank. Then on the final page, in a new script rough and angular, it read: *Found upon the ground in the locked abandoned cabin on this site, demolished.* A date followed, well older than the Courier's death.

Our ancient city has steadily swallowed the surrounding country by centuries, as we uncoil from the city's timeless center. Underfoot is that ancient and rural ideal, the child's paths worn running through the grass and shrub, the kind and pregnant mother shading her eyes on the rustic porch, the toiling father bringing life from the fields. Underfoot now are their lives. But the child's scrawl was perfectly free, unspoiled, an endless landscape that reached outward forever and would not be consumed. A childhood innocence, a paradise, that could not be improved or replaced, that would not be buried, would not retreat into structure, that was beyond shelter. That would not, against all odds, stay in walls. A nameless Eden.

My guess is that one of the workmen constructing the building must have preserved the journal, wishing it to remain on the site where it belonged, in the place of a lost past that the journal itself preserved. This workman enshrined the child's simple beauty in the architecture that would destroy it—a structure that, itself, could not stand forever. My room is the temple of the Courier's life that my book, this book, preserves; it is the place in which he lived and moved. But this child's book preserves a more distant past before that temple. Another book, simpler and more honest.

"All right, then, let's move on to the floorboards," said the city official.

Nobody asked me for the journal, so I kept it. I still have it today. I look at it and listen to the birds outside my window and the children that still play in the streets, treading their own paths over the same ground. I do not look outside; I listen and rebuild our city in my mind from nothing. I create as I speak. I fill the wild ideal with a city of the heart, the eternal city of the worn myths. It is a beautiful citadel lush with soaring stone arabesques, where people are free from falsity and toil, to stroll the promenades hand in hand and vibrate with the all-speaking beauty.

"Go ahead," prodded the official, barking at the reluctant crew of workmen.

I had not realized that they intended to tear up the floorboards. Everyone looked at me in case I should protest, but I held tight the little leather journal and decided that I could say nothing so eloquent as their failure.

"There's nothing under there," said the leader of the demolition team. "These boards are all tongue-in-groove, held with their original square nails. The nails are the same; the boards are the same. They're tight. None of the tongues are cut. There's no sign of anything unusual."

"Tear it up," I said, "Tear it up. You won't find him." And I left my home at their mercy, Clement and Cat at my side.

†

GLAUCUS SPOKE RAPIDLY AS he rounded a corner, striding out over uneven cobbles. Several members of his loyal cadre orbited him. "The gems were not there. He brought us there, he expected us."

"A perfect ruse, no?" responded another officer. "If he knew we would eventually come, why not feign cooperation?"

"No," said Glaucus. "He would anticipate our instinct to search. He would expect it as protocol. Feign cooperation, I will allow. But to do it, he need not take the risk of having the proof of his involvement right there with us. If the jewels were ever there, he had ample time to move them somewhere else before he put on a show for us. Rather than look like dullards who only ransack and accuse, respect will make this man talk."

"Sir," ventured Melic, "you were like the old man's confessor. No one knows him or listens to him, except maybe this person who brings him food. He wished to tell you about his life more than he wished to tell you what he saw. Can we expect that a man who wishes to interest you would tell everything, accurately?" For the first time during the investigation, the thoughts of the junior officer made Glaucus pause. Instead of the prideful reaction I might have expected, Glaucus savored the thought.

"He may. He may also be cryptic enough to hold that interest as long as possible. Cryptic he certainly was, but his type of solitude can change a man. He may also exaggerate, to create more interest than is warranted, but how would he know that the happenings on the west side of the bridge are just now critical to us." At last Glaucus said, "Here is Bacca: a poor man who may not be poor, an old man who says he is trapped in his strange home but moves spryly about its awkward kilter, a hermit in the heart of a sprawling city, who lives half above water and half below, a penitent who makes lengthy confessions that tell us nothing. It is possible that Bacca went up to the bridge and Faton went somewhere else, and Bacca told a story about the vacant west end to blind us with the impossible. Or perhaps Faton did go to the bridge, and he bought an alibi from a poor man who does not know how to lie. Perhaps Bacca tells the truth, and no one was on the west end of the bridge—in which case, I am glad that we keep our tight grip on Percy and the Lamplighter. How do we know what is true? But I think," he paused, "I think you may be right, that Bacca wants to be important. But that means he wants to share what little things he has that may be important. And since we have little else, we might as well begin with the girl who cries."

They stood before a grey door with four rectangles in baroque trim, smothered by many coats of spalling paint. It was not hard to discover the identity of the girl seen crying outside the train by Melic upon the Courier's Bridge. The police went to the railway with a description, and now they were outside her door.

Her name was Meda. She lived in a one-room apartment carved out of the rear second floor of a stately, deteriorating row house. The present home owners were not as wealthy as the builders, so they walled off their second staircase and the rear room upstairs to make a rental. A gate between two similar houses led down a narrow brick path to her side entrance. Gaps in the wood of the door showed it had been kicked in to evict a prior tenant; the separated wood was nailed together loosely. The trim around the door, curving and swirling up to a demure roof, was tumbling down in splinters. Glaucus rapped quickly. Little footsteps, light and fast, tickled down the stairs, then delicate hands fumbling with the chain and lock.

Meda looked elegant and wholesome, beautifully simple and direct. Her fresh unblemished skin was scented cream and strawberries, and her elusive face seemed ever to bloom to a final look, then continued to bloom. Fleeting expressions, where she wore plain emotions, transformed her from wise woman, to mischievous child, to hopeful girl, and back again. She danced the door open and was surprised to discover the officers. The thin fabric of her frayed dressing gown swayed to a rest. Her perfume wafted into the dirty street.

"I'm sorry—I was expecting someone," she said.

"I am Inspector Glaucus of the police. These are my associates. As you might expect, we are here about the death upon the Wayfair Bridge."

Meda seemed to shudder.

"May we come in?"

"Yes, of course."

She turned and led them up the tall and narrow stairs to her room above. The compact stairs had high rises and shallow treads, and the men nearly crawled up them. Ahead, sunlight streaming through the apartment windows lit Meda's slender form. Her shadowy silhouette surfaced inchoate through the translucent gown, swaying in the febrile fabric. Glaucus stared at the mirage until a ray of sun caught him from between her knees and hurt his eyes.

Meda pulled on a cloth robe when they assembled in the small room above. She motioned for Glaucus to sit with her at a café-sized table, and his two companions took their places, leaning gruffly against the wall behind.

"What can I do?" she said, to break the silence.

Glaucus gave her a solemn look while calculating her honesty and his approach. "I will be fair and direct with you, as you deserve. You are a maid on the regular eight o'clock train out of the city?"

"Yes."

"But you did not work the night of the murder. We know because we interviewed everyone upon the train. We have witnesses who have seen you with the Courier," he lied, "and now you weep on the platform where he was expected that night—again, we have seen you. Why don't you tell me what happened." He spoke with a paternal sternness. In Glaucus's estimation, persons of Meda's clarity wished to do right, even after they had done wrong. He thought she would return to authority.

Her raw well of sorrow reopened, and a single, shining tear fell like a star from her jeweled eyes. "What do you mean?"

"To begin, where were you the night of the murder?" Though he sounded assured, Glaucus was struck by the thinness of his words. While his hard, bright eyes fixed on Meda, he reminded himself that he did not know who was dead. He did not know if someone was dead.

As he stared motionlessly at her, a familiar panic coursed through Glaucus regarding near-infinite possibilities upon which he did not speculate openly. They raced around his restless mind. Someone may have been badly wounded only. There was a lot of blood upon the bridge, but there was no body. So far, the dredges had found nothing in the river. Could someone have been stabbed but escaped? Could someone survive a fall from the bridge? Did the Courier fight off a robber then run or swim, injured, with his parcel, only to collapse and die in some blind end of the city's interminable labyrinth? Was his corpse lying there now, curled about the jewels? Had some unknown and unknowable person taken the box from his dead hands and disappeared—had they taken the box with a promise to the Courier's dying breath that they would return it to the owner? Would you break a promise to a dying man for those jewels? Or what if the person who took the box from the Courier is yet to step forth? What if he steps forth today? What if some unrelated person was stabbed but lived, in sheer coincidence with the Courier's decision to abscond with the jewels? But where did he go? Did he jump? Can the witnesses be trusted?

No, thought Glaucus, that is the genius of the Killer. That is the brilliance of bridges. That is the victim of two-faces, who is alive and is dead, who is known and is unknowable. The Courier who carries but does not transmit, does not make it across the bridge—and yet there is a message here in blood. I am lost just exactly as the master Killer wishes me to be.

Everything reduced to the same simple point for Glaucus: one or more persons had to exit the bridge—the Courier, the victim, the Killer, or some combination thereof. Either Percy and the Lamplighter, or else Bacca and Faton, were lying. Someone had to be lying. And as all these possibilities mercilessly assailed Glaucus's brain, he kept his eyes fixed mercilessly upon Meda, tightening his jaw to conceal his perplexed mind. As the Killer preyed upon Glaucus, he preyed upon her. Each ravenous mystery consumed its smaller questions, as large animals eat small. As the Courier himself consumed the Killer.

"I was here," she said.

"Alone?" asked Glaucus, after a length of vacant staring that conveyed incredulity.

"I was waiting for someone."

"The same person you expect today?"

She hesitated. "Yes."

"We'll see if he comes. Why does a woman like you weep?"

"Because someone is dead."

"Is that all?" When she did not answer, Glaucus asked her to tell him about the Courier.

Meda composed herself, wiped her eyes, tucked her hair behind her ears. She studied Glaucus, as a hungry person looks at food unsure of its safety. Glaucus was the law. "He was very good," answered Meda brokenly. "I believe he loved me, but not like that."

Glaucus encouraged her to go on.

"I thought I wanted to marry him," she blurted out, pained with embarrassment, "though he never asked me. And, I loved him—I loved him, but I was afraid to marry him, because of how much he carried. There was not enough of him, I thought, to carry me alongside the secrets that he carried, day after day. I was afraid of a man labored with secrets. Innumerable secrets throughout a life." She added haltingly, "A short life."

"You would meet him on the train?" asked Glaucus.

"I haven't worked there very long. But there were a couple of times that he would take the eight o'clock. I would wait for him, hoping that he would be aboard. And he would find me at my work, making up an empty cabin—where we could talk alone. I told him we could get married, just before things became hard for me. You found me in this tiny room, and it is tiny, but this is like heaven to me. I should have died. This city is very cruel, and that changed everything."

"Tell me your story."

"Well," she hesitated, "I would not have told anyone before, before he died. But I'll tell you now. And maybe, you'll understand everyone, and it will help you to know who is innocent."

"When I was little, my mother died," she began, "I don't know when exactly. I remember her feeling, not her face—a feeling of absolute certainty and safety. My father married another woman. She is young, and she is jealous. When I was still little, I didn't matter to her. But as I grew, she noticed me. She noticed how I looked; she saw how others noticed me. In front of my father, she praised me, but alone in the house, she scowled at me."

"It is difficult for me to say," Meda went on, "I don't know how to describe it but that she wanted to be supreme. And I believe she hated me for my youth and for my looks and for my father's love. One day, when we were alone, she told me—I can hardly say it. I don't believe it." She choked, "She told me my father was attracted to me—as a woman. She told me I should leave the house because she could not restrain him. I didn't believe her, but one day he was looking at me and told me, 'what a woman you've become.' I would have always thought it was a father's pride. I never would have even considered . . . but she poisoned everything. And I became unsure and afraid. Every time he would hold me or come near me in the kitchen or in the hall I felt ill, because of what I suspected and, even more, because I suspected it."

"Meanwhile," Meda continued, "my father's wife told him I was promiscuous. She told him I had given myself away to boys around town, for fun or for money," anger rose through the dampness of her tears, "and that I shamed him and shamed our family. She swore to him she caught me at night in my room with . . . with . . ." They understood she could not say the Courier's name for sadness.

She stiffened. "I know because my father told me when he threw me out of the house. First, his kindness stopped. Then it seemed like he never touched me, ever. I could see how she kindled his disgust. I denied everything, but it was useless. At the threshold, my father kissed me on the mouth as he told me he would never see me again." She sobbed, "I was put out into the street with the clothes on my back . . ."

Glaucus asked her, where was the Courier.

"Carrying his secrets. They were his bride. I was alone. I couldn't spend the nights in an alleyway. My youth and my innocence trampled, raped, the little life in my mother's arms destroyed, made a ruin by the cruel death of the world. I would die like my mother. I would give birth in a pool of blood in a dark and blind alley, and I would die awash in the cries of an abandoned child."

"But you did not die," said Glaucus.

She composed herself again. "Percy found me. I went around the cafés, to stay in a clean, lighted place until they should kick me out. To stay as long as I could in safety. You wouldn't believe how guilty they look when they ask you to leave."

"Oh, but I would," said Glaucus.

"I stayed awake several nights like that, in the ones that never close, shooing away the shabby men that hovered about like flies. What they must have thought of me . . . And then Percy recognized me somewhere, I don't remember where, alone and without a coat. I had no make-up, and my eyes were draped in shadows. He pays for this place where I live. He bought me clothes and sends food, when he can, and for the rest I get by with the little I make on the train. But I am a good seamstress, and I think that will be, maybe. We've talked now about marriage. Percy is also good. He misses his friend."

"So now you love Percy," observed Glaucus.

"Percy saved me."

Glaucus thought of rivers—when they join. How one's name is given up. Its life drained into another. And a new river is formed. He saw faces in the tumult of the flow.

"What do you know about Faton?" Glaucus spit the question suddenly, and it seized her.

Meda's eyes turned to scorn, "An arrogant man. What about him?"

"How often have you seen him?"

"As I did my work, the same as anyone."

"He did not see more of you, then, on the train?"

"I have no interest in an arrogant man."

"Faton did not also wish to find you, making up an empty cabin."

Meda's eyes were lucid wells. She said, distantly, "He is a powerful man. But I do not love him."

"I understand," answered Glaucus, who became easier. "Do you know anything about Faton's actions on the night of the murder?"

"No. I wasn't on the train."

Glaucus gripped her in his beneficence, a beneficence he himself caused her to need. It was his own caress of Meda. And from the favor, the ownership, of his discretion, he asked the things he wished most to know.

"Why weren't you on the train that night?"

"I was sick." She answered as though she had no idea it could implicate her.

"When was the last time you saw the Courier before the murder?"

"At Percy's," she sighed, but now from a depth of discovered shame.

"When?" Glaucus repeated.

"That day."

Glaucus kept his rhythm without showing surprise. "How did it happen?"

"I was visiting Percy. I made just a little lunch. He came by unexpectedly and found us there. But he didn't stay long. He excused himself and said he had a new delivery. Something to carry."

"Was he surprised to discover the two of you?"

"I don't know."

Glaucus asked, with precision, what the Courier had said about the delivery.

"Only that it was sudden and that it was important. He was supposed to meet a man by a fountain in one of the squares, and he was taking the eight o'clock."

"And so you did not work?"

Meda said nothing. How could she have gone to work—the pain of the Courier was too great, of telling him, the sight of him, coursing with vitality, the wish of his voice caressing her in secret, in an empty cabin, in every vacant and empty place. Her modest maid's uniform, her cheeks and neck efflorescent in the moonlit landscape racing past the large windows. She shone upon the river of the coursing world, too limpid, too directional to invade her nakedness.

"And all this was said at Percy's that afternoon?" asked Glaucus.

"Yes."

"And then?"

"He left."

"Did he know what he carried?"

"I don't know."

"Did you?"

"No."

"And Percy?"

"Returned to work."

"And what did you do?"

"I waited."

"Why didn't you come to us?"

"I didn't think you would know me."

Despite all she had laid bare, Glaucus wondered if he did.

†

WE WERE TRAVELING TO Percy's old room as I crossed the Courier's Bridge for the third time that day. Clement lingered behind, scuffing the ground, while I walked with Cat.

"I only agreed to this because you did," she said. "I thought you would get some good material to write. I didn't realize it would upset you so much."

"Thanks." I smiled at her. Her eyes were twinkling as the sun cascaded off the river.

"I didn't think it mattered. You seemed so certain there was nothing to find."

"Well—everyone has doubts."

"I'll stop them," she resolved, valiantly. Her genuine way of speaking, its lightness, and the purity of it—I adored her.

"Let them go," I said. "They have their own doubts to deal with. Maybe someone will find something, and it will cure me."

We walked behind my cousin, Rabbit, whom we discovered unexpectedly at the bridge. He leapt into my arms when he recognized me. He clamped hugs on Cat and Clement as he brimmed with joy. His mother, my aunt, now led him by the hand, corralling his tireless and un-directional wonder. Rabbit is in his mid-teens, but no one would know because of his smallness. He is unchallenged in the ways that everyone else is: he loves selflessly and immediately, and he forgives effortlessly. He holds no grudges and cannot stay angry. He trusts everyone.

Rabbit lives in a world in which life and story bridge seamlessly. In ordinary places, he looks out for monsters and heroes and his favorite fictional characters. Unreal things frighten him, like grotesque statues found on old architecture about the city. But a person would not frighten him, no matter how grotesque their suffering. His perception of the world must be like our city's myths and gods that live inside our modern time—or our stories in which heaven comes to earth.

Rabbit attends a school that teaches him life skills, such as handling money, making dinner, and speaking effectively. He is the most popular student in his school. He excels at math and loves to be in the school performances. He is a natural entertainer, who sings terribly and without shame. He memorizes whole performances of plays, concerts, and dances. At holidays, he performs them whether someone is watching or not, singing and dancing his way across crowded rooms from start to finish. He packs more excitement than seems possible into the monotone of his voice.

Recently, Rabbit's class was learning about the city's history and its related myths. His teachers omit the violence from the myths and teach versions more like those used for young children. But one of the students began talking salaciously about the Courier's murder as though it were myth because it remained unsolved. The school grew abuzz with the centennial investigation. Rabbit became enthralled with the Courier's story and could think or talk of little else for the past two weeks. My kind aunt did not appreciate his fascination, or fixation, upon an ugly crime, so she endeavored to make the story and its modern events more about holding people responsible for their actions and about the truth coming out in the end. For those reasons, my aunt had brought him to see some of the day's search attempts. Rabbit also wanted to see the Courier's Bridge, which was the same way I insisted we walk to Cat's. That's how we all met unexpectedly. Now we followed him across.

"How funny we should run into you like this," said my aunt. "We wanted to surprise you at your apartment, but we just couldn't get ready in time," she glanced lovingly at Rabbit. "And here we caught you going to the next house."

"It's my house," said Cat cheerfully.

"Oh! How funny you two should know each other," said my aunt.

"Everyone else is still behind us," I said, "tearing my room apart."

"Oh," she added, with concern. "Oh my."

Plodding along beside his mother, Rabbit sang to himself in an unassailable world of joy. "Hi!" he yelled again to me. He threw his free hand in the largest arc he could muster and then went on singing.

Rabbit's actual name was something of astounding solemnity. His parents had given it to him right after he was born and before they learned about him. His gentle eyes were a crystal clear nutbrown. They were large and wide in the roundness of his face. He had a little chin beneath a mouth that twisted with hope and question as he spoke. My aunt kept the bristles of his stiff hair cropped close to his head. Though he was small, he was fast, and bounded with excitement when a new idea seized him. Then he would try to talk more quickly than he could manage, and would sort through the jumble of sounds as he held my hand imploringly. Sometime years ago, when he was in regular school classes because of their simplicity, the other children gathered up these traits and called him Rabbit. That was before any of the children understood. Rabbit loved the name, and still insisted upon it.

"Who, who are you?" Rabbit said to Clement.

"This is my friend Clement," I said.

"Hi," added Clement, characteristically curt but inviting. He used the same tone to meet anyone: authoritative, exuberant, and curiously nonplussed. Usually, a wry smile followed, and then Clement would launch into highly animated and nuanced thoughts about an off-topic opinion of his, to test how the newcomer to the conversation would survive. But on that day, Rabbit was too fast for him.

"Here," he said to Clement, "havesome. Havesomemarbles."

Rabbit loved marbles. He played with them constantly, gave them names, organized them into classrooms and armies and cities. He could tell them all apart even though they seemed indistinguishable to anyone else. He always had some with him and now pulled three from his pocket.

When Clement looked at me inquiringly, I told him, "It's okay, as long as you're going to keep them."

"Thanks." He accepted the marbles flatly, watching Rabbit like he did not know what Rabbit would do next. I thought it was good for Clement to have the experience of meeting himself.

"Now, now, now we're friends," said Rabbit. "Like us!" he added, and flung his arms around me.

"That's right," I said, encouragingly. Rabbit made me ashamed of all my selfish lust for my own stories. Even this story. He made me feel there was little to do minute by minute but to love others simply. My face burned with this shame as he embraced me long. Clement pocketed the marbles and said nothing.

That is how I crossed the Courier's Bridge the final time on the centennial: Rabbit bouncing between us lobbing questions about what we might find, new questions before the old could be answered. And that is the final, wonderful characteristic I should add concerning Rabbit. Rabbit asked questions. And he loved answers that were stories. One of his favorite pastimes was to ask questions about the old myths of our city, playing with our imperial stories come down from time immemorial as though they were his toys. These stories made our founders tremble but, with time, they hardened into fossils of culture, matters of identity only in a broad and diverse world. But not for Rabbit, in whose fantastic mind all things were possible. When Rabbit seized on a line of questions, he was relentless. And his questions were so simple that they could not be answered.

The river flowed beneath us like his questions, much of the view unchanged from the Courier's a hundred years ago. Upriver, the reflected single-arch of a bowstring bridge, its strings at a distance like the pluck of a lute. Its reflection made the mouth from which the river's questions poured. And downriver, the lenticular truss, the two eyes, the only witness, full gorged on interminable questions.

†

GLAUCUS WOKE PERCY IN the middle of the night, so that Percy would be unprepared.

"Yes?" he asked in a wreck awash at the threshold.

"You were with the Courier on the *afternoon* of the day he died."

Percy looked down, hid his face behind a tousle of brambled hair. His dejection equated to admission.

"You did not tell me, Percy. You did not tell me," sighed Glaucus. "And how does that become you?"

"If you will listen long enough to understand, you will not blame me."

"I am here only to listen. It is my duty to learn the truth. You are implicated—very well, let's see if it is so. Tell your story."

The men exchanged an ancient look, one older than men, older than survival.

"Should you invite me in?" asked Glaucus. Percy turned and led him inside. Another officer, concealed outside the door, jumped in step behind Glaucus. The three sat at a little kitchen table, Percy's resignation as the meal to divide between them.

"I was with a woman when I saw him. I did not want her involved."

"I know you were with Meda."

The name startled Percy.

"But it's not her that should cause you concern."

"How do you mean?" Asked Percy.

"You were with him; you learned that he was carrying the package that night. You are also both with Meda, no? The girl is between you; it is upsetting. You drink. You wait for him. Now he has the parcel. He is terse with you. You do not think you will make amends. You haven't much, now that you are caring for Meda as well, and there is the promise of what the Courier carried."

"You twist the truth into something it is not. You take different things and make a story that is not real."

"I stated no conclusion. I only related a series of facts."

"From the way you arrange them, it's clear what you think."

"You don't like how the facts of your life arrange? You had two faces, wealth and rivalry, before your eyes that night, and I myself smelled the liquor on your breath. It is weakness, only weakness, that makes men rash. Everyone is weak, but some men are also unlucky. I understand, you know, that two weaknesses at once will make you desperate."

"He was my friend!"

"You did not hate him for leaving you the obligation of Meda?"

"No."

"You did not hate him for failing Meda, whom you love?"

"I did not say he failed her."

"How is it that a man is killed upon a bridge," interrupted Glaucus, who again silenced his own doubts, "but according to you—the only eyewitness with any connection to the man—according to you the Killer never enters or leaves the bridge?"

"I don't know."

"Do you not see the impossibility you have created for me? I have evidence from people who did not know the Courier, who do not care for Meda, who swear the other side of the bridge was vacant. And you tell me no one came or went until the Lamplighter found the blood. Understand that I have a case against you now, and tell me the truth! It is in your interest, to make everything plain and dissuade me from my current thoughts."

And Percy finally ate the meal that was between them. He opened himself on the knife of mystery. For some the meal is sweet, but for Percy it was bitter. The same bitterness as the meals shared by the poor on our streets, who have to find, who have to scrounge. "I put Meda up because she was relying on Faton for money and it was a disgrace."

"And the Courier?"

"By the time she told him that she had left her father's house, the whole thing was done. She had done what she did, and I had done what I did. He and I never had the chance to talk about it, so I can only assume what he felt. If you've met Meda you can understand how easy she is to love. That's part of the reason I didn't want to tell him all the truth. But I swear on every god of this godforsaken city, I had nothing against him, and I did not know what he carried."

"Did the Courier know what he carried?"

"No."

"How do you know?"

"He didn't open the box. He carried it."

Glaucus went home from his midnight interview with Percy, but he did not sleep. Was Faton looking for Meda when he left his post? Meda who was not there because she could not face the Courier. Was it Faton, more than Percy, that despised her love of him, and if she had come would she have suffered in his place? Was it Meda who brought Bacca his meals, and did he feel the Courier should have set free a girl who weeps? Could it be the man and not the jewels that mattered all along? Were there such coincidences?

And what should he make of the implication that no one on the bridge knew what the Courier carried? Was it possible, he wondered, that someone would steal the Courier's parcel without knowing what was in it? It seemed there was too much risk for uncertainty. And murder—to kill for an unknown? But yet, there were desperate people in the city. At last, Glaucus resolved upon the one person who certainly knew what the Courier carried, perhaps the only one who knew. Glaucus resolved to see him as soon as the sun rose.

When Glaucus arrived at Melager's home, he noticed it was mostly empty. Melager had sold many of his possessions.

"Planning to leave the city?" asked Glaucus, striding about the empty space.

"Just old things I'm becoming free of," returned Melager's hoarse and patient voice, more elderly than of late. "I don't need them anymore. Necessities have become my priority."

Glaucus came to the point. "Did you tell the Courier what he carried?"

"Of course not. All the precautions I described to you, and you wonder if I told him? That would be imbecilic." Melager's inflection changed but not his pace.

"Is there any way he could have opened the parcel?"

"The box had no lock and no key. It was made of thick hardwood, assembled with dovetail joints. The joints were held by wooden pegs pounded flush and tarred in place like a ship's hull. There was no lid. There was no hinge. You would have to smash it or cut it open."

Glaucus recalled that Percy had seen the box intact, moments before the murder. "Not something that could be done on a brief walk across the bridge?"

"I think not."

"Could the Courier have opened it after leaving you and before being seen at the bridge?"

"It doesn't matter the time. Without any lock, without any key, without any opening, the box would have to be destroyed to access what was within. Besides, he was rushing to catch the train. By design, I met him so he was able to catch it only if he hurried."

"Could he have opened your parcel but replaced it with another?"

"Why? Why go on?"

"You don't think he knew what he carried?"

Impatiently, Melager answered, "It's not for me to say what he knew or didn't know. What I know is that the box would have to be destroyed—that was its purpose to transport something precious. You told me he was seen crossing the bridge with my parcel in one piece. Where was he going? To destroy it? To destroy the fruit of my life?"

Glaucus went out again, to watch silently the dredges working the river and to blame the waters that would not yield a face. Melager was strange, he thought. Melager would not exonerate the Courier, yet he gave good reasons to believe the Courier had not opened the parcel. Perhaps Melager was smarter than Percy—he knew not to tell impossible stories. Perhaps Melager did not want to send an innocent man across a bridge to disappear.

But could it be true about the box? Incredible as it seemed, Glaucus thought it was true—Melager had reason to protect the jewels through to their destination, whether he intended them for their end or for some other circuitous route. Considering it, Glaucus instead decided that Melager would have raised suspicion had he said the box was vulnerable. It would be unusual if Meleager, for all his precaution, had said something to make the theft more likely, if he created less challenging explanations. If the gems could be plucked anywhere along their path, it would be as though he lost hope in a solution—perhaps the act of one who did not want the truth discovered. But, Glaucus asked, in which way would the box be more vulnerable: if it could be opened and shut or if it required destruction? He compared Percy and Melager: what was the difference between a mystery that was impossible versus unsolvable?

And did that exculpate the Courier, if he could not open the parcel himself? Perhaps the uniqueness of the box, its beauty, its creation, its puzzle—perhaps the mystery was enough to compel the risk that something more wonderful yet was within? Glaucus realized, too, that absolving the Courier meant that Melager could be the only one left with knowledge of the parcel's contents. And could Glaucus take his word that the jewels were ever there?

Glaucus's eyes traced across the naked bridge in thought, following the path of the Courier already on his way to becoming myth, setting out across the majestic balance of weight and air, between earth and sky, in twilight between day and night, at the symmetry between the seasons. At the equinox, when light and dark are balanced before light overcomes. Setting out into the uncreated. Setting out to shut the telltale mouth of time. To walk the fractured city into one, across the opening sword of the river and its silver fire. Setting out to be opened and destroyed, on a blade-tongue of silver, to pour the fire of his blood. A man walking, a temple laden with unknown beauty. Carrying unseen beauty, ineffable beauty, that shines now where it lies hidden, awaiting ransom.

†

RABBIT'S QUESTIONS THAT CARRIED us across the Courier's Bridge on the centennial were the same questions as ever. Rabbit had encountered history at school, that is, what remains of history: our myths. He was overwhelmed with the diversity of stories, especially creation stories and stories of immigrant cultures from other cities different from our own. My aunt had no quarter from his questions; Rabbit assailed her at home, often asking the same question in many variations. He wore her down. When I saw them on holidays, she directed Rabbit to me for answers. When she saw I didn't mind, she then directed all Rabbit's history questions to me. Soon, Rabbit was saving questions for weeks, ready to spring them upon me while his arms were still around my neck, with the fuzz of his face and a gentle kiss on my cheek.

In the years before the centennial Rabbit brought to me many times his hunger for beginnings. Visiting me in my little apartment, on a walk home from school, in a calm corner of my aunt's crowded house on a holiday when he stayed up past his bedtime, Rabbit forced his way through his level stutter, surmounting the trouble starting his sentences, then finishing them by crowding all the words together, "But where, where, where didtheycomefrom."

And I told him every time, "You remember the story."

Rabbit, who had learned what his innocent charm could accomplish, looked at me sweetly and said, "I I think I forgot." While all the world lies maliciously for pride and power, Rabbit told his little fibs to hear his favorite stories.

"All right," I said, "In the beginning . . . " According to our city, there was chaos, but in that chaos were the elements of all things that are. The chaos separated, opened, and fire in the chaos sprang upward, as fire climbs and leaps in other forms today. It put lights in the sky. Air rushed into the empty space below it. The earth gathered together, and rose above the waters. From nature sprang the birds, and the fish, and the animals, and magnificent giants that had the purity of nature, so that they lived forever. They ruled creation, which was very simple: a life-giving river encircled the tiny world and fed all the lesser rivers and waters. The sun and moon and stars rose out of the river and returned to it. The giants lived on mountaintops. And somewhere in the north there was a place, inaccessible by land or sea, where only peace and happiness reigned.

The children of the giants became the gods of nature: the life and the power of the sun and the grain and the water and the earth and the underworld and every other manner of thing. The giants also made man.

They scooped up earth that still contained some of heaven because they were so recently separated. The giants formed the clay into human beings. So man has heaven within, even though we are creatures, not immortal like the giants and the gods. Then the giants took fire from up in the heavens and gave it to man to make us noble.

And that was when the gods rebelled against the giants who gave them life. The gods felt that the giants were elevating man to be like the gods. The cunning gods overpowered the honest giants and defeated them, and though the giants were immortal, the gods condemned them to timeless suffering. They remain stranded in isolation, bearing forever the incompletion of impossible tasks, in a tedium that destroys the heart and the will.

Man takes after our gods. The gods made the seasons, and forced man to find shelter, and to toil for food and clothing. And man became rebellious. Creation was in revolt, and misery existed. We overthrew our own mortal parents, and rivaled with our siblings, and the world was plunged deeper and deeper into decay.

That was when the gods decided to make a new start of the earth. They shrouded the skies in darkness, rain poured, the waters advanced, and a great flood raged until only two lovers remained on a mountaintop. In our city, mountaintops, the creators' homes, are sacred and places of transfiguration—wait and see how all things in our city are married. The gods relented for the innocent lovers and let them start humanity again.

We looked at one another, my face expectant, Rabbit's with a blankness that showed he was thinking hard—we looking like creation stories that need two reflecting attempts at creation.

"Are are you serious?" he asked. I laughed, because he made his face so smart. But I understood what he meant.

"In the past, they believed in all the gods and giants, in the past, when there were temples and feasts and sacrifices. But nobody believes in them anymore. Or at least," I added, "there are no more temples."

"No," he blurted out, long and incredulous, like he had caught me. "Where, where didthey *come* from?"

"Who?"

"Allofthem!" Because immortal is not eternal, he wanted to know what knife opened the chaos.

"Well . . ." I went on to explain that our old myths admit there was another unknown before the chaos and before creation, who gave breath to a limitless void and brought everything else into existence—a prevailing genesis from which spring the endless forward rays of our immortal myths.

"Who?"

"They didn't know."

He opened his mouth and nodded his head, as though he had heard something sweet.

"So, so, just, just the one then."

I remember his mother was watching us from across the room, but she said nothing, smiling contentedly.

"Tell me an—another!" he invariably sang. And who could resist? I thought of all my unfinished manuscripts and wondered if they were dirt compared to my telling of these stories.

"All right," I would say, veering toward the myths of our city's neighbors. Others believe that, a long time ago, a prophet gave new voice to a very ancient story. Nobody knows how ancient it was—it might have been the genesis of many ancient stories. This prophet and his followers have no temples, but worship on mountaintops. To them, fire represents all that is pure and illuminating. From fire on mountaintops comes the truth of god and the decree of creation.

They believe in two powers at work in the world. The first is supreme good, all-faithful, the source of life. The second is rebellious and was cast out of goodness because of rebellion. From his aloneness he brings war and strife and discord into the world as revenge. We live in the conflict between these powers. But this separateness will not last forever. A day will come when good will be victorious over all, and the sun, the fire, the symbol of light resplendent, will rise over a world of peace, and evil will be destroyed.

The prophet saw the beginning and the end of this story all at once, one day when he came up from beneath a river. He went down into the cleansing of the god-created waters. He came up and saw the light of god, and the immortal rays of life that are not god but spring from him. And the fire, the child of the good. And the prophet filled his lungs and sang god and beauty and creation.

"Was was there always the the good one and thebadone?"

And I told him that evil had a beginning; something eternal cannot be destroyed unless its end is its beginning.

"Where, where, didtheycomefrom?"

"The good one and the bad one?"

"Yes."

The story says they came from the one supreme being that was always, and created all others for goodness, but the one rebelled.

"So. So. So justtheone." Rabbit paused. "One," he said laughing.

Another time, on a visit to my aunt's for dinner, he marched up and said to me, without introduction or salutation, "What, what about the people from the thesouth? Wha-what are theirstories. Inthesouth?"

And I told him. Many people in our city come from the south, where runs a long and ancient river that they say is just as ancient as our own. And though it flows amid the desert, the land is fertile because the river floods. Before the flood, the earth is nothing but parched clay, harsh sand, and burning rocks. The river floods, and it destroys anything in the path of its powerful waters. Then, when it recedes, the land is quenched and rich with dirt and silt. And immediate life springs abundant from the ground. And pools of water remaining from the flood teem with miraculous life.

The river floods annually, so its people have witnessed its destroying and lifegiving again and again, and the river has spawned many stories. All creation stories may have come from flooding rivers. The people there have many different versions of the same creation, and many different names and relationships between the same creators.

They say the world began in a chaotic waste of floodwaters. They filled everything. Then wind blew over the waters and separated them. From the flood, a primordial mound rose, the first land, filled with the gods that were everything in nature. A mother god filled the sky and bathed the sun. She was imagined as a fertile cow that stood over the horizon. The earth god lay prone, with the vegetation upon his back. There was a god of the moon, and of law and wisdom, and a god of the flood waters from which life emerged.

The sun was born every morning, and he had many names: names for his ascent of the horizon, arising from the river waters, names for his almighty zenith, names for the path that he flew through the sky, names for his setting beneath the liquid night. In night he descended into the under-world, to be reborn upon the horizon of the new day.

In the first time, the gods and their families reigned supreme, and it was a time of peace. Among them a god-king ruled and civilized the world and taught its people truth. But his brother betrayed him, closed him up in a box, and drowned him in the river. His wife, a life-giving goddess, col-lected his body, which was lodged in the growth of a great tree. But the jealous brother tore the body apart. Undefeated, the god-king's wife found the pieces of his body, honored his death, and the king-god returned from death to life, his form situated among the stars where he waits resurrected for all, the ideal king holding a promise of paradise.

Our own myths know these same stars: the form of a man in the heav-ens. To us he is a child of the gods, who walked upon the water. A hunter, who was blinded because of lust but was restored to sight by the sun. His enemy, the brother of his goddess-lover, drowned him also, but the love and the tears of the goddess raised him up among the constellations.

Near the mouth of the long and ancient river live other people who came from some of the first cities like ours. And they recognized in the god-king their own king. You remember the first kings I told you about? They were considered the savior of their city. They ruled destined to die, to go down into death and become the love of the life goddess, to taste death in her place, to ensure her fertile and sustaining return each spring like the cyclical floods of the river. In death they made the throne of kingship.

"But w—wh—where did they *come* from?"

For all the names, for all the myriads of creations as numerous as the yearly floods—there was the unnamed, unknown, everflowing source. The single creator, the complete one, who existed of his own will. He spoke his own name; and so he was. A lotus arose from the cosmic waters, bloomed, and in its calyx was the divine infant, divine sun-child, who stood upon the life-engendering land, which was him, that rose with him from the chaos, and he created as he spoke.

He ruled outside of time and was forever all things. He could create even his own creation, which was not a beginning, but forever a manifold reflection of his presence and being.

His symbol was the sun, he who comes into existence, bringing light to disperse the chaotic darkness. He had all power to create, without the need of any other. Humanity grew from his tears when he wept for love of his children.

He sat on a throne above the immortal but uneternal. The fullness of all sexes, he was the source of fertility worshiped from ancient times. His creative will was manifest in his word, his heart and tongue, which he gave to fill the human form to rule as king.

In time, the people came to know the creator more anciently, and they called him the unseen, the hidden one born in secret, represented by the supreme breath of life that first separated and stirred the chaotic waters and animated humanity. All other gods were his manifestation only. Crowned with the sun, he was at once all mystery and all light, all secret and all life. And like the king-god, he descended to the secret of the underworld, to collect souls and bring them to the afterlife.

"So just the, the, the. One."

I never told Rabbit what Clement once told me about the cities to the south. "Didn't you know they dammed the river—ended the flood, the cycle, the rebirth behind almost every myth that exists. It will never flood again. Until the rain overpowers the headwaters and bursts the decaying dam above the populated floodplain. And there will be countless deaths, and the vacant desert will bloom."

Rabbit thought long behind the blankness of his face when I shared these stories. I could see the syrup of his mind was racing as he twitched his stubby fingers. He once rested his little chapped hand on my forearm, in a way he must have seen an elderly woman do when confiding in an old friend. Head bowed, he raised his eyes toward me and said with all soft-ness, "Tell tell me another." Then a broad smile spread over his face, and he winked at me and raised his eyebrows. "I love you."

"All right, Rabbit. All right," I said. There are also people who worship innumerable gods that live nearly everywhere and in almost everything.

They honor gods of the sky, of lightning, and of storms, gods of fire, of the underworld, and of the sun, and countless others. But the myriad are overruled by the ultimate three: creation, preservation, and destruction.

The creator, they say, made humanity from his own body, and in each body is an emanation of the divine. The preserving god comes down to earth throughout the epochs to sustain humanity. He came in history during a deluge that flooded all the earth, to protect the ancestors of humanity from destruction. He came as an invincible warrior, to rid the world of the tyrants that oppressed it. He will come at the end of time to put all that is evil beneath his feet, and free humanity to its virtue and purity intended for it from the beginning. The destroyer will come at the end of the universe. But the great mystery is that the end of all things will be a regeneration, not a destruction. The destructor is not evil but necessary to the creator.

"Where did, did theycomefrom?" asked Rabbit.

The gods creation, preservation, and destruction are three personifications of one supreme god, who is timeless, who made everything, and to whom all things return. All other gods are in time, manifestations or communications of the one. Within humanity lives a spark of the supreme.

"Tell me," pleaded Rabbit.

These people possess a lyrical story about a warrior on the battlefield of the soul. On the battlefield of life, in a war among brothers, god appeared to the warrior, weak with impending destruction. Between the charging armies god lifted him out of time to a higher field of truth, and said to him on the high wave of life's tumult:

Do not doubt. Doubt wins neither heaven nor earth. Free yourself of despair and arise like all-consuming fire. Grieve not the living or the dead— life and death shall pass away into eternity. My spirit dwells in all things, in your body, in creation. I dwell within your heart and dispel darkness. My spirit is the kingdom of light. This eternal kingdom in man cannot kill and cannot die. We are born to die, but through death in truth comes life. Freed from the bonds of birth, we go to salvation.

And the warrior asked, who is god? What is the source of this promise? And god told him:

I am not seen by all; I am hidden in mystery. But knowing me, there is nothing else to know. Whatever is good comes from me. My spirit is the fountain of life, in which the universe has its being. I am living waters. All things have their life in my life; I am their beginning and end. I am the fragrance of the earth and the light of fire. I shine like the sun beyond darkness. I am the seed of the eternal, the intelligence of the intelligent, the beauty of the beautiful, the strength of the strong. I am the gift of memory. I am pure desire. I am time and the serpent of eternity. I am the temple of supreme joy.

I come to the earth with life-giving love to sustain all things. Those who love the gods go to the gods, but those who love me come to me. I am pure and ever one and ever one are those in me.

"Sojustone," said Rabbit.

And in the eddies of the river's flow, we churn in echoes, echoes, spun about in ruined templed shafts of light, starry-eyed at the sameness of separate peoples, their mysterious sameness, and the criss-crossing exiles that carry them to themselves. As the god said to the warrior: I am one in all though it seems as though I were many.

"Another!" Rabbit sang. "Anotherandanotherandanother."

There are those who come from colder lands, who say that there was once no heaven or earth but just bottomless deep, full of mist. There was a fountain in the center from which flowed twelve rivers. When the rivers traveled far from their source, they froze, so that over eternity ice formed on top of ice, and the infinite flow filled the infinite deep. Apart from this cold dark, there emerged a world in light. And as the rivers flowed on and made ice, the light blew a warm wind that formed the ice into clouds. The clouds took the form of a lonely frost giant and a cow that gave him milk. The cow licked the salty ice for food. But its tongue slowly uncovered a man frozen in the ice. This first man was a god, who sprang to life full of beauty and power.

The giant created children, including a daughter, who the man-god took as his wife. Their children became gods. But they revolted against the giant, the first living thing, and killed him. Then they used the giant's body and blood to form the seas, the earth, the trees, the mountains, the clouds, and the heavens. The clouds are still charged with the snow and cold from the frost giant.

From the body of the giant sprang a tree that supports all the universe. Its roots reach into the dwelling of the gods that lies across the bridge of the rainbow, they extend into the dwelling of the giants, and into the place of cold and nothingness. And in-between these places is the region of humanity.

The gods ordained the times and seasons, and set the sun and moon in the sky, which caused the human world to blossom. But the world was incomplete without us. So the man-god and his descendants made humanity: man and woman in the man-god's form and likeness. They carved the man and woman from the tree that supported the universe, and gave them life and soul, reason and motion, senses, feelings, and speech. They gave humanity the world between the eternal places, but the gods kept for themselves the fruit of everlasting life.

And now the eldest son of the god-man and the giant's daughter sits on a mighty throne and rules over all, while his brothers and all their children live in the paradise of the gods, promised to those who die bravely. There is a powerful god of thunder, one of rain and sun and the fruits of the earth, a goddess of music and flowers and lovers, and a god of poetry. Among the gods prowl descendants of the giants, rulers of death, mischief, anguish, and starvation. The gods watch in defense against them. The tree that supports the universe is tended to by three fates: past, present, and future. And a serpent who lives in the river at the borders of the earth, with its tail in its mouth, encircles the world.

"But but where d-did they *come* from?"

According to the story, all these beings found their beginning in the time before the world. But before them and before all time is the almighty all-father. From the almighty sprang the fountain and the life that filled the abyss before time. And they tell of an end time, when the giants and death and destruction will attack the gods. So the gods ride continuously over the battlefields of the world, taking the most noble of the slain for themselves as warriors for the great and final battle. And it is foretold that the gods and the giants will destroy one another, the world will be engulfed in flames, the earth will sink into the sea, the stars will fall, and time will cease. Then the almighty will create a new heaven and a new earth, where evil and misery will be unknown, and the gods and men will live joyfully together forever in abundance.

"So just. So just. The one."

Yes. The ineffable, the eternal, the first, the one.

"Who?" asked Rabbit.

On the centennial, Rabbit and I bantered on as ever before. I crossed the bridge with him and the others, my net woven of words flung into the fathomless depth, to catch the way an open grave fills with water, to catch the way the dredges searched the river for the body. Even the way we went now, to open victim architecture. And little Rabbit leapt into my arms in thanks. Jokingly, I flung him over my shoulder and carried him off the bridge.

There we were in a moment of joy, at the apex of our city and at the center of its unsolved desolation. Rabbit across my shoulders, across the river the opposite hillsides spoke the language of the bridges that joined them. It was as though we were lifted, carried upward, like the warrior suspended between the two charging armies. You know, according to the story, he and his god had a conversation there.

God said: I will tell you my supreme mystery. All visible comes from my invisible. I am beyond those that perish, and I am beyond the imperishable. My spirit is the river of creation from the beginning. I am the fire of life in all things that breathe. I am victory and the struggle for victory. I am the goodness of the good. I am the silence of mystery. I am the supreme treasure. I bring forth the new day of time. I am the father, the creator, and the purifier of all. All beings rest in me, as breath has rest in the vastness of space. I am the sacrifice and the offering, the sacred gift, the holy word, the holy food, the holy fire. I am the way. Consider my sacred mystery: I am.

And the warrior asked god, how am I to do the work that is to be done?

And god told him: whatever you do, or eat, or give, offer it to me in adoration. Whatever you suffer, suffer for me. Even if you give me only a little water, I accept it from your hungry soul because it was offered with love. Offer in your heart all your works to me, see me as the end of your love and find rest in me, and you will overcome all dangers by my grace. Surrender to me the fruit of your work and give up selfish desires. Love your friends and enemies the same. Make your home in me and not in this world. Love, and have faith, and come to my waters of everlasting life.

Hear the glory of my word: at creation god made both man and sacrifice, commanding that by sacrifice man shall multiply and obtain their desires. Only a thief would take the gift of life and not offer sacrifice. And holy ones who eat the remains of sacrifice are freed from their sins. In my body I offer sacrifice, and my body is a sacrifice.

So by your sacrifice bear fruit. I own all worlds and have nothing to obtain because everything is mine, yet I labor. If I did not labor all worlds would end in destruction, and all beings would die. Offer to me your labor, and contemplate my good. Be free of vain and selfish desires, and labor in peace. In labor is freedom, for all sacrifice is holy. One who in labor sees me then comes to me—his life is offered by me to me in my fire.

Of his sacrifice, god said: though I am unborn, everlasting, and lord of all, I come to my creation and through my power am born, for the salvation of man, for the destruction of what is evil, and for the fulfillment of my kingdom. The foolish do not recognize me in my own human body. But those who love me take refuge in my divine—they love me with love's oneness, they worship me with love.

In my vastness, I place the seed of all things, and from this union all beings are born. One who knows my birth as god, and knows my sacrifice, does not go from death to death but to life. In any way that you love me, in that way you find my love; all paths and all good come to me. See yourself in the heart of all beings, see all things in your heart, and see your heart in me. See the infinite joy of union with god. Love me in whatever you see, and live in me. Even those who worship other gods in faith worship me because of their love. I accept every sacrifice. I shelter all those who come to me. Even the greatest sinner may come to me. My love is ever the same.

The warrior asked, how do I come to you?

And god answered: there is an everlasting tree, with its roots above in the highest, and below in the depths, and its branches in the world. Its leaves are words, and its fruit are pleasures. Its roots extend far, to entangle man in selfishness. On this tree, souls migrate through lives and deaths. But with the sword of the spirit that sets you above worldly things, cut open this tree, and seek the path to my life from the beginning.

The warrior cried, I am never tired of hearing your words of life—I long with all my heart to see you.

And god responded: surrender earthly will, and seek me. The seeker knows eternity's joy, and vision beyond the senses. The seeker abides in my vision and does not move from truth. See in me all that you yearn for.

And, saying that, god revealed his divine self to the warrior: full of awe, facing all ways and containing all splendors and mysteries; the creator on his throne of lotus, wearing his crown and scepter, serpents of light streaming in rivers, illuminating the universe, infinite and incomprehensible; the spirit that was at the beginning, the vast offering of god. The warrior saw terrible things, which taught him fear. He adored god in man since man began, the consummation of all, father of all.

And god said: you have seen what all long to see. Only by love can you see me, and know me, and come to me. Your constant yearning for my spirit within you leads you to this freedom. This body, our body, is this field of battle. I know the body and all the fields of my creation. Whatever is born is born of the union between me and the field. God within you is the same god in all that is.

To those who do not have my vision but instead many words: they may devote their lives to every letter of their words and know nothing more; their heaven is selfish. All their words are like a well of water in the flood; such is the meaning of words to the vision of my creative word. Kill with the sword of wisdom the doubt born of ignorance in your heart.

Hear my word supreme, the deepest secret of silence: fear no more; give me your heart, your mind, your sacrifice, and your adoration; leave all things behind and come to me, and I will free you from your sins.

And the warrior replied: Your will be done.

I sometimes dream of carrying Rabbit upon the bridge that day—except his little body is my own tender and precious self. I rise in the morning to a clean world glistening with storms of the past night and terrible thunder. I rise and shake stories from my locks of hair. I play with myths and lives in my hands, these hands, skin chapped and bit clean through to red and dirt that fills the folds and prints and cuts. And from them I unfurl the ineffable. Outside is the river. Follow the river either direction and find strife. A final battle rages always—a battle of myths, fought amid distant mythical worlds, when all stories are stripped from us and we are made to stand naked again in the first time.

I visit the museums of our temples. I visit the houses of our paganism. I lie on millennial floors where we worshiped vacant names, where the effigies are gone and the fires out. The echo is in the temple of my own heart. I stand for hours at the edge of the river's power. Do we approach the divine, or fall further from seeing mystery we once could—when we were children, who made gods as we made kings, children who gave names to the silence in their hearts, and who venerated the awe of a miraculous world that surrounded them. Children waiting and waiting for the word of truth.

†

GLAUCUS WANTED TO FIND the Courier's mother. Because every child has a mother. Because the Courier did not seem to know what he carried, and Glaucus wished to know who had carried him. Because family are often rife with motives that remained, in this case, an utter question. Because Glaucus had found no one who loved the Courier disinterestedly. Glaucus was determined to go to her wherever she may be, but he did not know where that was.

"I thought he left his family when he came to the city," Percy had told Glaucus.

When he inquired of Meda, she said, "I know nothing of them. He didn't talk about them."

"You didn't ask?" said Glaucus.

"You can ask, but . . . he left them behind. Many come to the city from homes far away."

Glaucus interrogated everyone connected with the investigation about the Courier's family and learned nothing. Public records of the day were scarce, especially concerning poor immigrants who came and went from one day to the next. There were none related to the Courier. He was a faceless individual, who came into the city and survived in one of its unoccupied niches—one that had been filled before he came and was quickly filled again after he died. So far as governance was concerned, he may well have not even existed.

Glaucus inquired of the Courier's landlord and neighbors, who never saw nor heard from his family. There was no clue among the Courier's meager effects, which I understand Glaucus kept in his study at home, to sift and ponder as long as the case remained unsolved. At last, Glaucus was content to wait. If the man had living family, they must eventually learn of his death or disappearance. Or they will wonder what has become of him. Then they will seek him out.

Glaucus and his team were busy while he waited. His notes from this period of the investigation are voluminous. They are locked in the city library's special collections, and I have held them in my hands. Glaucus considered his suspects, his opportunities, his theories, his motives, most of which emerged within the first few days of the case. And he plodded on, interviewing key persons in the suspects' lives, confirming their stories and searching for weaknesses. He looked for anything to unbalance the facts, to pull in one direction or another the pall that covered his eyes, to strip the truth. But a solution remained locked—or rather, lock-less—where there is no lock there is no key. When there is no answer, there is no way to work backward to the question. And day after day, as Glaucus peered down into the river, no face answered his. No victim up from the waters like a prophet. No reflection of the Killer looking down. The solution was shut tight as the Courier's mahogany case. And how to smash it open when the contents are an unknown beauty?

"That is the brilliance of bridges," plodded Glaucus over and over again, "they are open and the victim is trapped. They are locked and they are unlocked at once."

Glaucus kept up unflagging, until he had no investigation left to do. Other cases crossed his desk, other deaths. These were eventually dispatched, but the Courier remained. In the months and years that followed, he had only to think, but he thought unceasingly. The police found him burdensome because he had lost his zeal, his work on other matters more akin to trial and error than his former vision. He assumed everyone thought him a failure in this most preeminent of public crimes. And his difficulties followed him home. His wife was unhappy because he was distracted. Glaucus was growing older, and he had less patience with her. His wife reminded him often that she had wanted to have a child before it was too late, a child they had been unable to conceive.

Into this lengthening, deepening morass, a letter came. A letter not to Glaucus but to the Courier, whose mail Glaucus had been monitoring all the while despite its barrenness.

The Courier had received only a few pieces of mail after the murder. For all the sensation caused by his death, he seemed to have known only a handful of people in life. Those he knew had presumed him dead upon the bridge, so there was no one to write him. What few letters followed were investigated and came to nothing: items sent by clerical errors, an uninformed acquaintance who was nowhere near the murder and had a substantiated alibi (though Glaucus considered whether writing a letter after the death would be a good way for a killer to protect himself). But now, long after those few trifles, Glaucus turned over and over a light-blue envelope with a fluid script both definite and frail. He treated it gently, honorably. He slit it open with a knife. Out spilled a pool of flower petals.

I miss you, my precious one. And I wonder, will you ever come back to me? I remember when you were just a little boy in my arms—small and innocent and vulnerable. I enclosed you, wrapped you, held you; the softness of your child's face pressed against my neck and fit into its curve. I kissed the light and fragrant strands of your unkempt hair. I remember how you raced and coursed with life. How you loved me alone. How I had all your moments, all your smiles, and each endearing mistake, all to myself. I lived for you.

I remember your arms billowing with flowers, when you picked them for me so I might become a bride. You stood with your simple hope in the full sun and breeze, waiting for me with these petals spilling from your arms (you see they still bloom). And like the story, you would spill your own beauty from your arms—tumbling petals unfurling sweetness from the place where your body fell. These letters are my flowers to mark the place where you went down.

I remember how you grew and I watched helpless. I ache for the springtime of life—for that time when all was young and new and beginning. When ending seemed a distant star that did no more than light our joy. There seemed endless time for all we loved. There always seemed another day when I would play with you and rock you to sleep. There always seemed another time that we would walk hand in hand. But youth courses like a mighty river. Time was stolen from me like a song in the wind. And before I thought these moments had passed, their joy was already a memory. I was not prepared to be a shrine of memory when I thought myself a shrine for life. But I do not want you to mistake me; I was proud.

You were strong, and you told the truth. You remember how I hated lies above all. You were afraid to lie, and that made you strong because the truth takes strength to carry. And that is when you wrapped me—when your arms enclosed me. I was smaller than I remembered. And my head pressed against your chest. I remember the day you came from your work in the garden. The sun poured down on your bent back, and the dry dirt kicked dust that clung to your sweat. You came to hold me, as though the garden made you sad, as though you missed me even when I was just inside. And you pressed me against your body swathed in labor. But you smelled like flowers. I breathed the sweetness of your skin and thought you perfect.

That was not long before you left. And now you have left me. You must leave—I said—to an unseen father, to a promised kingdom. I bid you to go. But I thought I would see you again. I did not know this kingdom would mean death. I did not know that flowers spill always when you have gathered them. And I torture myself in wonder: did you die upon the bridge, did you cry out, or were your words silenced in the cold rush of drowning. The lips I fed and kissed. The cheeks and brow I traced a thousand times and have traced ten thousand times in my dreams.

You beautiful little boy, with petals over your eyes, tumbling into the darkness like you were nothing. Like I did not love you. Your last words are here in my tears. They are in the deserted temple I am made by your life. An empty womb where your memory lives imperishable. I hear you as a child laughing. Your infant cooing, the gentlest breath, the most silent and serene life, I feel against the lobe of my ear where you sleep upon my shoulder, where I hold you forever.

Glaucus was on the next train from our city that flung him toward the sender's address—a small and distant coastal town of a similarly indeterminable age. Dawn marked the middle of the journey, breaking the clouds like an egg, gold pouring outward over Glaucus's tired and sleepless eyes.

He looked over the enlivening fields moist with morning mist and girding their winter scars. The mist glowed rose and grey, retreating from the heavy loam to a canopy of soft purple treetops, where a lighted secret looked all encompassing, but fled and fled with its fleeting veil that draped the coolness of the night. Dawn colors like a rush of blood retreated from the apogee of all-colored light. The sky was opening as if it labored to bring forth the coming day. The dull clouds broke wider, an entangled tantrum of yellow. The indolent sun lumbered behind a network of light, mounting the sky to burn away the liquid texture and make the world a crisp blue that sees forever.

"Can't I write a letter to the dead?"

Glaucus found her simple door among a village of simple doors. He knocked, an unexpected stranger. She came to the door herself; she lived alone. Saying nothing, he held up the letter before her inquiring eyes. And that's what she said to him: can't I write a letter to the dead? Her name was Thesia.

"Your son?" asked Glaucus sympathetically.

"Yes," and she added, "I should be embarrassed if you read it."

Glaucus introduced himself, and explained that he had devoted years of his life to solving what happened on the Courier's Bridge. He spoke as though his labor gave him license, and perhaps it did. But there is no labor like a mother's grief.

"Why did you write him?"

"I assumed it would be burned up or destroyed, or lost with other un-deliverables. Or I thought some unknowing stranger might read it, and it would be found among his or her things in a hundred years. I didn't expect to face anyone. I didn't know you would be haunting my son's death."

"So you wanted someone to read this letter."

"He's dead!" she cried.

Glaucus, of course, still wrestled with the idea that the Courier had not died upon the bridge, and he was calculating the meaning of this letter if that were the case. But he felt a fool inquiring of a mother whose grief seemed genuine. When she saw the perplexity upon his face she added, "I sent my word out to him. I might just as well have whispered to the night, but I sent my word out to him. He knows what I said."

"When did you learn of his death?"

"It's been months past. Someone I barely knew had been to your city and heard the news, and eventually he brought the news back, and eventually it came to me when someone realized. Yes, it came to me from someone I barely knew."

"I'm sorry," said Glaucus somberly.

"Why?"

He looked long at her. He could not place her age. She wore a mantle of wise motherhood, of one that knows the pain of bearing all stages of life. But she seemed also full of unyielding youth. The wrinkles about her eyes and lips had the effect of smiling joy and not age. As she looked back at him, full on and unhurried, the blue tunnels of her eyes seemed to secret a deep and tragic wound, but a wound that did not bury her hope with sadness. A resignation without weakness and without despair.

"Why haven't you come forward?" he asked.

"Why?" again.

"We've been working very hard to discover what happened on the bridge."

"I don't know who killed him; I wasn't there."

"You could help the investigation. Or maybe you wish to see the results."

"What does it matter to me who killed him? He is dead. That is what matters to me."

"But justice—" began Glaucus.

She scoffed and gave him a tremendous sidelong glance that became a wry and flitting smile. "What do you know about justice? What are you going to do, kill the Killer, and have two deaths, and have another child-less mother? What are you, courting death? You spend your time reading a mother's private letters, and now you say one death is not enough."

"Yes, but—"

"You have no right to my grief."

And Glaucus knew that he had no right—he did not yet believe in any death. He believed only in possibilities.

"Will you please," he said, trying to show patience in his face and in the draw of his breath, "help me. My task is to solve this mystery, for the sake of our city. For the sake of order. Help me to understand him. Tell me his story."

"You haven't the power to make order." Her voice was so gentle, Glaucus felt no criticism. He felt only her motherhood that wrapped him with the gauze of her words in a holy absolution, that knew from the communion of the womb the limits where courage can carry no man. In her voice, he felt he listened to his own secrets—the powerlessness of justice and of order that he was ashamed to admit, that he was afraid to admit lest he be purposeless. "But," she continued, "you have come far enough that you deserve to hear."

She motioned him to a small table made of layers of thin wood like papier-mache. The old wood had warped into hollow waves, and splinters worked treacherously outward. The wooden chair, used to Thesia's lightness, creaked beneath Glaucus's weight.

"His story is a history of emblems," she began. She spoke with the authority of a matriarch and with the abstraction of an oracle, like the ancient oral historians that preserved stories before writing. "You would not believe it to know his ending, but he is from a line of kings. They are kings without a throne. Homeless kings with no kingdom. They have the blood in them, but it is a blood that no longer rules, since we are all beyond the myth of kings. His fathers abdicated centuries ago, to the will of a people in revolt who wished to rule themselves. But you could see the ancient power in their noble faces. That was what made me love his father."

Glaucus stared in astonished silence.

"His father, Theo, was from your city. He was melancholic. I think he knew in his blood that his place in life was ruined. He was full of strength but had no will to fight. Or had nothing to fight for. He was full of art, but he did not have the peace to create. Or else he had no hunger. And he had no labor either—his family retained its wealth. He was blindingly brilliant, educated. He went pouncing around the world, rattling around in the echoes of an unwanted splendor. And I'm sure he buried himself in a thousand women. Where he could rule. Where he could go down into the dust.

"When he was young, Theo was raised apart from the family, which traveled often and was too opulent to be overly troubled with the education of children. He grew up in your city with a trusted nurse and the best tutors. This was said to be for his protection, to keep him and his lineage secret while he was most vulnerable. His father visited at distant times, to be sure of Theo's development. But boys change quickly.

"As a child, Theo was not told who he was. He did not know his lineage, and he did not know his family's wealth. But his family had left him an emblem: a jeweled knife passed down for generations, from the time that they had honor. When he was of age, and strong enough to lift the heavy stone in the floor under which the knife was kept, then he was to return to the family, taking with him the knife so that he would be known. When he was a young man, the nurse who cared for him could see that he was strong and intelligent beyond his years. She retrieved the knife, gave it to him, and told him where to find his father.

"By this time, Theo's mother had died. His father was married to a woman who, Theo told me later, did not want Theo to return to the family. Theo was his father's heir, and she wanted the family's inheritance as her own. When Theo arrived in the city where his father was, he did not find his father right away. People thought him a stranger. And Theo's father did not expect his son so soon. His father's wife discovered his identity first, because she saw the knife while he played with it one day, sitting aimlessly in a plaza and testing the point against his skin.

"Before Theo's father knew him, she began to turn his father against him. She filled his father with suspicion for the searching stranger, and was able to convince him that the stranger looking for him was a thief, jealous and capable of murder, who was trying to find and steal the family's wealth. When Theo at last presented himself at his father's house, it seemed to confirm all that she had said. Theo was invited in and given food and drink, supposedly to refresh him before his meeting. Before he drank the fatal poison, his father chanced to look in at him, to behold the enemy. Instead he saw the knife. He burst into the room and saved Theo's life. Or you might say the knife saved him. Theo's stepmother fled. Theo stayed with his father for a time, long enough to gain his stature and his means, and he went out across the world. I don't know that he ever forgave being excluded from his mother's death."

"How did you meet?" Asked Glaucus.

"It was then. He stayed in our town for a time. He was no taller than the other men, but when he walked down the street he seemed mightier—radiant, I thought. I did not know the wasted lineage that ran in his veins, but I saw it in the decision on his face, how he carried himself. For having no purpose, he moved with breathtaking purpose.

"I saw him in the square. I tried to attract his attention. I knew he was not staying, and I wanted him to take me away with him. In my own adolescence, I thought this place was small. I thought I wanted the wide world.

"I let him pursue me. It was springtime, and our city was in bloom. I was at a well, drawing water to do the wash, when he passed by like a gentle wind—a wind that is soft though you know it has power to destroy. He had a magnificent silk shirt with their dead crest small upon his strong arm. He had brushed against some blossoms, and pollen smeared the pure silk like a gash in the unblemished white. I said to him—let me wash your shirt. And he agreed. He hoisted the bucket for me, and carried it to the small field behind our house, where I did the wash in a little place by the stone wall. I helped him off with his shirt. I was so young, and I marveled at him. And he must have thought me a ripe fool, though I was beautiful. And he was taken with my beauty.

"I think that we did love each other. I know I loved him so that I would burst. So that I couldn't eat or sleep. He stayed on a long while, a year nearly, which must have been because of me, because there is so little here, peace only. And we were together, in front of everyone. He raised me up to him, a poor girl, and my old friends were jealous.

"I was asleep when Theo left. He left suddenly, in the dusk, in secret. He pulled away with his raiment, leaving a trail of dust and a wake in the waters. And the dust settled. And the wake spread out to the farthest reaches of the ocean and became unrecognizable among the million other murmurs of the deep. Out there, where my boy's body must be, washed from the river into the endless ocean, his body lolling in the ever-waking babble of the waves."

"Did you see Theo again?" Asked Glaucus.

"In a way. Theo left life behind, within me. But Theo brought death with him when he returned home. He arrived by sail at the harbor where his father was. Because they had been apart so long during Theo's travels, his father had requested a sign when Theo returned. The boat was supposed to fly sails with the family's emblem, so that from a distance Theo's father would know that Theo was alive and well. Amidst the revelry of return, and with the passage of time, everyone forgot about the emblem. When he saw the ship coming in, Theo's father thought Theo was dead. He stabbed himself before the party arrived at the house, so that he would not suffer the grief of his son's loss and the end of his royal lineage. And that is how Theo inherited all.

"It was after Theo left that I learned I was having a child. I don't blame him for leaving. I think he had his reasons. I believe there is an answer to that question, though I don't know it.

"I think it must have been the gods that warned him, his ancestors that told him to move, to save the line, preserve the blood that centuries before we would have worshiped. Once, long ago, they would have called

Theo a child of the gods, a lover of the city's goddess. He, a king we do not recognize, from gods to whom we no longer pray. But I think perhaps they are alive, guiding him.

"And we lived. I raised my son, and my family helped us. He was a good child. He was no trouble and did his chores on time, though he was always out late at night. The dusk seemed mystical to him, and it drew him away as I wanted him home. He explored in the woods with the starlight and fireflies. He ate very little. When he was old enough, I told him who his father was."

Glaucus encouraged her to go on. "How did he react?"

"As you would imagine, he wanted to know his father. So when he was grown, we prepared for him to go to your city. It was the only place where I thought Theo might be. Theo was raised there, and his parents were gone—he had spent more time in your city than anywhere on his travels. My son carried with him a letter from me, identifying him, and an armful of flowers. The flowers he took were the type that stained Theo's shirt on the day we were fated together. They are native to our city; you don't have them in your own. And away he went—down the dirt road from this house, with the clothes that he wore, my words in his pocket, and the long stalks wrapped in cloth, the color flung carelessly over his shoulder. It was the last time I saw him."

She looked out after the image she saw in her mind and waited a moment to speak so she would not weep.

"When he arrived he did not find Theo, who was away. He found instead a young lady. She was only a few years older than my son. At first, the way she answered the door herself, and so young and playful with him, he thought her a well-dressed servant. He treated her sweetly. He left the flowers and the note upon an entryway table, awaiting his father's return. He visited again after some time, and found Theo still away. The flowers waited upon the table, dry and surrounded by a halo of fallen petals, but still recognizable for their rarity. My note was propped against the withered stalks. During that visit, he learned who the lady was—Theo's wife.

"She tempted him, I know. He wrote me the story in several letters. And she was beautiful, of course. She promised him secrecy, and power, said she could overrule Theo, who trusted her and was victim to her. She said she could make Theo give them anything, even their aloneness. With power over Theo, youth could have its desires, because what is wealth and royalty compared to youth. 'Look around you,' she told him; 'all this could be yours.' They could take Theo's money and disappear to an earthly paradise. A modern plunder of a kingdom, same as of old."

With a look, Glaucus asked more than words. If the Courier could resist such wealth, what did he care for Melager's jewels? Or was it that he had come so close, and it changed him?

"I'm proud to say my son refused. He had to; that way would lead to deceit only, and lies lead only to self-destruction. All buds bloom only in the light of truth—I taught him.

"Theo's wife was angry at my son's rejection. She tore open the dress she wore, lifted her breasts to him and said he was rejecting the fruits of the kingdom. She said within her belly was his birthright, where a king should conquer. She grabbed his pauper's shirt, pulled him against her bared skin and extravagant tatters, and told him she married Theo because he could have anything but he was too weak and old to have her. She wanted my son for her youth."

"I know you believe your son," said Glaucus, though he privately remarked that anything could be writ in a letter. "But do you believe what she told him, the lengths to which she would go?"

"What I know is that my son returned a third time, much later, saw only some petals dried to little ingots floating in the corners of the hall, and had a glimpse of Theo from a distance as Theo disavowed having any son. Theo's hopelessness was the suicide of his father. And if that woman could not devour my son, she devoured his kingdom—kept all things where she could control them. And I feared for my son. But I feared also for her, when I wasn't angry. I didn't know. She may have been trapped, as I was when I was young.

"My son stayed on in your city. By then he had made a place there. As you can see, he didn't grow up with much and he left with less. So, when he went to see his father, we planned that he would find a place to live and means for as long as it took to gain some direction. When he found a position as a courier, he took it. Then he found a meager place, after spending his first weeks in the corner of a boarding house.

"He had inherited his father's love of seeing the diverse world. He wanted to be near all the people, in that dense web of life. I was afraid that—going out to find a kingdom and finding instead only labor—he would be discouraged. But I was so proud of him, and so pleased with him as a son, because he accepted his labor. He did not curse his fate or curse the gods. He did not turn a gift of life into a prison. He was no victim to his story."

Glaucus pondered all that Thesia said. For the first time he felt overwhelmed, not with limitless possibilities but with limitless truth that is unknown. At a loss, he asked, "What do you think happened?"

"Who can know?" she said, with an inflection that was not a question. "We wounded people prefer our half-blind eyes and a story. And the story eclipses the details the eyes never saw; it hides their questions. And after a while, the story becomes the well-trod path. No one—not even the people directly involved who made the choices to act or omit, to speak or be silent—no one alive knows what actually happened."

Glaucus went home, where he remained an unexpected stranger. Thesia's letter was found among his papers when he died. I have quoted it exactly.

†

Rabbit across my shoulders, Clement and Cat at my side, my aunt following behind, we left the Courier's Bridge and melted into the labyrinth of the city on the way to Cat's apartment. We passed old buildings, dear to me, and new ones that have replaced them.

Our city is full of hidden architecture. Enclosed in shells of stone and glass and iron, as in the womb. Outside, on the streets, there is no hint of these treasures. The buildings scowl with darkened time. Their features are within, or above, where rigid figures hold the roof, hold the watch of the builders. Above where no one looks, where an errant tree takes root in late-gothic gables. I like to usher my ragged friends through the spaces like dignitaries, and we touch everything as though it were alive, and we wonder about the mind and why and where and when it makes its temples.

Or I move alone, a ghost among the crowds, admiring my anonymity like the leaded windows and filigree in the marble. Staring up twenty stories of concentric white balustrades to a dome of stained glass. Directional people moving worn paths on directionless staircases that frame shafts of light. Polished brass. Tall, angular lobbies to speak the vertical modern. The stone-frozen flowers of the unrecoverable past.

Recently, our city has been demolishing these aspiring buildings for ones that believe we have already arrived at the end of time. A sterile blankness like a preservative. No dust. No sweat. No mothering nook or shadow. No movement. Just an absolute static assertion that all ghosts are elsewhere; that our hands are clean. When I prowl in these new buildings, I am transparent. I haven't even an identity in death.

For the sake of our city, in my own small way, I carry the memories of its finest buildings that have been destroyed—whole neighborhoods leveled, consumed by ever-hungry progress that will eat itself alive with insatiable starvation. I visit the places where our temples once stood, to pace out their scale, to see the new buildings that are their headstones. What is our city's desire to destroy irreplaceable things? Or if not to smash them, then to carve them up and lame their spaces, lower their ceilings and shrink their windows, wall up their mantles, hide their hammered copper, and blind their mosaics.

The new buildings of our city are brilliant. A brilliant feat undreamed of in times past. A great dare. A wonder. But they will be destroyed at the end of their useful life. They will not be remembered or mourned. We marvel at structures millennia old that are no great feat comparatively. But they are human, and so we grasp their size and their grandeur. We pilgrimage to them in awe. But fearless awe is not enough to stem the advancing tide, the flowing current, the speeding up. The destruction of simple pleasure for selfish pleasure that consumes. The ornamental for the efficient. The empathetic for the sterile. The outgrown size of our monuments no longer makes us feel glorious ourselves, but instead, minimal.

In ancient times, before architecture was human, even before it was imperial, it was exaltation. Entire temple complexes, structures of incomprehensible size, the design of cities, were intended to create a tangible participation in celestial truth. They brought the world of the gods to earth, where humans could sacramentally walk. Those mighty edifices, built over generations, were meant to preserve, not to function. Their size, orientation, ratios, murals enshrined our knowledge of seasons, calendars, feasts, history, and even religious belief. A temple that once stood in our old city was built so that, on the equinox, our old familiar serpent from the creation story was projected in light and shadow crawling down the temple stairs into the world below. Among stone carvings, animals and eagles contended for human hearts, and plumed serpents entwined with umbilical cords. Equal gifts of life and death.

It is a matter of identity—the question of the temples we make to enclose our labor and our freedom, our fruitfulness and our fleeting life. Make it a noble place in an unloving world, fashioned after the compassion of life. Make it a fine and unsolvable dream, as the lockless box carried across the bridge. Make it befit the sanguine drama of life's indomitable march.

As the years marched on, and the Courier's body and the jewels remained unfound, many people chose either to blame the Courier or to believe there were never any jewels at all. And so it is the same with the vessels that carry life. If there is no soul in the architecture, knowledge and places are destroyed. The buildings go higher and higher, overtopping the old but crushing the human scale. Or the scale of the soul, that makes our spirits soar to see that we are part of a surge up out of the earth and mud toward some great answer. Like our city is the thriving shoots of spring, pushing up from the ground in a riot of verdant breath, leaping madly for light. How does our city grow?

But all monuments are smashed. When upwinding towers are toppled the taller ones look downward. As I pace the clear, dry ground of this, our ever-changing city, I hear the break of glass and hollow knock of brick crumbling beneath my feet.

The past is gone. It is not the past that traps me, only its mystery. I suppose there is some little void that has lodged in each of us, that has come enclosed in the shape of our creating. And as we long for creation, we long to fill the uncreated. But the void longs for the void. So here I am, giving away my sadness. I suppose I have a strange and broken obsession for these decrepit things that were beautiful. It is like I am looking a promise of paradise in the face. Brilliant and battered, invaded and overgrown, but it stands; the great truth is there somewhere, beautifying in the way it weathers.

I suppose it is the same regarding my fascination with the Courier. I found myself loving him when I discovered accidentally that I was living in his home. It was like the sudden discovery of truth in an outworn myth that I had heard a thousand times, and it began to grow in me. I started to look for the places where he was, to stand where he stood, to imagine his breath and heat moving through the spaces of my current life. I found that, despite a centennial of time, or perhaps because of it, we know little about the man. What we know is his death. His death is his identity. And while every person dies, his death endures, and now endures again in my memory, because it is mystery.

Like our city's lost architecture, I found myself enraptured with the Courier's death. With the moment of it; with the necessity of it; with the idea of his long-arching strands of blood caught in the firelight, strands of time loping down to the river and fracturing in the ecstatic crash. It is because of his death that I know him. It is his death that makes him. That is what I have of the man that slept where I sleep. To have his mystery, I have his death. To have this city, I have what grows and what is lost.

I began this story by sharing our city's myth of the great flood and the few survivors spared by the gods whose task was to be fruitful and fill the world. They did not know how to revive the human race, since it was just the few of them and they were one family. They went to see the oracle, in its abandoned and ruined temple that had been tended to by drowned men. Those were the ancient days, when there were oracles. Now they have been silent for countless generations; even the places that the gods inhabited have been lost to forgetful time.

The lone family traveled many days through the hills surrounding our city, traversing ground stripped clear and soaked with receding waters. When they arrived at the temple, they slid in among the broken pillars that might topple and crush them, making for the ruined holy of holies. Since the gods had spared them, they presumed the right to risk their lives and go directly to the gods. They intoned the forgotten names in the resonant temple bones, and the sagacious stones rumbled them a message that they knew in their souls.

"Depart from the temple with head veiled and garments unbound, and cast behind you the bones of your mother."

The family set out, naked in a new first time, with heads and eyes veiled in homage that hid their shame and saved the modesty of the gods' creating. But the flood had torn apart the ancestors of these survivors and mingled the razed graves across the world, and the survivors would not desecrate their mothers' graves even if they could know them. Instead, they learned in their hearts to gather stones, the bones of the earth, and cast the stones over their shoulders.

In a mystery they could not see because of their veiled heads and turned backs, humans grew up from the stones where they landed, a newly-mothered race but with stony hearts. And they made new cities and new oracles, erecting the buildings of themselves.

But I must add that this creation story is not told alone—all things in our city are married. The companion to the myth, as the first woman and man to each other, says that another flood will come at the end of time. A flood that will raise all the waters of the earth, so rivers break their banks and unwind, bursting their walls and tearing down mountains and uprooting the cities that bind them like fetters. They will wash away this most recent up-stretching attempt, replacing our attempts with their attainment, replacing possession with truth. One day this will all be forgotten and only one thing will matter. No monument will stand to time. No solitary life, but life only. No story, not even this story. The return of the flood is to wash away all bridges. This was the flood Percy and the Courier spoke about on the night of his death.

The loss of the stone heart of architecture, and the hearts that moved in temples of stone; the loss of the Courier's heart of flesh; all of it is like the rising waters of this final flood within my own heart. And I make the bridge of this story to sacrifice to their final accomplishment.

Clement, Cat, and I stood in Cat's apartment that was Percy's—where Percy, Meda, and the Courier spoke one hundred years before. We waited for another sickening sound of yielding stone and mortar beneath the hammering blows of unyielding fever. Rabbit and his mother stood near the back, Rabbit bouncing and humming with excitement. I did not share his honest and laudable desire simply to know. Instead, I felt so heavy, contemplating our architecture and the Courier's death, seeking an understanding of why I was there at all. The same strange, unworthy gaggle that had gathered in my room was now in Cat's. They left some amateur to patch my walls and replace my floorboards while they were on to other discoveries.

"I'm going over to my place," said Clement. He hurried out and we could hear him shuffling around and singing on the other side of the long crack that linked his apartment to Cat's. When she later asked him why, he said, "I learned you through that vestal opening, and we loved through it. It is a birthing place. If I am going to hear destruction, I will hear it the same way as well. It is my oracle." We saw his shadow take up position on the other side of the thread of light. I imagined his head bowed against the wall, and his outstretched hands upon it, to feel it quiver, as he held his position like to take its scourging instead.

The demolition crew explored the walls, searching for voids. The walls of Cat's place were irregular; some were straight and looked new, some were crooked and made of piles of shale or sandstone, plastered over and washed white. "Very heavy walls," the workmen said, "thick, like a fortress. These are old walls. I doubt there's going to be anything." Behind me, Rabbit grunted in assent while his mother shushed him.

But then one of the crew pressed his ear against a stretch of stone, knocking. He stood at a segment about his size that seemed more regular than the surrounding stone, even though the type of stone looked to be the same. "I have something. There is a space here; it's like a door."

The crowd got excited. Rabbit inhaled so loudly with surprise that people turned around thinking he had been injured. Cat stepped back stunned and fell against me where I stood behind her. Her hips pressed into me and did not move away, and they were firm and tender and full, and her skin where I caught her arms felt like a spring breeze that cools a stagnant pool of sun. We saw Clement's shadow shift with the action and brace for impact.

In a moment, the gentle workman had transformed to a demolisher, braced on wide feet with upraised sledge. "Careful! Careful," shouted the leader of the crew as he rushed over. "There could be some kind of panel behind the stone. Don't smash it down. We must preserve everything." The man dropped his sledge and traded it for a light pick-hammer. Another came with the same instrument. With ticks and pocks and the sounds of spreading cracks, they peeled back the rock and plaster, and a large wound opened in the side of the wall. One of the men got his pick behind a large slab and pried it off. It broke clean away from a wooden plank behind it. The wood was old but solid. Among the spectators, a hushed excitement took hold. They did not know that ancient architecture is worm-holed with secrets. They hoped this secret was an answer, not another question in a jeweled string of questions.

Soon the workmen uncovered a door. It was made of hoary planks, hard and gnarled and dry, dusted white with plaster. Fingers of plaster littered the ground with tiny splinters of wood and specters of the door's deep gnarls. A shattered door in negative upon the stone floor. And the real one stood waiting before us, its planks banded with iron hinges dressed in dints of hammers from an old forge that must have disappeared many centuries ago.

The workmen swept away the stone and plaster to clear an arc for the door to swing. Cat gave a push with her body against mine that sweetly sprung her small form quickly across the room. She grabbed hold of the old door handle while everyone froze with surprise. As she tested the handle, I heard the lever raise a latch on the opposite side. She gave a majestic pull that swung open the door. A rush of long un-breathed air swirled into the room, cool and dry, stirring her dress. And I remember being stung by the taut ivory of her youth that cut like a bow in the waking old shadows. No memory past could topple the brazen heart of youth that cracks open all bleak shadows as it dares look bright upon its shrouded source. I leapt to her before I knew what I was doing. Against a rising wave of protest and dozens of reaching hands, we entered first. I heard Rabbit shout my name in terrible anxiety as we plunged knife-like into the darkness.

We found ourselves in a cave of names.

†

WHEN GLAUCUS RETURNED FROM his visit to Thesia, he investigated her story, but he could not find Theo and his wife. They had fled. Years later, with nothing else to do, he ventured alone to Theo's empty house in the outskirts of our city. All of his former assistants by now had other tasks, or they had risen in rank, like Melic, and were running cases of their own.

Glaucus had heard of the beautiful devastation into which he traveled, but he had never seen it. Remember that the Courier had lived in the city for years after visiting his father's house, and more years had passed since the Courier's death. Things had changed.

Glaucus arrived in a neighborhood of ruined and bygone wealth. Once the rich had lived there in opulence, in stone mansions surrounded by gardens and greens, where they held reckless parties, hiring orchestras to play on rooftops and smashing the necks of fifty-year-old bottles of champagne. But now the tide had receded from these stranded buildings. The wealth had moved. The orgies of the world were elsewhere, in other cities, as the trends of the glamorous would have it and as the whims of money demanded from its captives. Moreover, the generation raised among this wealth pretended to despise it. Their parents had scrapped in the streets to gain the wisdom and luck that built these enclaves of privilege and safety. But the children went out to wander the streets and chase the lost wonder of the poor. The upkeep of the giant houses became impossible; no one could supply the staff to run and maintain them. There was no market for such houses. They were simply abandoned.

But houses like that, isolated in their once grand fields, do not stay abandoned. The homeless and recluse came. Artists and thrillseekers came. Wild adolescents threw mad bashes in empty swimming pools. Animals slipped through broken windows. Rain infiltrated the roofs and soaked tooled plaster into mush and made the frescoes weep. Thieves came and stripped the metals and woodwork, cutting up whole staircases and ripping paneling from the walls. Today, I can't even visit these houses. After decades of neglect, they had to be destroyed. Some of the greatest homes that ever were now are empty fields, and the old faint outlines of the gardens are over-run with weeds.

Theo's family was one of the later ones to leave, but they had left, it seems, not long after the visit by the Courier. By the time Glaucus found the house, he pushed open the door that splintered where the bolt had been. Alone, he spent the day picking through every crumbling room. There was nothing. No one.

Glaucus stood in the spacious entry hall among the warped floor-boards and peeling walls, imagining the scenes between the Courier and Theo's young wife. He saw her barefoot in silk, fresh as dawn, her delicate feet treading down the destruction as though she walked on the finest wo-ven wools. The house had aged as she must now have aged. It decayed as her body, for all its beauty, for all the lives within it, was also destined for decay. And he thought how no one can imagine what may become of the seemingly-immortal places of their lives.

Glaucus made his way to the door over a blanket of leaves that had invaded the busted windows. He heard a crunch beneath his feet. Under the leaves where he had stepped, he uncovered the shards of shattered crystal. It had been a glass; the stem lay dismembered among the sharpness. Glaucus imagined Theo drinking off the house in one grand gesture and smashing the glass, while his sneering wife waited, already outside the door. That was it: the vessel was always smashed, like the homes where people lived, like their lives themselves. Glaucus studied the crystal blades and imagined the blood pouring from the Courier's wound. It was not blood but rainbows pouring from the prisms beneath Glaucus's foot. All the colors of spring.

Glaucus crossed the overgrown yard in the dusk light, its border blurred with encroaching woods. He had a long way to go through the woods to the nearby town where he could catch a city train. He carried the despair he had expected. Theo and his young wife could have gone anywhere. They were untraceable. The whole history was gone and broke-into and ruined, just like a broken and raided and eroded divine right.

†

IN THE FIRST TIMES, according to our myths, the names of gods were totems of power, because a name is how to call someone for aid. When a city was founded, its name was carefully chosen to invoke a protector. When a child was born, the same deliberate choice was made. There were many gods without names that, for all their interference in human affairs, were useless to humans because we could not invoke them. That is why, when ancient heroes encountered new gods, they always asked the god—what shall I call you, whom shall I tell my people has spoken. Having a name, the hero had power over the god, or rather, the god relinquished the power to entreat. The power to ask.

I learned this from Clement. When we met he said, "I'm giving you power when I give you my name." He was a man of contradictions, like the way he wished to mediate the destruction in Cat's room. "It was not for my eyes," he told me later. He was delicate, and he could be kind. He never refused a person who asked him for a meal, or else he thought his soul would die. But he could also be cruel. He was two-faced, and his cynicism made me wonder if his kindness was ever genuine. Somehow I felt we betrayed him there in the dark; I knew he would be angry. Cat clung tightly to me as we pushed through a narrow passage. We had to hunch down. It was only four feet high.

Surrounding us were swarms of names in a lace network like a veil over the stone. Old scars carved with dull knives, swaths of paint that aged to look like tar. The scrawls were heavy and deep and angular, with the darkness of long waiting. Others were light and fluid and feminine. They chased each other across the stone. Beneath the names were dates, days when all these people were alive and breathing maybe the patient dry air that filled my lungs just then. Modern names contended with old names. Some of the names and dates were indeed very old, older than I ever would have dreamed. It made me wonder again about the building where Clement and Cat lived, standing like a fortress for no one knew how long.

We discovered the names *Percy and Meda* scrawled in charcoal just within the door. I saw them immediately in the light that cut from the opening. As we moved along the tunnel, dust and loose layers of stone on the walls trickled down where we brushed past. The names flocked all the way to the end of the passage, covering its every inch. The deeper we went, the older the names became, like sifting through layers of sediment. Even the ethnicities of names changed, as different peoples lived in this part of the city during generations that shifted with the deliberate slowness of sand dunes. In the dim light trickling from the door to the end of the tunnel, charcoal pictures depicted a type of barque that had not been seen on the river for centuries. A network of rigging festooned the barque, drawn with a mariner's precision but hazy with years.

And there we were, paused, looking at one another, bent in half, with the sand of names coming free from the walls and raining down on the bare skin of our faces, necks, and limbs. In her sight, I felt that I extended far beyond the bounds of our city, spilled through its network of streets, filled the depth of its river and climbed to its towers. Nothing is as liberating as giving your life away. There is no other way to realize the entirety of what you are, or to possess complete dominion over yourself, than to exercise devotion, to take a vow. It is the feeling of engendering a child. A supreme moment, an absolute fullness of life, knowing that you commit yourself to something forever.

The passage was blind. The end was made of a stone that was different in type and size and cut than the surrounding walls. From its location and direction, it seemed to terminate at the exterior wall of the building. "I think that, once, the building extended further, and this was the way to the destroyed part." I turned around at the end. The passage seemed like a long distance when we entered, but looking back, it felt oppressively small. I could see the silhouettes of heads surrounding the open door, peering in.

"I want to lie down," said Cat, "and look up at these names like they are stars in the sky, and all these lives are constellations."

"That's all you could do in here is lie down." Speaking the simple observation triggered a new thought in my mind. I scanned the walls again and saw that the names at the end of the passage were masculine. The couples' names were toward the entrance.

"These names at the end all have ranges of dates," said Cat. The couples' names near the entrance had a single date. When I saw what she meant, I became certain.

"This was a prison."

†

BACK FROM HIS LAST unrevealing history, Glaucus was also laboring under the weight of names.

"It could have been Percy, Meda, the Lamplighter, Faton, Melager, Bacca, Theo, or his wife. Every one of them was there, or could have been. Every one of them had the opportunity. The gems alone are a motive for anyone but Theo and his wife—and they have motives of their own. Together, they tell a story that makes the death impossible; makes escape impossible. Any one of them could lie, concealing the single, simple truth that makes their stories fit."

Over and over he said, "I cannot eliminate them. I cannot prove any one of them is guilty."

And in his darker times, he dared to remind himself, "Then there is the Stranger, some unknown, some sneak-thief, some faceless immoral who kills for money, who could have walked by unnoticed while everyone recalls that they were looking. Such slaves we are to the certitude of memory." Slaves, as Thesia had said, to the story that becomes memory.

"The Courier has no face, and the Killer has no face. And in every one of these names I see them both."

†

"I DON'T BELIEVE IT," exalted Clement in the sunlit street. We had left Cat's. If the hidden passage-turned-prison once held the stolen jewels, they were not there now. Rabbit hugged me with deep satisfaction when I emerged and told me how he did not like the dark. Cat and I faced no repercussions because there were no jewels. The demolition crew poked around until the politicians were satisfied, and everyone moved on. Rabbit and his mother went their own way.

"This is the greatest and most wonderful thing," continued Clement. "Here where we sleep. We're sleeping on top of a mountain of moaning souls. They're squirming around beneath our feet. They're staring slack-jawed at our food from where they starved. No wonder I have such strange dreams."

"What are your dreams?" I asked.

"That I am a thief. That I am trapped. That I am sentenced to death."

"In my dreams I am already dead," I replied, "and I am alone and searching to see what lives."

"No. Not me. There is only my life that wanes. It is like I am trapped at the bottom of a dry well, hidden together with my crime. And I am willing to confess—my discovery would be my confession—but I shout and shout until I am voiceless and no one comes."

"Clement," said Cat, "I think you are breaking your own rules. I stopped remembering my dreams since you pleaded with me that dreams are foolish. Life, you said, is the present alone."

"Did I say dreams? By dreams I meant hope. Hope is foolish. It is captivity. Yes, we live in the eternal present. Look at us—we three should be out roving, devouring, grappling, while we can, with the infinite paths that lie open to us just now, and we are sitting around hoping. And I reinstate the rule that dreams, as hopes, are foolishness. But, lovely, what comes to me in the silence of my mind is only another present. It is my present, filled with pasts that will not relinquish *my* now. Not like my friend here," he slapped me candidly on the back, "who will not relinquish his pasts. Your writing, child, is a form of hope because it expresses a future. And you're filling the future up with a past that already was. See how he carries the burden of it—transmission." He clasped Cat around the back of her neck, his rough mitt enclosing her delicate stem, as he wrapped me gruffly in his other arm, pulling me tightly to his side. "You're bridging right over the present, leaping over ecstasies! You've disinherited it. He's living like a bum under the bridge piers . . ."

"There's a lot you can still see from the bottom of your dry well, I guess." That earned me Clement's most superior look.

While Clement accounted the nature of the prison, I fascinated myself with the passage—before it became a prison. I reveled in the missing part of the building where it once led. What had it been? Who had lived there? How was it destroyed and why? The answers seemed to float transparent and indecipherable in the air above me, treading destroyed corridors. The passage was small enough to have been concealed. Did it lead to a secret room, an oracle, a treasure? Wherever it led, the place had identity and purpose; it had stood where I now stand and occupied a time and place. And now it is excised from what remains; there is gravity and void in that space, even though it is filled with the modern, and singing birds pass through on boughs of sunlight.

The passage transformed to prison after it opened out into endless sky.

Clement, instead, was fascinated with the transformation of the prison into a hiding place for lovers, and their names.

"Oh, if it wasn't always a prison it was probably the tunnel to the prison," he dismissed me, as we walked toward the Lamplighter's house. "It's so small. You see how the men were captives. They marked their lives with ranges of dates. Dates of captivity. They began, and they ended. And what it must have been to carve the final date, on the day of ending, and look it in the face."

"What if they were carving the day of their release?" I asked.

"No. Freedom will not be enclosed."

"But is it shaped by their captivity?"

"Anyone subjected to a prison that small and dark is doomed to die," Clement answered sharply. "The point is that the range of dates transform to single dates, unbounded. To endless dates. From one's solitary captivity, in time, they transform to lovers' continuous day. A place of death is turned into a place of ecstasy: death to life. The lonely male becomes names male and female. One date that is an eternal date of being—was, is, and will be. That date is the date the lovers grappled with the haunting shadows, and with cries and shouts of joy they chased the dark away with beauty! You see, they made life of a prison, and that is why they are unbounded, except that they are bound together. And here, they leave their names. The names to pronounce their triumph. They give the power of the names, so we can speak how they chased out all the time and made it free. A network of names that over-laces and dresses the captives, exults their solitude, and hides their shame; the captives did not know all along, long ago, that they died for the lovers to come. Lovers that are gone except for their unbounded now. You worry about old architecture—these people were *here*." He was walking so fast that it was hard to keep pace. This was the face of Clement that found such magnificence despite his hopelessness.

I missed a lot more that Clement was saying, because all his talk made me think of Cat. Made me think of her soft, trim body, fit and shapely, laid in a glowing streak of pleasure that opened the grey and dust and stone. I saw her draped naked in the lace of names, as she turned the stone to silk and flung it gently over the hollow where her shoulder met her neck. My back encrusted with the grit of the walls where I pressed, eroding the names and taking them into my own flesh and vigor; her filling and filling the prison with her breath and sparse cries, until it was recreated an access to something lost and majestic where now lives only a void. Our rolling heat and breath to transfigure the frigid space, like we were liberated, warming the stone into the heat of womb. Or close the door, and in the absolute darkness, we would feel the abyss of impending centuries, the shrouds and shrouds of identities like a bed chamber, and be the first hot knife of life opening the unloving universe. Arms tight around her, hands gripping her slender back, curt breaths into each other's hot mouths. The knife thrust into captive promise.

And on my breath, my words, our names, would tickle her ears like the wet and gentle southern wind. But Clement was like the myth of the northern wind. It cannot blow gently; it must carry off its lovers and begets only warriors with wings.

And I knew what Clement wanted. He wanted his name upon the wall, to elevate himself to the devout ones. I knew he would try to lead Cat there that night, to try and make his mad claim upon his name, and he would do a dead thing with her, loving not her but the prison walls as they create his palette. I thought he might hurt her tender flesh on the stone. Not like me—not like I would take the cold and dirty stone against my own spine—a transition of the hard stone to arduous but tender man, from prison to passage, to her fragrant and mystical bloom. As Clement walked and talked, he was electric, and I scowled with the unpleasant taste of ill envy. I felt that I could make Cat alive as he could not—would transform her from his prison to my passage.

Desire and envy sped me to the door of the Lamplighter's old house, as I watched Cat's form move within her light spring dress. She hung on Clement's words and cooed back his excitement. And like the end of a journey, when I always wish to start over again, I finally considered that I ought to be happy for my friend.

To reach the Lamplighter's house, we had to pass outside our city's ancient walls—tall, deep bastions that once encircled the city's heart against a dark past of siege. Now, they are open to tourists and young lovers and teenage boys, who stroll for miles along their tops, looking down at rough stone often bled red. Like all things that are married in our city, our walls have a story. Orphae constructed them of song.

Orphae's lover died of a snake bite, and he went to the underworld by way of our river to retrieve her. Being a poet and musician unmatched, he persuaded the gods below by lyric song. I have not come in conquest—he said to the realms of silence and uncreated things—or to know your secrets or the secret of death. I come only in search of my love, who died untimely in her youth. Love led me here, Love who is a god all-powerful to the living, and if old traditions are true, a god all-powerful here as well. Let me have my love, and we will return to you at the proper time.

The gods that live in death wept for Orphae's love, or wept for themselves, and they allowed his lover to return on one condition. Orphae, leaving the world of the dead, was not to turn around and look back at his love. The secrets of life and of death, the mystery of resurrection, were not for his eyes but for the great, intentful silence of gods. For a living being, a being of love, a being of choice, such revelations would destroy him by overwhelming his human will.

Orphae led his love a far way, almost as far as where the river reemerges to the light of day. But at the last moment, he forgot himself, and looked back to see that his love followed. Because of this look, she returned to the dead, not for herself this time but for him, in his place, though she did not blame his impatience to behold.

Orphae sang his lament, a lament sweet and potent so that stones shaped themselves and moved by the slow dirge of his beautiful song to build the walls surrounding the city where he sang, to manifest Orphae's division from his love and seal him away from the world. But he sang until the living world could not bear his longing. At first, stones that people threw at him fell harmless at his feet, enchanted by his song, until the hateful crowds shrieked down his music and their unhearing stones finally crushed him. Now he is with his love again, the story says, where he forever longs to look and is forever free to look and is forever filled.

This story, and the walls themselves, are ancient. They say that Orphae's consecration of beauty made the walls eternal—that as his lyre raised the stones into place, only the sound of the final flood will tear stone from stone. The flood is like Orphae's music because all are buried in its level harmony. But you cannot speak death in the language of life—our city's growth long ago outpaced the walls' size and suffused them. New homes and industry spilled across the surrounding countryside and replaced the wreath of abundant farms that once encircled the walls. The Lamplighter's home was one of these.

Initially, traffic through the walls was sparse enough to use the existing gates. But as the precincts outside the walls grew, the gates themselves became outmoded. At the time of the Courier's death, the walls were formally opened to the spill of progress and commerce. Large segments were cut and removed for traffic and buildings that bridged the ancient divide between those within and those without. Clement expostulating, we passed out of one of these wounds into the Lamplighter's former world.

The Lamplighter had lived in a small and modest row house, on a narrow street, in a mosaic of matching row houses from the same period, bristling along the scrawling sidewalks. The neighborhood was tight, the fences low, the yards tiny, the alleyways no wider than a door. The Lamplighter had earned himself this little place of ownership from a lifetime of vigilance, carrying and multiplying his flame. It was not much more than a foothold.

By now the day's anticipation was stale. The notion of finding treasure hidden away in a place of such thin means seemed extravagant. The same tawdry group milled around, looking bored. More stragglers had joined them as the day wore on. When we were ushered inside, the local politicians and news persons intoned the same worn mantra. Rabbit and my aunt arrived mid-speech, causing mild interruptions as she shushed his unyielding questions.

"The centennial search is still on. Two houses have been explored and the final remains: the Lamplighter, the man who found the bloodstain upon the bridge but found—he claimed—no body. Was he the murderer, feigning surprise all along? Did he discover the body still laden with jewels? After he filled his pockets, the gems glistening by candlelight, did he dump the body into the river and cover the splash with the sound of his screams? Without the flicker of his lights, death was shrouded in darkness. Maybe," the politician added with a punctual thrill, "he was late to light the lamps for a secret purpose, to allow for the murder. Maybe he and the Courier worked together, the Lamplighter giving cover for the Courier's disappearance. Did they spill another's blood and split the proceeds? If we did not find them at the Courier's, perhaps they are here; wealth like that cannot be lost forever!"

The reporters took notes for an evening edition of the story. The crowd was so tight in the tiny house that they were breathing on each other and no one could turn around. The thin couple that lived there was forced into the back yard. I could see them through the window listening somberly as they held hands. Who knows what they were promised. The politician turned to the sullen girl accompanying him. "How was that?" he asked.

"Good," she said, unimpressed.

"I hope. We're out of houses." Of the remaining suspects, their homes had been destroyed in the intervening hundred years, or else stripped to their frame and rebuilt. If Melager sent an empty box across the bridge, any gems he hid had vanished with his house. The politician mused for a moment, I guessed about the jewels being buried in toppled debris and dumped anonymous into the gaping ground. Or else some poor carpenter picked them up decades ago and disappeared.

The demolition crew fanned out and went to their tasks. The crowd also expanded and got in their way. There was a long and impatient wait full of sordid whispers. During the search, the sun lowered enough to throw long rays of blinding brightness through the windows, raising the temperature and causing the restless crowd to sweat. Rabbit slid up to me stealthily and held my hand.

"So bright," he said. He was staring directly into the light, squinting his eyes until they teared. He did not wipe the tears. He did not shield his eyes. He did not look away.

The leader of the demolition crew burst into our silence. "The outer walls are solid brick. On the sides, they abut the brick of adjacent houses. The interior walls are plaster on brick; they're not framed. I don't know if I've ever seen a house built this solid. This house was made to last and last unchanged. You could let it sit here for a hundred years in the rain, and all you'd need is a new roof and some simple floors."

"What about the floors?" asked the local politician.

"Look above you." We all looked at his command. Rabbit's mouth gaped as he threw his head back ridiculously. He smiled when he noticed me watching him and gleamed back at me from the extreme corner of his eye. The floorboards of the second floor were laid across exposed joists, and little shards of light eked through. The joists sat firmly on a hollowed shelf in the exterior brick. "There's nothing to hide," the crew leader added.

"What about the attic?" insisted the politician.

"There is none. The second floor is open to the roof trusses."

"The basement. It's a dirt basement, right? They could be dug down into the dirt."

"There is no basement. This floor," he stamped on the terracotta, "is set on masonry right on the ground."

"They could be under the floor."

"If you broke up this floor, you'd never rematch the tiles or the mortar color or the wear on the mortar. There would be an obvious inconsistency, and there is not. And, boss," he leveled at last with the politician as he had been wanting to all day long, "I can't see no one committing murder, and stealing the jewels, just to bury them in the damned cement where they can't get at them."

I smiled broadly.

So in the Lamplighter's house all was in the light, and nothing was hidden. Of course, the politician had the men tear up the floor anyway, as a matter of pride, telling them that they will do as they are paid to do. While they argued, I explored the house and marveled for a moment at the meager hearth where began the fire that for years illuminated so many city bridges and revealed the Courier's death. When I turned around, I saw an unexpected sight. Clement had Rabbit cornered and was questioning him. Clement was animated, and Rabbit cowered. It looked like Clement was trying to be nice but failing because he lacked patience. I walked over to them.

"What's going on?"

"Oh," Clement drawled, "I was just asking him about school."

Rabbit nodded at me.

"Are you ready to go?" I asked.

"Yeah, let's get out of here," said Clement, and he headed for the door.

I looked inquiringly at Rabbit and received a fast waive and a "seeyousoon" as he darted over to the workmen.

Rabbit and my aunt stayed to watch, because of Rabbit's insatiable curiosity and his interest in the digging machines. Clement, Cat, and I left for that part, in time to see the owners pacing and wringing their hands and wondering whether they could withdraw their cooperation. But then again, you never know what you may find when digging in the past—often, not what you are looking for. What a shame. It was a beautiful floor; you would never have a floor like that in a house today.

The sun was drifting lower, and the heat of midday subsided. We had eaten nothing yet. The final site of the centennial was the graveyard on the hill overlooking the city, but we knew they would not be there for quite some time. So we walked to the little square where the Courier received his last charge. The fountain was still there, still murmuring. The crowds were still about, the benches still full. We found a little café at the corner of the square and started drinking, and our inebriated breath and laughter went up like incense.

We had made three strikes into the body of the past. And now there was nothing to do but take the body to its grave. The sunset of baby blue and citrus clouds piled high in dreamy spires. All the color reflected in the still river, so that the river was sky. From beyond the hills a bourn of silhouetted birds crossed the city. In such a calm, the river ascends, and looks no different from heaven above.

†

ABOUT THE TIME THE Courier died, there was another death in our city. The man worked on the river. He was a boatman who ferried passengers across at long stretches where there was no bridge. The Boatman also carried passengers up and down the river, if they wished to cross town while avoiding the traffic of the streets. He owned his boat when not many did. But the fees for ferrying were set by ordinance, and the fees were low. He lived mainly on gratuity at a time when people had little extra to give.

He was a large, coarse man, perpetually hungry from his size and his hard work and his too little pay. He was a simple man, who wanted little more than to be free of labor, to spend his days lounging in the sun with the smell of the water in his nose and the lap of the waves upon his hull, then to carouse with good friends at night. And he wanted to be full and not hungry. He was a strong man who rowed all day long.

The Boatman was not merely hungry but mythically hungry, as all rivers flow to the sea but the sea is never filled. He was hungry as a man who has been punished with famine. We have a story in our city of a king who felled a sacred tree to make room for the city's growth and was so punished. He ate ravenously and could not be filled. He was hungry even as he ate. He sold his daughter into slavery many times to pay for his hunger. Every time, by supplication or intervention or trickery, she escaped and returned to him. And ever hungrier he sold her again, until at last he began to eat his own body. Consuming himself, he died hungry. This is how the Boatman was hungry, in his heart.

One day he did not come home from work—at this distance of years, no one is certain anymore what day it was. His wife, pacing ceaselessly about their home, worried that his boat had overturned and he had drowned in the river. She worried no one would find his body. She was afraid that his appetites finally overpowered him and he was dead from drink in a gutter somewhere in the hidden places of the city. She feared that his will might have broken, if he was out of his mind with work and wished pleasure, and he found another woman. She feared that he might take his life, from shame. Or that he might have surrendered to his tedium and ceaseless hunger and pointed his boat downriver to escape alone into the unknown. Most often, she chose to worry that he ran away, because it was less painful to think that he was still alive, even if he did not love her anymore.

Day after day she went down to the river's edge, with her arms full of flowers that she wove into wreaths. She set the flowers afloat on the water and gently eased them into the flow, her hands wet with tears. And she begged with all her might that he would return to her safely, because she loved him, for all his coarseness. And the beads of tears on the delicate petals mixed brackish with the insistent scent of river water moving ever forward. She watched the petals plead their way into the current and scuttle out across the sun-decked ripples, until they tumbled down into the river's cryptic depths.

The family of the Boatman's wife believed that she was deluding herself with hope and that the Boatman was dead. Believing in the man's death, they advised her and then pleaded with her to pray, to mourn, but by all means to give up hope that he was coming back. These were ugly confrontations that served only to reinforce her belief as she shouted through defiant tears. Together, her family devised a plan to suggest the truth to her, a plan that seems cruel today but was viewed differently when our myths and superstitions suffered one less century of time's erosion.

They approached Percy, who lived next door to the Boatman and his wife. In the middle of the night, Percy opened his door to a slender, light-footed girl with a candle that gleamed on her cheekbones to make them high and precious. He led her to the crack in the wall that looked like a river unwinding a vastness of pure white sand. He watched her spry shape as she put her lips to the river, candlelight spilling over the wall and illuminating her loose white dress. Slowly she whispered, "Your husband is dead. Your husband is dead. The river has him. Mourn him and have peace."

In her dreams that night, the Boatman's wife saw her husband's stiff body lolling in the river, breathless sneer on the lips bobbing up as though to breathe, puckering toward the luminescent surface, ripples of light playing upon his blanched face.

In the still-dark morning, she woke gasping for air. She rose from bed, mad to reach the river and be united with her husband's body. In a long nightgown, she fell into the streets, and early breezes clung to her. She passed the sleepy café owners and bakers opening their bleary doors. The pre-dawn men who labored for manufacturers, sliding in speechless droves toward the furnaces in dusky silence. The young and the drunk who had not slept and purled their last vicious fantasies with voices like breaking glass. The wandering prostitutes whose eyes made love to the outpouring of the river. The encamped homeless who stayed awake for fear and warmth. They saw the madness of her lean white streak come hurried in tears, a rippling flag of mourning. Onlookers leaned their heads together to whisper about her desperation, and the desperation of a woman without the tyrant she loved so purely.

When she reached the riverside, she stumbled down the muddy bank and plunged in to her thighs, soaking her thin nightgown that gave away her body. Her hands felt wildly in the water, and she began to wail. And she cried the Boatman's name in the still night, so that the echoes could be heard at the far shore, upon the buildings and the bridges, including the Courier's bridge, which was well upriver. A crowd that had followed her through the streets gathered, and asked if they should intervene, so she would not be swept away with the current. But then, a dark form approached her beneath the waves.

It came impending like time itself, a husk of the past, a seed of the future. First a shadow, then like a shadow receding, it neared her, and its indeterminate hulk turned to something long and mangled like a fistful of broken threads, of broken hopes, a fistful of bridges uprooted like weeds and chaff. When it drifted to her, she bent into the water to embrace it, and fell to her knees. The water flowed over her breasts, hidden and exposed by the waves. Her long hair floated on the surface and fanned out around her like waves of grain. She clutched the body to her chest. It had been long beneath the water, and it was damaged and churned apart by the rough flow and the river traffic. It was unrecognizable. She held it tight to her breasts and her hair enwrapped it, and she wept upward to the sky as the river's flow crept upward on her and raised the body to her neck.

The onlookers feared to go to her, but they watched in case the river should swallow her entirely. She wailed again, a cry that rose like the caw of a new and wild and wounded bird. It spread its wings over the river, entreating the waves to be still, entreating the water to stop its flow.

When she began to rise, she let the body fall away from her breast, and she leaned over to kiss it. When she did, her eyes grew wide, and she shrieked as though she was the victim of some long and unforgivable lie.

"It's not him! It's not him! It's not him!"

At last a few young men entered the water, thinking she was a danger to herself. Together they held her arms tightly and stood her up and walked her to the shore, the water frothing about the men's powerful waists, her gown revealing her fullness beneath folds and ripples of white, like a marble Madonna, like the river was pulled endlessly over her bare skin in pure white satin. She let the men drag her through the water, repeating to herself aloud, "That's not him; that's not my husband."

They laid her down to weep for her husband, who remained lost to her even as an unknown person pulled the maimed body onto the river bank. A call went up and down the street in both directions for a doctor, and a beautiful man with a face like the sun came running. His name was Ask.

Ask had a reputation for skill as a physician, but after days full of house calls, he spent his nights on stranger things. He used electricity on people near death, and it was widely rumored that he had revived several patients thought to be beyond the brink. He shook his head at the wife's intense grief and the hopeless case. The onlookers begged him to do something, even if only a gesture. He examined the body as though confirming its death and offered, seemingly out of kindness, to take the body to his office until it could be appropriately investigated and buried. He led a group of men there, hurrying the body through the streets in a white sheet. Alone within the office, the doctor suffered an unfortunate accident, shocked to death by his own instruments.

It is presumed that he tried to explore the very limits of his craft—if not to revive a being capable of life then at least to make a beat, a flow, a breath, a tiny first spasm among the infinitesimal things that make us. To impart a momentary motion, direction, will. Some said that the haze of sleep caused a foolish mistake—apparently Ask could not wait and, whatever happened, it happened before the sun rose. Others said that the gods below were angry at Ask for stealing back the souls of the dead, and they petitioned him struck dead by lightning for interfering in the balance of life and death. Ask's father thought it was faulty machinery; in a rage he assaulted the mechanics that built the contraption to the doctor's specifications. For that assault, Ask's father earned one year of indentured servitude.

But remember that in our city all things are married. While in servitude, Ask's father helped his master to win a bride. And when the master grew deathly ill, his bride, in her abundance of love, chose to die in his place, so he would not be lost. All this strange future, as strange as any other, rode upward on the winged sobs of the Boatman's wife.

Now, a body found in the river just a few weeks after the Courier's death alerted Glaucus, who took charge of the investigation. "How can this be possible!" he cried. "Why didn't we find it dredging the river?"

He received several answers: "It could have been drawn down deeply by the current and caught in mud and rock at the bottom;" "It could have been pulled into hydraulics that churn mercilessly at the river's uneven bed—spinning and spinning for days in the swirling water and unable to break free;" "It's possible we damaged it while dredging." This last explanation was the deepest stab for Glaucus.

"We may have destroyed it?"

"Yes."

"Searching for it?"

"Yes."

"What kind of a search is that!" he snarled.

Glaucus visited the body where it had come to rest at the coroner's. It lay on a tile platform covered by a sheet. Under a sheet across the room, Ask's body also lay very still. Glaucus approached the body as he would a family member, heavy with somber breath. He also found it unidentifiable. The face and head, especially, were ruined. The limbs were badly twisted or frayed and missing. The torso was mutilated. It was impossible to discover whether the body had been cut or stabbed before it entered the river.

The clothes had also tattered and ripped away, leaving only one recognizable ornament. Tight around the body's neck was a leather band with a charm. The charm showed a circle with symbolic figures dancing around it. The figures represented the pantheon of our city's ancient myths: the nature gods, the humans loved by the gods and thus made gods, the heroes elevated to divinity for their courage and acts. Glaucus carried the whole long story in his breast pocket and travelled to the Boatman's wife.

"Was this not your husband's?" he asked, holding out the leather necklace with the charm.

"Yes," she said in tears. "He wore it every day for protection."

"Yes," affirmed Glaucus, "and his friends have told us the same. And did you not suspect him dead? He was missing for weeks."

"I did."

"And you say your dream of your husband brought you to find this body?"

"Yes."

"It seems, I'm sorry, that you were meant to find your husband, and that you found him. The only identifying mark on the body points to him."

After a long pause, Glaucus expected that the Boatman's wife would finally admit her unwillingness to accept the truth. Instead, she said the following, which Glaucus recorded in his journal: "When the shadow came toward me, I felt like it was my groom, and I felt like it was I coming toward him where he waited. And as he touched me it was like the touch of a lover, and I thought it the touch of my husband, his love perfected in death. I held the rotten flesh so tight I could feel the ribs loose inside it pressing against me, and I did not flinch; I would have bathed it in my tears and my hair. . . But it was not my husband."

Glaucus sighed and shared the rest of what he had learned. "Do you remember the woman with the twins that went down to the river to wash and draw water for her children? She was threatened by men who were bathing. They did not want to admit who was with them, but we have talked with them and, under pressure, they were willing to name the group. I am sorry to say your husband was with them. I don't say that he made any threats or advances; I don't accuse him. I say only that he was there. And when the river began to sweep hard and pulled the men away, there was flurry and confusion, and it was not certain who made the shore and who did not. It seems that your husband was carried below the water. And it seems he was trapped below, until the gods ordained in your dream that you should be reunited."

"It's not my husband," she repeated somberly, as though she almost preferred that it was.

†

THE BOATMAN'S WIDOW DIED years later without recanting, even though she was absolutely alone in her belief. The body she found was buried in a grave marked with the Boatman's name, and she was buried beside it. This was the grave to which we travelled at the end of the centennial, because the modern seekers thought they could tell something that Glaucus could not. The sun blushed the sky in hues of rouge and the color of feet that have not yet walked, when we convened at the graveyard on the hill overlooking the city. They had taken too much time searching the houses earlier in the day. No one intended to open the grave at nightfall, but that's how it happened. As a result, we exhumed the body during the exact time of the murder. Crossing the hilltop graveyard, Cat mentioned the hurt in her tooth, and I could see her tongue wriggling around inside her cheeks.

A speech was, again, in order. "Perhaps now we will have a final clue as to what happened upon the Wayfair Bridge this night a hundred years ago—and we may yet learn the fate of the precious gems. Who is in this grave!" the politician shouted, as though fecklessly demanding the man come out. "Is it the man whose name appears on this stone? Is it the Courier, mistaken

for another? Is it a stranger whom the Courier killed? We will probe the secrets of the body within. Let's see what light we can shed, to penetrate these
coiling questions that entwine the fabric of our city." The reporters jotted
spastically. The graveyard was better attended by casual onlookers than any
of the houses had been. I looked over the modest, twitching crowd, their
faces disappearing into the settling dusk. My aunt and Rabbit were con-
spicuously absent, and I concurred that Rabbit should not see such a thing.
I wasn't sure I had the stomach myself, but Clement was all sparks and hot
bolts of energy. He vibrated with the idea of looking death in the face.

He told me, as we crossed the Courier's Bridge that morning, "You
must face anything you conquer. Unfaced, unconquered. And this elusive
thing, death, so elusive that you don't ever really believe it's going to happen—today I am giving it a face. I am nailing it down and making it stick in
a place where it cannot hide. And I am going to pour my eyes right into it,
pierce it with my eyes. I am going to look on it where I have it nailed, and
know, you understand, *know*." He jabbed his fingers repeatedly into me. "I'm
going to lean right overtop of that face, and look right into the dead sockets
and pair my seeing to their blindness. And I'm going to gaze at the wasted
nose and breathe deep and pair my breath to that breathlessness. And I'm
going to look hardest, most hard for you, friend, who needs this more than
me, I'm going to look my very hardest right at the hard, thin, wasted tongue
in that motionless mouth. And I'm going to feel the fine and silken flesh
aching in my mouth and pounding at the doors of my jaws to split my teeth
and speak! And I'm going to pair it to that tongue of ash and silence and
know. And then for me, for all time, death will be the knotted thing they put
back in that grave. And I will have liberation."

"Here's your chance," I told him, as our circle cinched around the rent
earth, next to a headstone, laid flat, that did not bear the Courier's name.
The sky turned dark flame and the trees quivered in an evening wind burst
that blew thorny down the tangled spine of the river. I could see the tiny
hairs on the backs of Cat's arms stood on end. In a wave her skin turned
smooth to rough, chasing the chill in flocks like seductive butterflies. An
exhumer crawled out from the lair where he had been carefully removing
the last handfuls of dirt. He lifted himself into our halo of artificial light. I
peered at the narrow wooden box.

My whole knowing poured into that tear in the earth and refracted. All
of creation, all stars and planets, suns and moons and celestial wonders, all
skies and storms, painted clouds, lightning and thunder and wind, all mountains, all stones, all caverns and secret places, all monuments, great oceans
and crystal pools and trembling mirrors, water in immeasurable quantities,
all forests and flowers, all animals, senses, spirit, survival, all breath, all that

breathes, all struggle, glory, triumph, all sadness, all speech, all words, all languages, all song, all ineffable, all life. All pulled from the ends of creation where existence meets and penetrates the void. All poured in symphonies through the open ground in its ever-ordained, inescapable current. Into the dark lens that gravitates all, rent with all, then bends all, pulls all, focuses all, contracts all, refracts all, ennobles all, delivers all now from this enclosed moment when existence is compacted to a great dissymmetry, erupting to an open fountain, gushing ever-opening trumpet blooming song and light and breath and multifoliate harmonies and ache of indescribable sweetness and theophany.

They pulled the coffin up with ropes and set it on the upchurned dirt. I heard the dry rotted sound of rusted nails breaking as they pried the lid. The weak wood splintered in two from the leverage, and I thought I smelled pungent lavender.

I saw only a black clod through the narrow gash in the wood. Then two men lifted the halves of the lid away. All I heard was breath. Shared breath like the wind forced itself into the mouths of the crowd. There lay the naked ewer that was an unknown broken man, his identity echoing within the collapsed skull, offered with the mangled limbs. I could trace the hollows in the clay where the power of his heart raced jets of life, eruptions of hope and awe and pleasure. I heard the departed strength that moaned in the maimed and broken bones. There was the necklace, the leather rotted, the metal pantheon unchanging. There was no face for Clement.

A ripple of illness passed through me, like a rumble of thunder, suddenly chilled and stiff-necked and aching. I had a notion of our old story about curiosity—when a woman opened a box belonging to the artificer of humanity and containing all the unused and ill-suited materials. The unloosed plagues descended upon the world: toil and death and violence, lust and greed and pride and envy, sloth and gluttony, vain self-pity and self-destruction. I thought of the first sin, the first desire to become gods and myths, to know all things, consume all things, eradicate all mystery. I thought of the tragedy of what the Courier carried: the Courier killed, the Killer mired forever and chained to the rock of his guilt. Of course, as the story goes, along with all the ills the woman discovered the virtue of hope, unneeded by humanity in the paradise before we troubled the river's waters. And she cradled hope to her breast, a gentle and mending bird.

The body seemed to crumble before my eyes in the dusky breeze. Two doctors from the coroner's office rushed to the casket to protect the body and ply their trade. They took it to their laboratory, in hopes that they could determine more details about its identity or discover microscopic marks on the bones showing the body had been stabbed. I learned afterward that they found neither. The body was reinterred in the same grave. The name on the tomb remains unchanged.

And they failed. They all failed. They had the audacity to break open all our sacred secrets on a single day, a day that meant all to them and nothing to the Courier, a centennial that was an arbitrary mark of capricious time. They were assured that the day would honor only their success. They thought the answer would break clean away from the edifice of history—that at the light of their faces the clod of clay would crumble and reveal the form of man. That they could behold the man, put the wounds upon his hands, the wounds of the son of our city. That there would be a form to pierce with blame. They were wrong. They did not understand that the Courier was his death, that the treasure was the mystery. Night fell, and they had no answers. And the centennial was ending. And they went away to sleep in the darkness of cruel, unfulfilled fame.

†

THE OPENING OF THE grave shook me deeply.

I shook because I learned that there was not just a mystery but a man. A man whose life drained away like a river, when he exhaled at the crown of the bridge, and his animating breath fled up the high stone towers and out into oblivion. And the brilliance he carried vanished.

Maybe it is because I tread the floorboards where he trod, and maybe it is because I lay my head where he lay to watch the children below the window—but when you have come to love a mystery as I have, there follows a need, a physical need like a rising tide, to unite in the body with the thing that captivates. There is a need to eliminate the remoteness of mystery—mystery that cannot be destroyed, only brought closer or denied.

I recognized the pain of the Courier, metastasized in that unearthed body. I recognized the brilliance he carried as something personal that I might carry. I saw his death as my death. As he was opened, I will be opened. As he bled, I will bleed. I will be pierced. I will vanish—into the mighty river that swallowed him.

He was vulnerable as I am vulnerable. But I am afraid I will not die as he did, plunging across the bridge in darkness carrying beauty, full of life's ebullience. Transmitting his duty, obedient until the end, like the lover that long ago died swimming the same stretch of river, reaching toward his beloved. Transmitting not that which he carried but instead his very identity. Death was his immemorial self. He is forever crossing the bridge, because his life and his death persist.

I wanted him. I wanted him actually and tangibly. To know him. To share him. To share his endless trajectory carrying beauty into the void. I wanted him as a mystery alone cannot give. I wanted him as my stories are incapable to relate. As all stories are incapable. I wanted him as the river of stories cannot carry away. Cannot erode. Cannot cripple. Cannot cough up the hacked hunk of flesh they withdrew and called a name. I wanted him indestructible. I wanted him chaste and eternal. I wanted him unconquerable.

I wanted to love him. To embrace him. A familiar temple, like a spouse, that renews. Like a steadfast friend who understands. A parent who forgives. A lover thought to be lost. A love from across the bridge of the void. A love to fill my own love of void, that recognizes my own empty body pouring and tumbling in wind-drawn strands from the precipice of the bridge. Bone of my bone and flesh of my flesh. A bride to the bridge. Bridled in its unbreakable cable that dances across chaos.

I wanted his blood to remain upon the bridge. I wanted to kneel over the stain and stare into the depthless red and say—you will not destroy me. You could destroy me—you could show me the truth and unveil the mystery and destroy me. But I look because I trust you. You will not destroy me. Captivate me.

I went to the bridge in the first hours of morning, so the dark would hide the nakedness of my desire. A new day began as the city slept, and I christened its creation in my searching. I started where Percy would have said goodbye, drunk with wanderlust. He sent out his hope with his friend because he wanted to fly with him, with a real secret in his hands, to a place that ached in wait, even as Meda in her home ached for him. I processed up the solemn arch as my hand clipped the peeling paint of the rough iron railing. I paused at the peak to assure that the bridge was deserted. A fresh wind lulled along the river valley. I closed my eyes and inhaled a wet dirge of cut wood and dewy leaves, rusted metal and algae and earth—dark and fecund. And faintly, behind it, a hint of the city's stone and brick, of old ashes thrown out into the garden, sulfur of the city's beating heart. The river murmured its strange and indolent language that has no translator. Solitude enwrapped me.

Looking back, I traced along the bridge until the east end dipped below the bow of the deck, remembering how the Courier like a departing ship, like the sun to the west, descended from Percy's sight. This was where the Courier sank below the horizon and dropped from time. I dropped to my knees.

The entire deck of the bridge was wood in the Courier's day. Since then, the roadway has been replaced with metal grating, but the walks at either side have remained intact. I lay my face close against the heavy wood, grey and pitted with time, the timbers' raisined bodies worn deep at their centers beneath the pulsing flow of foot traffic. But near the metal lattice that separated the walk from the road, and near the wrought-iron railing above the river, the timber fanned its splinters like elderly skin, full of sharp hollows where the wounds of a man may hide.

I searched. I thirsted for him.

I went into the arms of the bridge because he was alone. I went because I was alone. His solitude was sufficient; my loneliness was not. Bent down low, so that my lips almost swept the planks and my back ached, I crept toward the western bridge tower. He must have died before the tower, or the witnesses at the west end would have seen him. I strained my eyes, pouring sight into each minute abyss. My pulse raced—I do not know why I was so afraid of discovery. I felt its heat. I felt its metered rush. My own pumping river, ticking out my days.

When the wind rose, it rankled the bridge, threw street dust in my eyes, and curled oceans in my ears. But as it subsided, my pulse was there. Regular and heavy and metered time loping toward a blood line in the tissue of the wood. Loping toward the sacred in its aged cradle. Pumping even as the pearled tide of life pumps into new beings and the wombs of new forms. As the Courier's blood pumped in jets of ebbing life into the waiting river. And the river received it as a cup: down from the bridge our river joins with a dry, steep valley, the empty bed of its own ancient course. The shape formed of the two, in the confluence of the past and the now, caught the life that spilled from him and fell.

I searched like a man hobbled with age and wrongs—my old-aged and failing self hidden within this alluring youth, myself old before my time—who loped his broken steps along the yearning bridge as if down the aisle of the oldest altar. His steps seem to come forever. I think his stuttering legs, his broken gait, are just about to appear above the crest, are just about to fail, but on they come. Advancing the aisle toward enshrined fate, paced and metered as my heart. Slow and numbed by pain, as everyone waits and watches, awed at his determination. He comes, a brave but feeble pulse, on a fickle tide. On and on I plodded in the nakedness of future. A crippled man, who can hardly stand, but by his god is going to kneel when he comes before his manhood.

He comes. And I come. And come Time, you Killer, come and confess from the terror of my words that flock on you like cranes. You wish to drown me in the river. But I live. And my sight convicts you. Confess, Time! Or if you should kill me, kill me like a jealous lover, and let me be the river flowing endless into you.

And there. There, a distant black infused a halo of the coarse and bitter, knotted grey. A whisper, it faded like the day to the west. A crumbled black that waited deep in the deepest hollows of the wood, where the bread of night, torn, shed wisps of sinew tinged maroon. A pensive softness, like a delicate moss, a waiting spring in the pale and sap-drained wood. A breath might stir it, a breath into the tangled husk where the bluntness of the wind could not dare go.

I knew, of course, it could be any rubbish—any dirty thing waiting to consume a foolish heart. And the time. Of course, I know the ravages of time. Towing us in current, pulling us with ever-long fingers entwining muscle and pinions, and lengthening us on the rack of centuries. Its great avulsion deposits us on the far bank of myth, where we are all potential and no flowing, no echo when I pound the courage of my full chest.

I blew very gently into the cleft of tortuous wood, the way I might have filled the lungs of an infant. And with my lips so close to the planks, I drove a fine powder up from the profundity. It splashed my face, speckled my cheeks and nose, a playful life that, unhinged, flung spurts of life serum into vacuum. I did not wipe the douse upon my lips.

My eyes fixed starry, penitent, on the constellation of rent earth. Earth of infinite forms, of dirt and flesh, trees and wood and ashes, that sprays magnificent and vast as oceans in pumping human arteries, in the artery of our city in the circuit from the depths to the shore—flows its passing form into ever-new flesh. Collapsing into the embrace of its other self. I was scattering like dust. The wind blew me back to nothing. I grappled with the clots, with the crumbs of a life, a fibrous thrush with the power of the killer and the killed in my hanging form.

I stared with the absurdity of staring at bread.

The absurdity of being given to stare at this man's blood. To stare into the dazzling watery eye of mystery, the purchase and the power to lift me from my knees. I know the taste of blood. I have had my own blood in my mouth. I know the menses. Iron and mucous, citrus and seasons and shed petals, the must of pressed grape skins and rain. I know it.

I wet my lips. I brushed them so very close, so only my moist breath filled the slender distance, the tempting of a kiss. My being cried out to the infinite outpouring of life and flesh and divinity that had led to that precise moment. Cried out to the cloud of myths and untraceable pasts, and to their cloud-piercing height that made me feel upon the mound of buried history that there is something more. Cried out to the wound in my own heart because I cannot but also do not want to see the truth of time laid bare and broken. I moved my lips toward the mystery.

When I am weak then I am strong. When I am weak I know my need, and in the knowledge of my need I have the strength to surrender. I surrender to that which brought me here. You will not let me disappear into the uncreated. Into the air above this bridge where I cannot fly. Into the plunge below where I cannot swim. You will not give me up to this consuming emptiness. You will not destroy your creation. Do not let your created go into the darkness, into the loneliness. Do not give me up into oblivion. Do not let me go into the nothing. Do not abandon me! Open my lips and make me speak! Do not let me suffer for nothing. Temper me. This is the potter's hand. The shears to the vine that bears fruit. Wring it from me! Wring the blood and the words from my heart of stone. Give me the fear that is the beginning of wisdom. If you take my breath away, I am dust. Give it back and renew this earth. Give me breath. I howl to eternity with the bellows of my voice, out of the raw garden of my lungs. I am pouring out my life, spilling blood like wine. Spill into the river that sweeps down into this buried city, brings its purity and purpose to the buried, to carry us out of this delirious waiting. Open my lips, and I will speak! This is the day; this is the last day! Out of the mouths of infants bring the cry of life, the defense against avenging night. Let all things that have breath open!

What I see is not made out of what is visible. Everything exposed to the light becomes visible. Everything that becomes visible is light. Awake, sleeper.

I put my lips upon the wood. I tasted first the bitter dust, the silt tang, astringent leather of innumerable trampling feet, the bleak, burgeoning soil that makes the mouth feel full of cotton, illness like my teeth wished they were loose in their sockets, and the desert-dry exile of the wood. And beneath that was the taste of toil that drove my own feet across the planks day after day, and all the sweating toils of an entire city driven ceaselessly across bridges. There was the taste of my own beloved suffering, where I keep myself from joy to frame an image that I venerate. And beneath that there was the taste of struggle for the unattainable, the unquenchable thirst, the taste of a whole suffering world that is dying for a reason to suffer, the taste of loss, abandonment, loneliness, infinity, and eternity so great that they isolate me in a static and everlasting stillness, whole universes and all uncreated potential stranding every love upon itself alone. And beneath that there was the love that dies crossing the river to its beloved, that is the creation of bridges. But then faintly, beneath everything. Faintly, so that I may never know if I tasted. The mediated glory.

†

WHEN THE ANCIENT KINGS of our city were expected to shed blood for certain ceremonies, they went to holy rooms atop our temples; they pierced their tongues with a sharp reed—a bloodletting for the gods. It was only the kings who must bleed, and it was the blood of kings to be offered in the place of the city's people. As it was the king who led our city into battle.

These ceremonies were marked by celebrations that we should have a king, that we should have his blood to give to the gods. For a time, games also marked the event, games in which contestants played for their lives. But here is the great riddle of time: we are not sure from the old texts whether it was the winners or the losers who were killed. After the model of the king, it may be the winners who played for the honor of dying, who went to the gods via death to return with rain, sun, fertility, life, and favor for the people.

At the heights of our ancient hunger, we practiced human sacrifice—first with prisoners and enemies, but eventually in highly-ordered ceremonies with special victims set apart from birth to belong to the gods. These victims were raised as royalty, honored, kept in luxury, kept pure. They were instructed from infancy about their destiny, their divine role. They mounted the temple above a hushed crowd by torchlight, certainly afraid of death but also imbued with certainty and purpose of this appointed time. They mounted the temple like they went to their wedding bed to make life.

During one era, they were pierced through the heart with a ceremonial dagger. Their hearts were removed. During another, they were thrown into wells, weighted with gold and precious stones: the stones sank down to the underworld to appease gods below, while the soul lifted up to appease heaven. Even the souls of sacrificed criminals were expected to go upward to appease the righteous gods.

†

DAYLIGHT CAME, ONE HUNDRED years and one day after the Courier was killed. It was the centennial of the first day the world and I lived without the Courier.

I had stumbled home from the bridge in darkness and did not have a good look at my repaired room until I woke. In the morning light, I found that the apprentice left to fix the damage had not put my floorboards back in the same order, so their trod paths and worn faces were all a mangle. There used to be deeper, darker trails from the single bed to the window, from the window to the desk, from the desk to the bed and to the door. That is why I had arranged my room as I did, in hopes I might walk his paths. Now the paths are scattered, a puzzle without a solution. As I write this, I retrace the old ways and try to reform them, but there is not enough time, and I have too few steps.

I can tell you all about myself in an instant. There is a story of a prophet who offered his prophecies to the king for a price. The king refused. So the prophet burned several books on the spot and offered the remainder for the same price. When the king refused again, he did the same, compelling the king to buy.

That morning, I had a restless desire to visit the Courier's grave, but there was no grave because it was empty, just a hole in the ground. I had notions of going back to the cemetery to lie in the open pit—seeing that I lived also in the rooms where he had lived—but I had an overwhelming sense that once I chose to go in I would not get out again. The walls would be too steep, with no foothold, and I would be trapped. So instead, I submitted to an expedition that Clement had been planning for a long time.

We have a buried bridge in our city. It is a grand stone-arch bridge with intricate carving and detail, lined with urns bursting forth stone flowers, frescoes of gods and battles, and an arabesque balustrade with voluted pillars paved in mosaic. All that labor and beauty, however, waits entombed. The buried bridge was the first in our city to bear the text: *Yield not to disasters but press on more bravely.* The text was renewed upon the Wayfair Bridge, which was built long after this first was buried.

A man named Ania built the bridge, and he buried the bridge. His story is worth telling. Ania was a refugee from a city that had been destroyed by its enemies. He travelled in search of a new home with a small group of families loyal to his leadership. They arrived finally in our city after an arduous journey of many years that led them to many diverse places.

Before they reached our city, they stayed in another, ruled by a queen who was beloved by her people and renowned for her kindness. The queen welcomed them because she was once a refugee herself. She had been royalty in her homeland, and was married to a man of extraordinary wealth. But her brother coveted her husband's wealth and arranged for her husband to be killed. Under the law, her deceased husband's wealth would pass through her to her brother. When she learned her husband was dead, without time to mourn, she fled the city with a group of faithful subjects and as much riches as they could carry. She promised them all titles in a new and just kingdom. She was queen of the prosperous and peaceful city they founded when Ania discovered it by accident.

The two refugees fell in love. They found themselves together in exile, in a place that was not their home but where love still bloomed. The queen overwhelmed Ania by her goodness and intelligence, mingled with a decisive and enduring strength that is distinctly feminine. She admired the humility with which he accepted the trust and leadership of his friends, setting out through the wilderness with courage tempered by compassion. Each watched how the other exercised the power life had strangely granted them. In her court he knelt before her raiment, eyeing beneath his brow the hem of her dress, the gold bands on her tight and slender arms. In her chambers he pressed her perfumed skin so tightly against his own roughed, tanned skin that she felt she could not breathe, she felt she needed not breath but his embrace, and she smothered herself in the muscle and heat and smell of forests.

But Ania did not stay. He was going to a place that he thought destiny and gods decreed, a promised land of his own kingship, a place where his own blood and the legacy of his followers would live on infinitely. The queen was tender but unflinching as she watched Ania and his people prepare their ships. She fell in love with him again to see him in command, but she would not be alone with him, now that he was wedded to destiny. He last saw her as he knelt again before her in court and thanked her for inviting and preserving his people. He kissed her hand lavishly, but she remained controlled. Then he mounted the bridge of his ship with steps that shook the shoreline, and the sails were up. She watched Ania disappear over the curvature of the earth.

Ania traveled to our city to build the bridge that Clement and I set out to visit. The queen built her own funeral pyre, climbed upon it looking the most regal of all her life, and fled to the gods in a pillar of flame. Her last thought, as she lay upon the dry wood that pressed on her gentle skin was that she lay upon Ania's bones. Some said Ania lost a child to the fire, but only the queen would know.

Ania arrived in our city, fledgling as it still was, unaware of the tragedy left in his wake. He married into our royalty and, in time, became king in his own right, which he would not have been as the husband of the ruling queen. His blood mingled with our own ancient line. The families that came with him melted into our own. And though there were skirmishes and differences, the people adored Ania. They had been convinced by oracles before he came that a foreigner would uplift our city. His claim to the throne and his succession went unchallenged.

Ania undertook optimistic building efforts that became some of the glorious public places of our old city. One of his projects was to solve the problem of a deep ravine.

I mentioned before that our city has a dry riverbed, where the river once flowed in ancient times. Some ancient cataclysm, some small detail for the earth but incomprehensible for us small creatures, perhaps the ancient flood itself, shifted the river's flow. One story says that the river winds like the snake but charges like a bull—the present riverbed and the dry bed make the bull's horns. One bed is dry because that horn was broken off by a hero who once struggled with the bull, and this broken horn is represented by the horn of plenty that spills food and life upon the family table, or the horn some wear around their neck as a sign of fertility. Others say the dry bed is where the gored earth remembers the death of a woman, executed when her hair was tied to a bull and the bull was let run.

For a long time, the gully was arduous to cross, so the city grew around the edges of the crescent-shaped gash. Ania determined that he should bridge the depth. It was fate for him to reconcile this fertile place, because of the child or the death he had left behind him.

In his heart, he built the massive stone-arch bridge in honor of his former love, expending the highest talents of his stonemasons. He marked the bridge with a text representing the high destiny that caused his flight—the text now upon the Courier's Bridge. At the two ends of the bridge, among the frescoes, were two faces. To all the city they looked like unnamed watching gods, but to Ania they represented the distant queen's two loves: her husband and Ania himself. Ania did not know he was building a monument to the dead.

Ania also buried the bridge, after it stood nobly for over a decade. His plans for city improvements grew more ambitious with time, and he decided that he should fill in the entire dry riverbed, so the steep gully would be reclaimed for streets and houses, making the city contiguous. This plan would cover the bridge, because it sat below street level. It crossed the precipitous center of the ravine, and the roads wound down to it. To accomplish his feat, Ania moved a steep hill that was impeding expansion in another area where the city was just then growing. There was some discord about the hill, as some figured it for a place of prominence in an old military victory, but the men with picks and shovels came anyway.

Ania laid low the monument of the hill, employing for years hundreds of people who moved piles of dirt in wheelbarrows. His militia ranks were full of powerful workers, strong from moving dirt day after day. The men enjoyed the camaraderie and exercise—they were fed well, worked reasonable hours, and, for the most part, the work was not too dangerous. Only one thing bothered them: when they overturned their wheelbarrows at the edge of the ravine, and watched the dirt pour in, the opening was so big that it seemed they had done nothing at all. Still, the brazenness of the project became a celebrated tribute to Ania's endlessness, and the ground slowly rose with the flow of earth. Only the end of the riverbed remains unfilled, where it meets the present path of the river. The confluence of the valleys holds up a chalice to the river's flow, and at night the promontory between fills it with an outcropping of lighted homes.

In hindsight, some believe that Ania buried the bridge because he discovered what happened to his foreign queen when he left her shores. Perhaps another refugee brought the story to our city by chance, as Ania came to her. As the Courier's story came to his mother. To me, it is a grave either way, because of the bridge. Supposedly, they filled in the gorge from both sides, leaving the bridge in the center for last, so it could be used. It looked, I imagine, like a sacrificial victim, long and bare at the bottom of a sacred cenote. Ania, it is written, threw the first shovel onto the path of the bridge.

Though the chasm was closed, the streets and homes that lined its rim remained untouched. Ania simply built a regimen of parallel streets across the new distance, and new homes followed. Looking at a map of our city, it is easy to recognize the older streets that reflect the crescent outline of the ravine, a great old stab right in the making of our city, right in the plot that is its identity, with parallel lines running like sutures crossing the closed wound.

The bridge has never been unearthed, and its magnificent art has not been seen for many, many generations. We have in our library only feeble sketches, the architects' plans being lost to time or destroyed. More recently, the city commissioned a fountain to mark the spot of the buried bridge. From research of old plots and narratives, the fountain is supposed to rest approximately over the center of the bridge, spilling water that does not run beneath the arches.

Clement and I made our excursion to the site of the buried bridge on the day after the centennial. Having nothing but time, which is the only thing we ever have, Clement and I took the long way, watching the sights and the throngs of people at their myriad occupations and distractions. On our way, we passed Ania's ruined mausoleum. Once a magnificent circular monument of flowered tiers and breathless apses enclosing urns of gold, it lies overgrown, long ago sacked and collapsed, surrounded by a vulgar fence. Some say the graves were scattered; others say they are the very dirt beneath your feet. Like all the eternal glory we once were, there it reposes, empty.

That was when Clement began, "You know how they buried this bridge—the dirt didn't fill the spaces beneath the arches. It piled up on either side. As long as they filled the ravine to the top, who cared—it meant less dirt. They left huge, sealed underground vaults. And, you know, it doesn't take very long for people to discover a thing like that. And you know the people like me who wanted to discover it. They say that for a couple of hundred years there was a network of tunnels connecting the vaults, filled with torches, and that the arches were occupied by brothels, and bands of thieves in hiding, and poisons and hallucinogens and clandestine stills, where every illegal thing had its price. And then they say vagrants and the poor of the city eventually moved in, the poorest families that had no shelter. And they had to band together to secure their tunnels, so that the children living under one arch were not stolen by the brothel in the next."

"Imagine," he said, "the tall stone arches, forming bastilles like heart chambers, pumping with moans and cries, full of acrid smoke and the dirty ferment of cheap alcohol. And the stale air full of humid breath, and the smell of the sweat of slums teeming with orphans, with no running water, and the sickly salty smell of adultery and the drugged sighs of the girls fumbling around in their overworked bodies smeared with false floral scents where no flowers grow. And maybe slum children fighting and playing and singing where no birds sing and no above-ground sounds penetrate, and everything, everything of course, tempered with the smell of the trampled earthen floor, living in the packed damp clay odor of graves. That's what they did with the bodies when the prostitutes died—the dirt was right below them—and why take a slave into the light when the rich man comes below to break the wounded girls with his power?"

"You see," Clement continued, "this is how it is in time: all us poor orphans go beneath the bridge, bastards of time, bastards of myth, sniveling little brats, selfish for the bare needs of breath and hunger and life and light and heat and flesh. We go beneath the bridge. And the shadow of the bridge enfolds us in its pitying wings. It's not those old great stone arches, those triumphal arches that bear up the weight of the way. No! It's the orphans beneath who bare it up on their stringy backs and tortured ribs and calloused hands, and all our stolen lives and stolen hours, and all our stale breath and all our giving away."

We reached the fountain, where I dropped down to one knee. I pressed my palm firm against the ground with my fingers spread wide, and I tried to let my body read, in some ancient way, the size and depth of what lay silent below me. I tried to sense the bridge with the same solemn architecture buried within myself.

There is an ancient relic in the human, and it remembers things that cannot be spoken. It is the thing that makes me want to dive into solitary forest rivers and lay bare in the sun atop boulders, to dance wild with unbetrayed freedom in the midst of a pounding circle of drums, to smell the salt of the sea, to look from mountaintops; it is the thing that makes fire beautiful. This relic is still spellbound and overjoyed with the realization that life exists, and thought, and beauty. It is the thing that feels a long lineage pulling a present body in tow up out of the muck and moss, up into a wind that pours scalding down a gulping mouth into a cathedral of light and sky, mountain, wood, savanna, and sea. This relic has no appropriate language, but articulates itself only as kindred to other ancient things, a brotherhood and sisterhood that is before expression. It must come out; it must come out and you dance.

That is how I tried to know the buried bridge: to press into the earth that enveloped its patient husk and to vibrate with its spacious silence and latent power. Like a great, lost transmission lodged inside my manhood. A potentiality. An entombed link.

It's down there—I thought, trying to discern its weight and curvature, to feel the delicacies of its stone frescoes, as though bridge cables came up like pinwheels from its corners to my fingertips. I stayed there a long time, thinking on the man who built it, whose unseen face was frozen in unseen stone below, thinking on the love or death he honored, thinking on the monumental undertaking of a monument's burial. As I knelt there in the center of the crescent wound in our city's atlas.

"My father will be in there."

"Clement—" I answered.

"When he's finally abandoned his intoxicated life."

I remained at the fountain, leaned against the cold stone, and listened to the rush of water against a lucid bronze body flickering up to the sky like the creation of spring. I wrote some of the first notes that I have transmitted into this book. Meanwhile, Clement pursued the neighborhood. He said the tunnels to the vaults had been backfilled a hundred years ago or more, and no one remembers where they were. Still, he couldn't help but say he looked. He milled the streets adjacent to where the bridge lay, especially the alleys and closes. He knocked on doors of houses near where the bridge ended, to ask what the homes were built on and whether there seemed a walled-up section in the foundation stones. He claimed that he dropped into a sewer and went a ways by the light that penetrated the grates above. But he found deep wells and tunnels where the light did not penetrate, and he had to give up. He was convinced the sewers would somehow connect to the old tunnels.

"Imagine what could be down there," he said with wonder. "Maybe there are people who already rediscovered them hiding there now."

Eventually Cat joined us at the fountain when she got off work, and we three strolled the neighborhood together. The warm sun was a pleasant contrast to the coldness of the spring nights. We sat al fresco for lunch and coffee. And, unexpectedly, we noticed Rabbit, smiling in the sunshine like all the world was a great and happy pastime and everyone loved one another no matter what they might do. My aunt was in the store behind him, but he preferred watching the street roll by.

He made a wide-eyed face exaggerated with surprise when he spotted me. I waved, and he ran over. "H-Hello," he said.

"Hi, Rabbit," I answered.

"You know what? You know what? They—they—they didn't find anything. Yesterday."

"I know."

"They were in—y—your house?"

"They were in my house, but they didn't find anything."

Rabbit thrust his hands in his pockets, threw his head back, and laughed like it was the greatest news in the world.

"Hey. They, they should have known—they wouldn't find anything."

"They should have known," I repeated. I could hear both his pocketed hands clicking together his beloved marbles. He always had them with him.

"They were looking in the in the wrong place!"

I had to smile at his fantastic excitement. "Oh yeah?" I asked, giving him an inquisitive face. Cat and Clement sat beside me, leaning together with their shoulders pressed tight. They held still so they could hear. Clement gathered his brow above desirous and judgmental eyes. His hand rested heavy on her forearm.

Rabbit got on his toes to approach my ear. I leaned toward him. He gently patted the back of my neck and took me into his love affair with the gentle world. Very softly, he whispered, "I know where they are." He stepped away. "But guess what. Guess what. Guesswhat!"

"What?" Clement yelled impatiently.

"I'm—I'm not telling!" And Rabbit laughed again. A laugh of such great confidence as only a child can muster. The type of laugh that does not believe in death; death has never even occurred to it. Then, solemn again, he added, "Know w—what I think." He took a proud breath and looked upward dramatically. "S—some—someone was supposed to, to get the jewels? R—right?"

"Yes," I answered.

"Well." He paused as though we should know already. "Well what. W—what if t—they didn't *want* them?"

At first, my heart was tickled at his naive idea that someone would not want something so precious. Until I thought on the great apathy of it, possible because of its greatness, and the possibilities of despair, pitiable and fruitless. I thought of our talents and duties, the heights of ourselves buried. And a peculiar simplicity of the idea rang out, a simplicity that gave it clarity.

I realized that I did not know who bought the jewels the Courier supposedly carried. I would think that Glaucus must have found that out, but I never came across it in his notes. Perhaps it was taken for granted that the buyer wanted to buy the jewels Melager sent. But want takes different forms. What if the buyer, by killing the Courier, obtained the jewels for which he did not want to pay? Or what if there was some other benefit that materialized out of the freedom from their burdens? I remembered the buyer called the Courier's employer, complaining that the jewels were not received as planned. Perhaps it was an easy ruse.

But now, the symmetry of it: the two men, the two cities, buying and selling the beauty, like a convict passed among sovereigns, the confined fire. The conviction. And what of Melager's brothers who fled, who shared his business in other cities? Was this his peace to them? Was it their vengeance? Did the man receiving the jewels conceal that he was Melager's brother? I imagined the buyer speaking to the Killer, "I have a package coming by courier—I don't want to receive it." He might have let the Killer take his cut and then filled his hands with the free beauty, the free fire.

But would the Killer share what he had got by blood, when it was in his own hands and he could flee alone? What if the Killer never delivered the jewels? What if, to avoid this possibility, the man to receive the jewels was himself the Killer?

All of us were musing to ourselves on the sidewalk when Rabbit asked me, "Wha—what do do you think?"

"About the Killer?"

"Yeah."

"I always like to imagine that the Killer was successful," I said to Rabbit but for Clement. "I imagine him in a remote and exotic place, where he is untouchable and at peace. I imagine him bronze with sun and wearing white linen. His long hair afloat in the breeze. His bare feet playing in pure white sand. Where the warm wind strips off his clothes. He is alone and naked, diving again and again into the clear water. Wanting for nothing; waiting for nothing; surrounded by light and purity. I imagine him completely in love with the man he killed and living a life of beauty for the life he took. I imagine he gets drunk at night beneath the stars and feels the whole world vibrating with his pulse, utterly grateful that one would die for him to have a paradise."

Clement exhaled, and I pushed him further.

"Euphoric, he spills wine into the sea as the name of the Courier spills from his intoxicated lips. His fire on the beach devours the sea air, plaits his hair with gold, and shields him from the night. It shadows and accentuates the muscles of his struggle. That overpowered his victim. And before he sleeps, he pours his abundance of wine over the coals to quench the fire, blood upon the embers of the gems. He pours and pours, and the simmering sweet aroma goes up like incense, so he can smell the sun-baked vines, the quenched loam of the fields that lie in mist, the must, the sweat of the worker, the flesh of the vintner, and the oak where the vintage waits for perfection, like the Courier waits unmarked and unknown in his oak coffin. And at night the Killer sleeps in his victim's blackness. So when he awakes, he is almost blinded by glory."

"Sometimes," I added, "the Killer I imagine is not even wealthy—he has only the wealth of life. A saved life that should have been lost. Sometimes I imagine that the reason no one found any jewels is because they weren't in the box the Courier carried."

Clement laughed.

"Melager didn't send them like he claimed. Listen, why wouldn't Melager have arranged for a courier in advance if he was moving his jewels? Why was it done at the last minute? It had to be something else. Maybe nothing. Maybe a note to make amends. Maybe he lost the jewels. Maybe he didn't have any jewels and took advantage of the disappearance to pretend he did, for his pride. Maybe he thought he could recover something for the loss . . ."

"We know how that works," said Clement, who could not wait to speak. "Everyone says it's not their problem. Especially the Courier, whose company doesn't pay for, what's it called—an 'act of god.' Besides, the old man died poor like everybody else. You can have all the money in the world, but you die poor."

"I think there was a message," I said. "I think the message was the thing of great value but it was incomprehensible to the Killer. I can approach a Killer who finds something different than expected. Maybe the jewels were the Killer's motivation, but all that burned up in the life that came after. He learned something that let him flee toward simplicity and mercy."

They say that even gods can take irrevocable oaths. It is essential to having the fullness of their power. They are not all-powerful if they cannot keep their promises. That is the lesson of our city's story about a human woman who was lover to a god. She was tempted to see the god as he is and not in his mediated state in which he loved her. She made him take an oath that he would grant her unspoken wish before she asked it. And when she had her wish, when she viewed him arrayed in immortal splendor, she turned to ash, as we cannot bear to be made choiceless in the fullness of revelation.

Rabbit seemed to understand me without understanding. He nodded generously.

"You think about this too much," said Clement.

Catherine looked like a rose, flower-heavy, that is turned toward the ground.

"I think about it every day," I answered somberly. "I have written the scene a hundred times." When no one spoke, I continued, "Of course, the reason I think of the Killer this way is because it means a great deal to me to think of the Courier dead. If you're right, Rabbit, did the person receiving the jewels kill the Courier?"

"No."

"Then what happened to the Killer?"

"He didn't go far."

"Well where did he go?" challenged Clement abruptly.

Rabbit backed away, then pantomimed that he locked his mouth shut with a key. Then he threw the key. His eyes followed its arc through the air to where it landed in the river. He threw open his hands in a timid little motion that said *Splash!* He intended it only for himself, and he looked down at his shoes like he forgot we were there.

"Well you know what I think," said Clement, gathering momentum. But Rabbit did not look at him. "I think the whole epic story was a fraud, front to back, which is why it was never solved. I think the Courier died happy in a hotel in a faraway city much better than our own, next to a gorgeous fallen angel who served him like a slave. And I think he strolled the avenues and gorged on dinners and liquors with friends, and had what other things and persons he wanted. And if he preferred to be alone, I bet he stayed up all night in the cafés with a fine cigar that trickled its little dance into a smoke-filled room while he unburdened his mind with oblivion. And I bet he looked out at the sea of night, over in our direction, and thought about what a bunch of believing idiots claw around this old river, in this old city that has been dying for longer than people can remember, filled up by graves with dates washed clean away, like the fools underneath that worked themselves to death for nothing. All the trusting fools that the Courier had beaten. I think they slit the throat of some mangy dog on the bridge, a dog so worthless that it didn't even have a master to miss it, and all this time, everyone's been laud and honor over some bastard mutt, over a murder that never even happened. And maybe Melager got some piece, so as to set it up, and maybe they didn't feel like paying him and that's why he wasted away. What's the old man going to do? And maybe the police got theirs too, just to keep alive the great fabled treasure hunt as the perfect haven for the truth."

"W—where did he go?" spoke Rabbit so softly that we ignored him.

"Or one other thing it could be," said Clement. "Suicide. The Courier couldn't go on carrying anymore, and he slit his own throat and tumbled into the depths with his burden."

Even Glaucus had never proposed that.

"And the grave?" I asked.

"Look whose name is on it. That old dirty Boatman fell in the water because he was crazed ogling some young girl. The body had his necklace."

"But the Courier disappeared at the same time. You don't think—"

"No. I don't think. Your myth and your mystery are like a war where victory goes to the first slain. You're like empty cities built for dead kings. You're built around a stolen idol. You're infatuated with the impossible because you think it means something about who you are, what you are. It's not going to change you, and what's more, no one's listening to you."

"Clement—" I began.

"You have a lot of talent. You could be making money, but you don't write what people want to read. You're laboring to create, like your vision of gods, but your stories don't want the way that you make them, and they don't want what they make you. They're a mother that doesn't want you."

Rabbit squirmed while Clement spoke. His eyes grew ill and teary. He ran into the store where his mother was.

"Look what you did," I answered Clement. "It's not like that. I am an ancient lake at the source of the world's longest river, with scattered temples to every dying myth on my shores. And it rains in me like the world is weeping. And I am stripped to my naked self in the rain by the world's false hopes. I am taking all the tears to myself, and I need to pour them out. I am building temples in an ungrateful world, and that makes me sick with fantasy. At my writing desk, I dream I am in a cottage by a rough-hewn shore, in a peaceful retreat I have taken for the season. I dream I am waking up in a different city, turning my traveling eyes with confidence toward a garden of newness, wearing a key around my neck to a little typewriter I use to record the stories of the world. I dream I am in a solitary and eternal youth, that I can get anywhere and meet anyone. But it's all fantasy that I hold myself up against, because I am broke, and broken, and have responsibility. And I wake up in the same place every day because I can't seem to muster the change I want. There's all this rain and I am destroying myself with thirst. That thirst is a well of fantasies that, instead of drink, are drowning me. And full to bursting, I need something to pour my hopes into. Some river to join them to, to speak them, and give them life if only to watch them die at last. To kill the false, find the true, and not resign myself. Or to accept and not lose hope. And when I open, the world floods."

After a pause he said to me, "Well, add the Courier to your list of fantasies to let die. You think you have a monopoly on this story. You don't have a monopoly on this story. This story's been in bed with a thousand greedy men already, and you're one-thousand-and-one and I'm one-thousand-and-two. And I know everything that you know, and I haven't found nothing."

Somehow I loved him most when he frustrated me to blindness. I knew his wounds as well as he knew mine.

"You want it too, don't you?" I mocked him. "Listen to you, 'I haven't found nothing—' like a child throwing a tantrum because the parents who gave him life won't give him a cheap toy. You want the treasure. You want the knowledge. You want the brilliance. You want to touch it—truth. You're no different than me. We just think two different things are treasure."

Clement turned from me and said nothing.

"Cat?" I asked.

But she kept her round face in the petals of her locks of hair, heavy with rain. After a while, Clement told her, "Let's go," and pawed at her dress. She turned submissively.

"I'll see you tomorrow," I said.

"See you tomorrow," said Clement. We could part as sour as we pleased, but routine always put us back in one another's hearts.

†

So that was what we thought. We had not advanced much in one hundred years and one day. He died; he did not die. We still felt, as Glaucus did, that everyone was suspect.

Glaucus's later journals—kept with less care in a cardboard box in our library's stacks—are filled with his ranting about the case, reviewing every angle just to prove that each came to nothing. "Everything has two faces," he seethed in heavy script. "The bridge has two faces: it is captive and it is liberating; it is captivating; two ends, both watched. He goes from east to west, like the sun, everybody can see. It is radiant. But then the sun is below the horizon, gone, and what happens to it under the blanket of horizon? It's unseen. Then comes a man carrying fire, and it lights the blood. Two faces and two more unknown faces: the Courier and the Killer."

He ran over his list, forever etched into his identity, "Percy, Meda, the Lamplighter, Faton, Melager, Bacca, Theo, his wife. The Killer. I cannot release them. I cannot convict. And there's more. Ask—how strange this doctor is on hand so quickly when a body is found. Why? Does he watch for the body? Does he conceal his deed? Does he change the body, alter it? I saw it only after his work. Does he die from guilt . . ." And so on.

But Time is judge. Time can do things that Glaucus could not with his short life. As Time destroys, Time creates. Remember the story of how Time's wife gave it a potion to disgorge its children. Time devoured the suspects in turn and in that way freed them; it made them forever unconvicted. But Time alone could not make them innocent, as people have a deep suspicion of Time. In the eyes of the city, our circle of names remained forever suspects. Their stories, their sight, and their memory perished with them. The cold earth kept its counsel, and key interrogations remained unfinished.

Faton was first. He died a young man, only a short time after Glaucus interviewed him. Pathetic Faton had become a conductor only by begging his father, the General of Railways, for the position. Faton had not endured the patient trials of coming up through the ranks, which earn a conductor the respect of his crew and teach him mutual respect. That was the condition in which Glaucus found him: both a fortunate and an unfortunate young man, a man with position and income who earned not the least loyalty of anyone. Even after Faton became a conductor, he only continued to beg from his father. He wanted appointments to prestigious lines, with luxurious coaches and new engines. His father denied him, to try and teach the impatient boy, but Faton would not be restrained.

Faton's jilted peers devised a rumor that would strike at the heart of his pride. The story circulated around the time of the Courier's death: Faton was not the son of the General of Railways; his mother lied to a man of wealth and power, in order to secure an unfair future for the boy. Faton carried the insult to his father and demanded proof. The son had inherited his father's pride, and both of them wished to silence the story as foolishness. Faton was elevated to conductor of the fastest and most powerful engine in the fleet, and he drew wealthy clients in rich coaches across the interminable country. Nepotism, they felt, was beneath infidelity.

Insatiable Faton drove the brimming engines hard, obsessed with their strength and wanting to set records. On a long stretch downhill he at last pushed the train past its tipping point, when its brakes were useless. On a long following curve that lipped a steep valley, the train wheels separated from their tracks. Sparking where they grazed the rail, the wheels glowing like suns bit the metal with heat and speed. Fear seized Faton's haughty eyes, weightless as he realized his impending destruction. The momentum of the heavy train turned to shreds the capsized engines that blazed with unbridled power. The wreck of flame and metal plummeted into oblivion.

The General of Railways saw that Faton had a proper lie upon his grave: that he was a symbol of motion and progress; that he sought the great human promise, faithful always in its triumph; that he died in pursuit of glory.

And so Faton remains, unjustified. His possessions were discarded and lost, and his home has been destroyed. Though the jewels were not among them, that is not enough reason for the city to forget him. Or the murderous strength of his jealousy. Was it Meda or the gems he left to see that night? If he had the gems, his short life was sufficient to hide them but insufficient to spend them. Perhaps they still wait where the hands of a long-dead man laid them in their own tomb at the river's edge, waiting ignorant of Time for a long-dead face to reappear, for an irreplaceable past to whirl and spark again through their light-stained prisms.

Another suspect that died shortly after was Melager. Without the sustaining fire of his gems, his health began to fade. He became poor. His body waned. He finally showed his age. A starved ghost, he appeared at his usual fine cafés and bought as little as would let him stay the long day. He shunned their sharp windows and melted into drapes that lined their back walls, and he listened to the unmentionable intentions of the other desperate people who gathered there.

"A heel of bread," he would ask. "Just a cup of wine—the dregs of yesterday." The servers pitied him and would not take his money. But he pitied himself and would not live on charity.

He sold his fine suits and silks. He ate curds of cheese with honey and spoiling apples, leftovers from the grocers. One day, a little girl watched him upon the street: a crescent moon for a face in anemic silver, shrouded in sallow shadow, curtains hung from his bones. "That looks sweet," she said, eying his honeyed apple.

"Little girl, it is not sweet to me," he sighed, and handed her his best apple slice from an unwashed hand. He remembered the power of his hands, their tendons as they clutched his relic: the jeweled dagger that slew the wild boars in the old days long ago. How the fine edge would open any adversary. And his brave hands washed in hot blood: precious brilliance, hard and visible and invisible, transmuted to the animal soul, the vigorous steam that rose in the cold, springing from the rainbow of color, the lens of life-giving. The steam opened in his nose, a scent of hair and sweat and stone and iron, like blood in sand, and the butcher's metal, and the perfumed silks torn asunder, and spilled wine, and mashed fruits with their bitter pits crushed to powder on the cobbles, and the splintered balsa wood of their crates. And ashes. And ashes.

The little girl took the apple, the last food his hands would touch. His preserving embers extinguished; he perished.

He died as any gem-seeker would, when his treasure is forever lost, when the search is gone and the mystery does not burn. They found him in his empty home, where he had sold all he owned and slept on the floor. The cupboards were bare. Six men who did not know him wrapped his naked body in burlap and carried him on their shoulders to an unmarked grave. They buried him without ceremony but not without reverence. He was a pitiable man in whom they could see themselves. Their silence, born of fear, mimicked the torrents of his brilliant gems that were quenched.

Now no one can visit his remains, as I did the bridge, to try to understand. The location of the grave has been forgotten. The young men who opened its earth have fallen in. What has not been forgotten is Melager's tremendous strength into old age, or the jeweled dagger he possessed. His death alone is not enough to quench our city, and some say he died of conscience, not hunger.

After the body found in the river was buried in the Boatman's grave, Bacca stopped answering the portal of his sinking barge. One day Glaucus knocked and heard no sound but lapping waves. The portal was bolted from within. Glaucus ordered an officer to return daily, but no response came. Thinking Bacca dead inside, they finally broke in. One of the other portholes, hidden beneath the water line, was open, and the cabin lay awash in river water. A search discovered no body and no jewels. Melic, who had met Bacca, insisted that he was too old to swim. Melic thought he opened the portal to drown, and his body floated away.

"A suicide from guilt?" asked one of the other officers.

"Would he take the jewels with him?" countered Glaucus.

"Only if he wished to save his name."

"A name no one knows?"

The hull full of water unbalanced the barge's rest against the shore, and the barge slowly began to pull into the river. As the flooded end sank, the grounded end began to rise. The trees growing over it gradually uprooted and toppled at the pace of seasons. The barge scraped off the bank, an inch a day, pulling taut the grape vines that wound tightly round it. The vines could not hold the weight once it edged into the current. During a heavy rain, the rising river tousled and clouded over the bow. The grape vines pulled until they snapped or uprooted. The hull slid gracefully off the slick mud into the tumultuous water. By the strokes of lightning and the starry window lights lining the river's banks, the outline of the old hull could be seen hovering just at the water's surface, with one noble and erect tree outspreading its branches. The weakened frame broke up several miles downriver and went to pieces in the current.

Glaucus, who kept in touch with the Courier's mother, Thesia, learned afterward that she had taken on a boarder: a spry, elderly man who arrived one day and said her son had brought them together. Glaucus made the long trip to meet the old man, in hope of any revelation however inconceivable.

The old man was spry indeed. Every move he made burgeoned with vigor that defied his frail form. His eyes were clear and bright and somehow much younger than his years, and so different, like he had thrown off all past shadows in a way men cannot do at such an advanced age. Glaucus searched his face intently but did not recognize him.

In the short time that he had lived with Thesia, the man already cultivated an impressive arbor of grape vines that cascaded in fragrant bunches behind the house. He rested in the shade of the perfumed vines for an interview with Glaucus. But the man was so drunk. His steps were sure, but his head was swimming with delight and exuberance, even about the smallest bee that browsed his arbor, laden thick with trickling sun in amethyst and jade. He was occupied threading cut vines into a crown. "It's for her," he cried jovially, showing how the shy leaves would drop sumptuously about the woman's eyes and ears. "It will be a crown of stars!"

Glaucus made only nonsense from the man, whom he deemed crazy with age and the charity of a good woman. Certainly no Killer, it would seem. But his madness was intoxicating. When Glaucus himself felt lightheaded and giddy, he decided it was time to leave.

Glaucus's instinct was probably right. Nothing happened to the old man and Thesia. They did not become suddenly rich; they did not flee. They just stayed home, laughing in the shaded and drunken fragrance of their always-ripening vines. Meanwhile the parched city asked: what is the cost of the finest wine? What is the need of this inebriation? How is there peace after tragedy? Could she who carried her son be content only to possess what he carried?

The same story could be told for each of the other suspects. Though they lived, their lives and times never produced satisfactory answers for Glaucus, or anyone. Percy kept his job, and kept on with Meda, and they shared a little place they could afford until he became ill. The Lamplighter kept on making his lonely rounds, scattering light divided but undimmed. They did not do anything that Glaucus would have expected from someone who had the gems. They showed no outward signs of wealth. They did not escape the city. For years he thought he could outwait them.

"One of them will run," he told an inattentive underling. "They may yet be mastered by guilt or fear, but no one can reject an opportunity like that— freedom from toil—no one can last with that temptation. One of them will run, and we'll be waiting. I'll be waiting."

The underling answered, "But might they be trading one freedom for another, sir?"

And Glaucus scoffed. And he waited. And no one fled. They simply lived, under a gauze of whispers, under ripples of suspicious gazes.

Glaucus's journal observes, "It's like the stories of those who treat kindly the gods that come in disguise—and they are given as from mortals what mortals cannot give. Or like those who stay loyal to the gods despite persecution—the chains fall off believers in prison, and the doors are thrown open to them. Every time I've nearly trapped them, they are absolved. The doors are thrown open again to innocence."

As time's relentless erosion wore on, Glaucus lost faith in the ability to find the truth. He wrote: "Someone is lying. Even if they think they are telling the truth, they must be lying. They must believe a lie, even if it is a lie that they told themselves. They cannot all be correct, because they are all convinced of an impossibility. They tell their stories. Their stories are mutually exclusive. Even so, if they are all convinced that they tell the truth, then the actual truth, though perceived, is lost. The truth becomes intractable."

The moment immediately after an event is perceived, the truth of the perception is replaced with narrative. And the narrative becomes memory, because who we are, or at least how we identify ourselves, is language and narrative. We are stories. And when our narrative is reflected upon, repeated, repeated, it becomes the full vehemence of conviction. Sometimes, even, the narrative precedes perception.

"Everyone has two faces," Glaucus raved, "not just the Killer." Who they actually are, based upon the authentic things they have been and said and seen, and who they say they are, based upon what they believe they have been and said and seen. "They all have two faces like time and a bridge."

And Glaucus was right. I confess that even I have two faces, like time and a bridge. Here we are, you and I, communing, talking and listening, perhaps across many years and far distances. And we are communing with the past. And you wonder where my fidelity lies. Maybe you can still ask me and maybe you cannot. At the same time, we are looking out together into the boundless and nameless, the incomprehensible, for the face of an absolute answer. And when you and I together find ourselves peering into time-worn and time-blinded eyes, you will wonder whose face I have dragged us toward. I am like the Courier; he lives and he dies. He carries. A man, the ark of all stories.

But, returning to Glaucus. After more fruitless years, well after his loss of faith in his witnesses and in finding truth, and even after the loss of faith in himself, he at last lost faith in the Courier. He wrote: "I do not want to dishonor the dead . . . well, if it is so . . . I had always thought him innocent in my heart. But there is no other clear way to the solution. There is no other way to make sense of it. I have criticized others, I cannot fall prey to my own narrative and defend a man when the evidence condemns him. He must have faked his death."

This surrender inspired a new wave of activity for Glaucus, who forgot the true grief on Thesia's face. Glaucus retraced the Courier's possible steps and secretly intercepted the mail to his mother's house, in case he should try to reach her. After much effort, Glaucus found Theo, or rather, stood over his grave. Theo's wife denied that he ever had a child and denied that anyone had ever claimed to be Theo's child. More surveillance, more intercepts, came to nothing. A fresh sweep of case documents produced no new leads. Glaucus tried to trace sales of jewelry at merchant centers, alerting the merchants to the types of missing stones that might have been traded by the Killer or intermediaries, but this, too, led nowhere. There were too many gems.

"Of course, they would have been traded on the smuggler's market," said the shrewd merchant to Glaucus. And Glaucus had to admit he was probably wasting his time.

This is how a man becomes his mystery, as the ancient Glaucus became the river in which he swam. Obsessed with solving the crime for many years, Glaucus finally became obsessed with his inability to solve it. He loathed himself and reveled in his judgment. He took pleasure in the absolution of pain and self-pronounced failure. His marriage suffered, his wife wounded by his growing cynicism, and the old wound of their childlessness, and the loss of respect for him by his colleagues. Frustrated, he fiercely re-interrogated witnesses with no results. There were rumors.

More than any of these things, however, it was Glaucus's hollowness that made his wife leave him. He was always a hard man, and she could love a hard man even when he was temperamental or unaffectionate, wrapped up in his work. But his determination was always tempered with purpose— it would swell his chest on proud days and he would lift her off her feet when he came home, he would be free and voluble, he would over-tip at restaurants and astonish their guests with stories from the police just mischievous enough to feel like a sensational and upright secret. Now, he wilted. She could not live with a directionless and dissipated man, even though it had softened him. Afterward, he was forced to retire, because he would not take on any new cases.

When asked what kept him busy, he said only, "I contemplate the mystery."

But his colleagues liked to remember him when he was fit and heady. They recalled him pacing about in the weeks after the murder, his mind churning and churning. Once he stopped the bustle of the busy station when he pounded on his desk and shouted, "A murder on a bridge, with witnesses watching both ends, and nowhere else to go. This should be simple! It must be simple. How can something so simple become so intractable? It is like heaven itself."

†

THE THIRD DAY. Two days after the centennial, one hundred years and two days since the Courier died. The dawn filled with quiet color that the breeze cooled into azure. The river lay a furtive snake, low and golden. The city's valleys lulled with patient mist, erecting shadows of spired buildings, monuments, bridge towers, mulling the river's glow. Flowers bloomed in full. Trees rained petals down in the wind. The empty streets were strewn with their delicate curtains, tumbling over the old dirt, the trod-down paths, the ancient worn plan. The city, millennia deep, buried itself in sashes of color and perfume.

In some basements near the center of our city there is another basement beneath, and sometimes beneath that one a deeper basement yet, dating back to ancient times and the old street elevations. Some residents have cut through the foundation rock and dug out the lower rooms, finding old plates and knives and lamps, icons, or an old rotted ball of linen that might have been a blanket, or animal bones, or even graves. With temples this is especially so. There are temples upon temples upon temples. One torn down for the next more prevalent. On sites deemed forever sacred even before the haze of myth. They host tours, where visitors wend down ten or fifteen meters below street level, eventually to see a wild old stone face, some unworshiped deity millennia-blind, in a niche in a rough-hewn wall, and marks where candles burned dribbling down the coarse stone.

I went once, deep into the cold dank must, to prowl the buried catacombs, the raided tombs whose bones did not keep. And you know what I found, even beneath the catacombs: an old, simple house, with a little altar, and a spring that still ran in a stone-hewn kitchen trough. A spring, miraculously cold and mineral sweet, that nourished the unknown family. A spring I splashed upon my face and let trickle down my chest and neck, and I swabbed the sweat of my long hair back from my face. A spring as where every mighty river begins. A fountain as where the Courier took up his final charge. In a room that once was filled with daylight, until the city went on burying itself, and the worshippers became subterranean.

Ascending from the depths of time comes the dawn to make contractions of night-trained eyes. Dawn after dawn piles day after day upon our city, light after light endlessly, as sun after sun accepts its way across the blue arch of heavenly waters. And there was me, the singularity of existence, in between like the open grave of two days before that contracts and funnels all earth to sky, all sky to earth, lens of all transmuted light, looking out my open window, traipsing the shadow of a thinking man behind my empty head. And above me were other tombs, high on the hill above the city, where one still lay flayed open with flanks of heaping dirt settling in the moist and killing the grass.

I watched petals roll on down my street. There must have been a storm in the night to shake them. They were extraordinary, as though collected they had dropped en masse from the hem of the dress of a little girl who plays with storms. And there came down the street a little girl ready for school, collecting petals by herself, taking handfuls from the corners of stoops and street gutters where they lay thickly.

A long time I kept my vigil as the city came to life. The city seemed the same as ever, timeless in its preoccupations. People flitted into the streets, bustled to work, kids to school, spouses waving from open doors and windows. All-night revelers sauntered home, treading on a ghost of the evening's joy and weary. The religious made their offerings. The cynics grimaced over their al fresco coffees. I saw in some faces the love or hope that made them strike out in the new day. I saw in others the hatred of the toils that kept them from what they felt they deserved. I could hear fights in some apartments. Amorous cries in others. All the windows open to the temperate world that listens at them all, and in the city nothing is really private.

Many lingered resignedly, buying time before they delivered themselves into another's authority. They were already thinking about the evening, even as the day began. Inevitability denied them peace. Others rushed on in a press of fear, torn between too many intelligent things and convinced of their importance. So many things that cannot all be done. And I watched and I watched and I watched. It looked as though the failures of the centennial had already been forgotten in our eternal city made from innumerable transient lives.

I lay my head against the worn spot at my window, where a century ago the Courier rested his. I let the hours pass. This is what I do when I wish to destroy myself with time, and let the precious seconds flow over me and drip from me delicious and unfulfilled.

I stayed around the apartment, writing and reading, until I met Clement at noon, to talk. That's how we spent most of our time. We rounded out the usual subjects: women, his impediments to belief and to institutions, what we were reading, what I was writing, the status of art and its striving, historical curiosities, and our usual dose of braggadocio. And then we had the rumors, what happened to whom, and why it was hilarious, and whether it was drastically in or out of character.

It was as though yesterday had never happened. When apart from Clement, I wanted to be with him, to talk about things that matter and escape frivolity. But when we parted, I wondered what we had said and how we had whiled away so much time without action. He inspired me, but there was some height, some fruitfulness, I wished to ascend, where he was only weight.

We started in on coffee in the shade of an awning, but we cannot keep from drinking when we are talking well. That is another of his influences. We changed to liqueurs that glowed hot in us and spilt us out from our cool shade. We peaked when talking about creation and the power to create, our rising voices bubbling about the street and offending people.

We got on foot and met people and read them from a distance and prophesied and cut through the crowd like conquistadores. The sounds of the near river, and the bright fresh air, and the lives swarming around us with all their memories and preoccupations overwhelmed us. We marveled at the infinite possibilities of a moment, its infinite potential worlds, and the things we might do. We talked on the rapture of discovery, an ever-coming dawn. Then a note of melancholy was in order, to keep conscious of life's loss and struggle aside its ecstasy.

We sat down at a bar and resumed drinking: cool, tall lagers in the warmer afternoon. And Clement thus could resurrect his hated childhood, and revel in the mixture of admiration and disdain he held for his father— how he honored the image of the man and loved him in all the memories he had forgotten. And I stewed directionless, having only present loves, regretting what kept me from my assumed purpose, and lamenting survival and toil. Even as I was there and not at work. We thought we would have the futures we wanted because we wanted them. We thought we were poor, but we were not poor. The guilt I feel now, at all my selfish angst and posing. All my squandered time. And yet—later you ache for a day like that.

"Let's walk," said Clement, "I want to roll this buzz around in my head, and find out if it will open me up to see something new."

So we paid the bill and took again to the streets. It seemed a day like so many other lazy days we had before. But Clement was never still.

"Don't you sometimes pick your cousin up from school?" he asked, unexpectedly.

"Yes," I answered. "My aunt helps at the school, and he usually goes with her. But sometimes I stop by to surprise her and walk him home. If I happen to be nearby."

"Well you're nearly there now," said Clement, grinning.

I looked around unawares and found that he had steered us to the neighborhood. And I realized it was just about time for classes to let out. Clement had timed it well.

"All right."

"You don't think he really knows the secret, do you? I mean, he can't really figure those things out." Clement's dismissive tone inaptly veiled a strange curiosity. I was offended but numb to his intolerance.

"I seem to remember something about the pure of heart seeing."

We heard the school-bell, hand-rung, as we came around the corner and approached the stolid brick building with accents of stone in pillared arches about the entrance. A wave of children poured out, all of them similar to Rabbit. Brimming with joy over nothing more than the sunlight on their faces, they bounded into the arms of waiting loved ones with hugs and worship. Avoiding the stragglers that darted wildly for the exit, we wound through the wide and heavy old corridors to find my aunt on the second floor. Rabbit was sitting in a chair swinging his feet while my aunt arranged some homework. He saw me fill the doorframe and ran to me exuberantly. I made a futile wish that my aunt would not smell the drink on my breath.

"I was nearby," I told her, "and thought I might help by walking him home."

"Oh that would be very helpful," she said kindly. "I have so many things to finish before I can leave—he'd be waiting here bored a long time." I held my breath when she came over to hug me and did not kiss her. Rabbit had settled to the ground and locked around my shins. I was wrapped from top to bottom, as Clement stood behind me grinning. It was as though he was not there. My aunt finally shot him a "Hello" after we had finished discussing arrangements for Rabbit. He nodded grandly.

In little time the three of us were off; my aunt was anxious to get back to work. We meandered through the sunny streets, Rabbit holding my hand and skipping at my side. Clement and I resumed talking about everything and nothing, in that way we do that feels like searching for its own sake. And I told Clement that he was jealous because he could not possess a happiness like Rabbit's, who smiled at the sound of his name. Rabbit did not listen to us, and I'm sure he did not care to follow our burdensome concerns anyway. He was perplexed by the piles of petals he kicked into light plumes where he skipped along the roadside.

"Ah!" Clement interrupted, "I forgot—I told Cat I would meet her." It was as if his memory was a punishment for my accusation. I thought of Cat standing there lonesome because Clement had drunk their afternoon out of his mind. "It's not far, just over by the river. Come with me," he pleaded.

I protested on the grounds that I did not want to interfere with their plans, especially bringing Rabbit along when I was supposed to take him home. In truth, it was growing harder for me to see Cat with Clement around, and I feared I would make a fool of myself or insult someone.

"Just say hello; it's not far," he insisted.

"What do you think, Rabbit, you want to walk some more?" I asked.
"Yes!"

So I relented. And the walk was, characteristically, much farther than Clement had indicated. We went, not to the bank of the river near us, but down into the city center. We passed through one of the narrow closes of the old city, under a sapphire sky rent between the teetering rooftops like a rift between continents. Then, at the end of the street, the panorama of the river opened splendidly before us. It lay there lolling blissfully, dressed in the blue of the sky, as sunlight tripped and frisked over the calm. The city's brigade of bridges stood stately in their formal spires, their strength, dressed in their epochs. The trees rained blossoms that settled like bouquets along the banks, in pink and white, and the backdrop of the city seemed washed clean. Old, maybe, but prompt and uplifted, like a colorful royal pageant watching the river's parade of time.

And there, to our right, waited Cat: her eyes sparkling behind a sunny squint, freckles standing out, her hair and her loose dress swaying in the light breeze that rolled down the river valley, to cherish her face and fondle her form. Behind her rose the Courier's Bridge. She shaded her eyes, watching us approach, and I developed the feeling that Clement had been planning this all along.

"Hi!" Cat waved to me.

"Hi, Cat," I answered.

"Hi, Cat," repeated Rabbit.

The length of our walk had taken us late into the afternoon, and the sun was low and long. As long as the day itself, full of waiting and nothing.

"How long have you been waiting?" asked Clement.

"Not long," said Cat in a tone that meant she had.

Clement scoffed and said nothing, and she looked at him like he was a criminal. In the awkward silence, I asked Cat what she thought about the abundance of flowers. She smiled—it was the first time I had seen her smile without embarrassment since the accident in the graveyard. Her tooth was still dark, but her mouth was made up a delicious shade of red that shimmered like a polished apple.

"I love them," she gushed. And I likely blushed.

As we talked, I let go of Rabbit's hand. Clement kicked up tufts of petals collected against the ornate stone wall at the river's bank. Rabbit still seemed frightened of him and kept his distance, but Rabbit was also curious. Out of the corner of my eye, I saw Clement hop up on the wall and sit with his legs out wide, leaning forward with his elbows on his thighs, confident. And he had a way of fixing you with a smile that said he knew all things, and that one could ask him anything and he would tell the truth. I think that smile lured Rabbit at last.

Cat must have watched Rabbit walking over, because I saw her eyes tracing movement behind my back. Bubbles of quiet conversation floated to my ears. Her eyes came back to me, satisfied. While Clement was talking to Rabbit, prying at his secrets, Cat slid her body next to mine in intimate confidence. She was either ignorant or had remarkable control. It was hard to accept that the innocence of her face and her curls paired with Clement's brutal decisiveness.

"Clement is having trouble," she confided. "He's desperate. He hardly eats; he drinks with you is all."

Behind us, "There should be no secrets," said Clement grandly, as though surprised at the very thought of it.

"N-n-no, Clement!" protested Rabbit.

"You are stronger than him," said Cat. Her placid face leapt toward my ear, where she whispered the words, quick and suggestive. I felt the swollenness of her lip beneath the vibrant color brushing against my skin. Then she stepped back and fixed me contentedly with moist, pregnant eyes. She looked as though she bit me with the words and taught me a needed lesson.

I doubted what she said though I wanted desperately to believe her. Strength requires trust. I persevere, but I'm not convinced that strength is merely to persevere in matters of necessity. Is it strength to thirst? And without satisfaction, don't you only thirst more? I wanted Cat in that moment, with abandonment. But Clement, he had a will of iron. Even when he did spiteful and ungracious things, it was because of the strength of his will that he could do them. Some people behave out of cowardice, which is ultimately selfish. Clement unabashedly wished things for himself and turned the world to his will, as he was turning Rabbit.

I was conscious only of Cat and that I could not follow everything that was going on behind me. I wondered why she chose to tell me this now, when she had not expected me to be there. But I ached to hear what she thought of me at last. I found myself, for the best, speechless.

Without turning her head, Cat's eyes strayed to the right and strained to catch Clement still busy with Rabbit. The tip of her tongue instinctively touched the bottom of her dark front tooth. I wanted to look myself but felt transfixed, like this might be the one moment of her transfigured, not Cat but Catherine, her real name, and if I turned or blinked I would miss it.

"The two of you are very different," she said, now laconic, speaking beneath her Madonna-gazing eyes. "You love him, I know," she turned to me, as though assured of privacy. "You're good to him, because nobody else loves him, not even his father, who cusses and swings at him even when

Clement brings money. You didn't know that, but I've seen it." She knew how to ask things without ever phrasing a question. "His father throws the money away. Clement can't change him."

Clement was fond of saying that his father saw only a heavy black curtain on a stage at the end of an aisle in an empty theater. He chose the mystery of oblivion over the mystery of ending.

"And he inherited the same callousness he hates." Cat looked sidelong at Clement again.

"You've never met his mother," she asked again without asking. "She's a frightened woman. Clement says she used to be able to sober him up. But that was when he wanted to be sober. Clement, I think, courts his father's terror. And his mother knows. It enables Clement. It gives him a reason to be forgiven for the way he acts. And you forgive him because you love him. You are the only one to love him."

"No!" insisted Rabbit at a distance.

"I'm not going to tell anyone," plied Clement as though hurting sweetly.

"And you," I asked Cat, finding only sparse words at last.

She fixed me again with smoky portends of her eyes. "You love him because you see him as an artist. Or that's how he lives. He's unencumbered with possessions, he sells as little of his time as necessary, he is ungoverned. Except by himself. He lays about all day, reading, smoking, bathing, watching—with his different girls that lust after his freedom when he shares with them all his same few climactic moments of prose. But he creates nothing. It comes to nothing."

"He has no secrets," she went on. "He steals, he cheats, he lies, and he talks. And all that you might allow because his personality is so big that there's no way to contain all of his life, he cannot focus." She collected her indictments. "Doesn't he tell you everything? You knew I ruined my mouth in that ghoulish place where he took me."

I looked down and said nothing.

"You know exactly what's beneath my clothes," she dared me.

Again I said nothing.

Satisfied, she said, "You see: Clement carries nothing. He has no mystery." She leaned to me—her healing lip a tangle behind the red before my bowed eyes, her breath in my face. "I cannot live in a barren world." Then, "I know how you work. You work too hard. You expect too much. But it's okay because you're after something beautiful."

"I always thought I was lazy. The only thing that moves me is envy— envy for . . ."

She put her hand to my chin, to lift my eyes that met her own. There was a great stillness about her. A certitude in her eyes' unspoiled harbors rich with repose and pleasure, eternal hidden coasts preserved for one who holds their unseen secret inside a seeking heart. I had never seen her iris islands so close, burning so hot with a green-gemmed flame, like a sword, like a seed, a springtide genesis.

By now the golden sun that lit the scene when we arrived had lowered, first behind the skyline, then behind the hills. Outlines of rooftops crept across the river contrasting its glimmer. Then the shadow of the hills tumbled down upon them, eradicating all shape. The dark hills leapt the riverbanks and climbed up opposing buildings. The river continued now in a mute blue, a sleeping titan.

"Why don't you show me how smart you are?" Clement was saying to Rabbit. I turned around when I heard. "Why don't you show *us* how smart you are?" he amended.

Beaming, Rabbit toyed with a rock between his awkward shoes while we came to a small half-circle around him. At last, he looked up and said, "I n-nowhere the Killer is!"

"I know knowhere, where he is!" Rabbit repeated proudly when we did not answer.

"You are so smart, Rabbit," cloyed Clement, and I looked at him crossly. But Clement kept on, "You're smarter than all of us, than this whole city. No one else knows. Why don't you show us how smart you are and tell us?"

Rabbit looked at me with watery eyes that upturned, his mouth slowly opening. He looked like he was about to part with something very valuable, something private that he had treasured for its privacy, like fidelity, treasured forever. He kept looking further and further upward.

"He doesn't know," scowled Clement, and he pulled Cat around by the arm and began to speak in a whisper.

I crouched down to Rabbit's height. "You don't have to tell—" I began. But suddenly he was out with it.

"The, the Killer is. Is the man they f-found. In the river."

Rabbit spoke carefully but certainly. He said it like he was recalling a memory. And even I was surprised, admittedly, to hear an answer so direct and simple, though it seemed directly wrong. I expected him to say something fantastic, like his questions that usually included myths and creatures and fictional characters that had their own living place in his reality. I could not help but want to know what he dreamed in the innocent carnival of his mind.

"How," I asked gently, "could he be the Killer if they found him in the river? What do you mean, Rabbit? Do you think he fell in with the jewels after the crime?"

"No," he said, beaming. "The the m-man they found. In the river. Isn't, isn't in the river."

"Where is he?" demanded Clement. He came up from behind me where I did not realize he was listening. He pushed past and held Rabbit firmly by the arm. Rabbit winced at the big hand that enclosed his waifish bicep. "Where is he, Rabbit?" Clement lowered his face to Rabbit's and looked intently into his eyes. "This is important to us adults." Clement tightened his extortive grip, and Rabbit squirmed.

I hated Clement rawly in that moment, with a hatred I recognized as a close and unacknowledged friend. I sneered at his superficial authority. How could he, selfish man, have a right to this? I asked blindly.

"Clement—" I yelled.

He whirled around on me; "I need this," he shouted desperately.

Turning to Rabbit, he demanded, "Where is it?!" He shook Rabbit's little frame.

"That's enough, Clement!" I grabbed his shoulders and pulled him away. I stood between them and put my hand on Clement's racing heart. "That's enough."

Staring full in my face, Clement's eyes overflowed a heavy pain and a heavier longing. His brow arched supplicatory. He looked his own trembling child.

Rabbit spoke behind me. "I'll tell you." I turned, and he patted me on the chest then laid his head on me and started to hug me. "I'll tell you," he said again. "Not him. You." But he did not seem to understand that Clement was right there and would hear anyway.

Rabbit released me, turned to the bridge, and pointed. He stayed absolutely still, with solemn face. Authority, command even, throbbed from the true line of his outstretched arm, as though this were his act of creation. At first, I did not know where he was pointing. The whole sweep of river and city was before us, and the hills beyond. I struggled to discern if he meant a house or a hilltop cemetery, or maybe the direction of a distant city. Or did he mean heaven? His arm stretched, it seemed, too high for something earthly, indicating a truth that does not speak from its simplicity, or need not be seen to be believed. But he was not pointing up, as I could imagine him doing plainly if he meant "sky." He was pointing out. His gaze was fixed.

I leaned over and put my face next to his, to look along his outstretched arm from his own gaze. He leaned his head against mine lovingly.

I saw that he pointed to the western tower of the Courier's bridge. To the top of the tower. The tower that was shrouded in darkness, opposite Percy and the Lamplighter. The tower where no one came or went.

I remembered that Glaucus and his officers had considered that the Killer might have escaped up the bridge cables. I remembered his notes that officers walked the bridge cables themselves, all the way to where the cables passed through the stone arches. They found no one. I also remembered that the officers were present on the bridge for days after the murder and saw no one come down. I examined the heavy stone tower carrying the weight of the bridge. But it was Rabbit that stood like stone, like an ancient temple statue indicating the oracle. Or the depiction of the oracle itself, pointing seekers out from the temple with their answers.

Clement deciphered Rabbit's meaning about the same time I did. He began to move slowly away from us, taking a lead, leaning over the rail at the river to stare.

"It's solid stone," I whispered to Rabbit.

"It is?" Rabbit said disappointedly. He dropped his arm but blinked dramatically. I gawked at him, puzzled, with my lips parted and my eyebrows knit, so that someone unlike him would have taken offense. I could not understand if he was asking or telling.

Clement began to run.

"No!" Rabbit wailed long and loud. "I-I-It's not yours!"

Rabbit leapt from me with limber grace and sprinted after Clement. I chased Rabbit. Cat ran after all of us shouting, "Stop!"

True to his name, Rabbit was fast as well as small. Though Clement was faster than me, Rabbit was faster than Clement. He gained on Clement quickly. Clement fumbled through his long and ludicrous strides, looking backward with his strained mouth open. He dug in his pockets and produced one of the three marbles that Rabbit had given him on the centennial.

I decided then that Clement was ruthless, gathering us together with Rabbit and bringing Rabbit to the bridge to root around in his honesty. And another thought forced its way unwelcome into my mind: I looked at Cat with doubt for the first time since I met her. I hoped that if she agreed to help she had not known his intent.

Clement probably brought the marbles to bribe Rabbit into sharing his thoughts. But now Clement had a more desperate idea. With Rabbit steps behind him, Clement lifted the marble above his head, where it flashed like a little world. Rabbit gasped and shouted the name he had given to the marble. Clement sent it rolling backward down the street where we ran. Rabbit cried out and turned quickly, his brow bent down in determination, his open lips showing uneven teeth. His eyes fixed on the bouncing marble, and he plunged after it as I passed him in pursuit of Clement. Over my shoulder, I saw Rabbit picking up his marble and cuddling it to his chest, smiling. Cat asked him if he was all right.

"Hold this," he insisted, thrusting the marble into her hands. He sprinted again, passed me, and gained on Clement.

"Youdroppedsomething!" he yelled, the words mashed together in a frantic monotone. As he approached Clement, another marble appeared. Clement threw it backward over his shoulder, and Rabbit missed as he tried to snatch it from the air. He wheeled around again and chased after it with loving concern darkening his face. Again I passed him going the other way, Cat questioned him, he thrust the captured marble at her, and he raced forward. Again he passed me, yelling, "S-stop! You're, you're gonna lose them!"

We were almost to the Courier's Bridge, and Rabbit was at Clement's heels again. Clement held up the third marble Rabbit had given him, maybe forty meters from the anchors where the mammoth bridge cables tie into the ground.

"No!" yelled Rabbit, "That's my favorite!"

Clement drew his arm back midstride and whipped the marble far down one of the passing side streets. Rabbit shrieked wildly as it sailed through the air. His face was struck with a moment of indecision, but then he chased after the marble as it went bouncing down the cobbles.

"Follow him," I ordered Cat, and she nodded enthusiastically. By the time I neared Clement, he had already mounted the large stone cable anchor. Rising solid out of the earth and heavy like a mausoleum, it received the termination of the eye-bar chain that draped the bridge towers and carried the weight of the ecstatic arching deck. Gripping the spaces between the eye-bar linkages, Clement began ascending the cable. I looked around and no one was near. Dusk had descended, but the starry city lights did not yet seem bright. It was that moment like the Courier's death, where day and night are mingled and all things seem obscure, distant, and unstoppable. And no one would stop me if I began to climb.

I was furious with Clement and his obscene madness, but I did not want him to fall and die. It occurred to me that he might kill himself and leap from the tower if he did not find what he sought. Without thinking— for thought has caused many of my failures—I started up after him from compassion only, grieving both my love and my anger, cutting my skin and tearing my clothes as I clambered up over the impossible stone to reach the cable. I threaded my hands into the same narrow spaces between the huge links and plodded after him. My hands thrust into the openings felt difficult and intimate to me; I was touching within some dark secret as though I put my hands into a wound. My feet searched for a hold on the bulbs where the chain links joined. The angle became astonishingly steep, much steeper than it looked from the ground, but Clement pushed forward.

"Clement! You're going to die climbing up there!" But he made no answer.

There was an ornate ledge several feet above where the cable met the western stone tower. The cable passed through the tower on a saddle, then continued its long sweep downward to meet the crown of the bridge deck, descending to the place of the murder, before rising upward again to mount the eastern tower. The stone towers continued upward above the ledge, higher than the cable saddles, each wearing their mural crowns. Clement was on the ledge gripping the stone, trying to figure how to raise himself to see over the top of the tower. I caught up to him as he was thinking. Clutching the stone ledge and the cable, I focused on Clement to distract myself from the terrible height. He looked surprised that I had followed him so far. We were higher than any buildings, higher even than the graves on the hilltop, where we had seen the sun set two days ago.

The street lights were coming on below us as the city illuminated itself in the gloaming, donning the stars of its radiant mantle, and the dusklight kept us hidden against the muted stone. A stiff breeze rustled our hair and blew it over our eyes.

"We have to know," said Clement. "We're here."

I nodded.

†

CLEMENT FOUND A DEATH that night, but not his own.

He shimmied a few paces along the ledge until he could brace his feet upon the carved relief of the mural. He was above the arch of the bridge tower, directly over the bridge deck, so a fall could have but one outcome. I was dizzy with height, so that I was intoxicated. The lighted city below us swirled around our pinnacle, spinning and spinning and spinning with nature's dance of time. Shaking, I slid next to Clement. I drew his confidence like many waters. And this was Clement's glory for all his faults and all his doubts: he so wanted an answer, so wanted to hope even when he could not, was so restless until finding rest, that the danger to his life did not dissuade him. A greedy man would have turned back from utility. A sated man would have turned back from fear. Clement would have done this alone, whereas I needed him with me. With our raw hands straining to reach the top of the tower, clinging to the smoothed stone, we jammed our feet hard into the clefts in the crumbling carvings, until they hurt. Together, tenuously, we raised our eyes over the top.

The mural was carved into a parapet wall. The bridge towers were solid for only several courses above the cable saddles, because the stone above the saddles did not bear any weight but its own. The mural crown was ornament, and there was no need to enter this space for service. Behind the parapet was a chamber of smooth sides like a well—a well to draw water and the stories of the ages, raised above all other things, a pit into which to descend. It was not very much taller than a man, but tall enough that he could jump forever and not grab something to climb out. It was deep enough to hide the whole world from one inside, allowing only a single clutch of rectangular sky. And in that constrictive throat of stone, at this height, someone could yell themselves breathless, speechless, until they coughed blood; nobody would hear.

The bridge was old enough that the men who built the parapet were well gone when the Courier died. The Killer could run up the ascending arc of the bridge cables, use the carved mural to climb the parapet as we did, and hide there unsuspected. He could hide there maybe without thinking of the consequences and become trapped, drinking rain until he starved.

We gazed into the chamber: amid more than a century of dirt stirred by the wind lay a bleached mess of bones, clung to in parts by what looked like ossified remains of putrid flesh and cloth. For the most part, the bones were picked clean by birds. They set like a jewel in a ring into the dirt and stone; the bones had become one with the bridge. The skull seemed to look right into our eyes, as though startled when life at last broke the horizon and we peered over the ledge.

I stared back into the hollow eyes of the Boatman. For it had to be the Boatman we looked upon. And this was where he hid after he stole the Courier's life: trapped at the highest point in our city, staring at sky. He had an excuse to disappear when he and the other men were swept downriver during the incident with the young woman, and he seized it. He must have heard about the Courier's fated delivery through the crack in the wall between his home and Percy's, Clement's and Cat's. On that day, the Courier visited Meda in Percy's apartment, and the Boatman lived opposite the crack that spills down the wall in a river's torrent, through which lovers whispered whose tragedy made the bridge, through which they fed the Boatman's wife the dreams of his death, and through which the knowledge of the Courier came. Most recently, through which Clement loved Cat.

The Boatman determined the Courier was coming from the east and lingered on the bridge before anyone was watching, because he knew the Courier was going toward the train. The Boatman killed from the depths of his hunger, then put his own emblem around the Courier's neck. He expected the body would be wasted before it was found, and it would pass as the Boatman's own to explain him. His wife never believed the body was his.

And now, there he lay and there he died, like the myth of the rebellious god punished for bringing fire down from heaven and sharing it with humanity. He, too, was shackled, to die in isolation, because in our city all things are married. There lay the man who brought down the fire of the gems or the fire of the word—whatever you think the Courier carried. The man who dared himself to take that stolen fire to the world. The man who dared with that fire to be made his own master. Who forgot, maybe, the worn myth that gods speak in unconsuming fire. The stolen jewels' light bearer so punished: stranded, moored to the stone tower, his cries unheard, and the birds picked him clean.

And the Courier, whose history is his story of emblems, had the final indignity of being mistaken as his Killer, buried in a grave under a stone that bore his Killer's name.

This is the only solution that makes sense to me, though people will invent others. Some will say the Boatman bled on the bridge and we looked upon the Courier who tried to flee. Some will say an unknown killer drug the Courier's lifeless body there in the darkness of the unlit bridge and went free into the myth of justice. But I have given the explanation I have, and I keep it. Without it, I should be digging around in aging architecture for memories and prisons.

The Courier set off with the preciousness he carried; that carrying is the message he gives, is his answer to our aged question. He did not cross the bridge. That which he carried does not transmit. Some would say his task is not complete. I say that what transmits is his task, his obedience in place of the ancient things that did not come through time. The prehistoric forces that birthed the brilliance of the gems do not deliver their brilliance to my eyes. What we have in their place is the death and its mystery. As Clement once said, it's the carrying. I was surprised to realize that so much a mystery should come down to so base a question of one man's hunger. Then again, there is no hunger without a satisfaction.

Near the center of the jumbled bones, upon the crumbled chest, an askance litter of ribs, was a mahogany box, like the dead man pressed it to his heart as he died. The frayed wood was pitted and abused as driftwood. It lay broken open. And from where we stood we could see into it. There was no treasure. The wind stirred in its hollow chamber. It was filled with only breath and dust.

†

So now I've told you everything just exactly as it happened. Generally I do not like mystery stories, and I had to think about it a great deal before I decided to tell this one. I don't like mystery stories because they don't tell the truth. The only reason they work is because the author conceals the facts such that the reader may search for what the author already knows. If not dishonest, such stories are inauthentic. But I haven't done that. I have told what happened, just in the order that we discovered it. Because I do not create mystery. And I cannot solve it. I only preserve it.

I see in the Courier all the ancient myths that do not answer, that do not cross the river, that do not come through time. Scattered pieces that will not reassemble. As the message of the jewels and the Courier, the man himself, do not cross, so our city's ancient genesis and the truths of its stories, their source and oneness, will not come to our city's crown and bare her beauty. They are slain upon the bridge. They do not transmit their own splinter of truth, but instead the mystery of what remains. They are replaced with mystery, and the mystery of death. The blood upon the deck. And the beauty of this mystery compels my belief.

Beauty answers. Death shows that life is not the pretense of the ancient but the world that is forever reborn in mystery itself. The old myths are unbelieved now, devoured by time and not relinquished, because all the old myths are smashed in this death. Time is at its fullness, swollen with incarnation. All the old gods cry out for their hours. But our ears are overspilling with the noise of life. The ritual of us has crumbled before life. The mirrors of our crumbled selves have nowhere to lay their heads—least of all upon the breast of what we are destined to be. Supposedly, the last prophecy our ancient oracle ever gave, before going silent forever, said roughly: *This house has fallen. We have no shelter, no harbor, no sacredness. The prophetic fountains are silent. The water is dry. The voice is stilled. It is finished.*

The answer to our mystery is mystery. From the temples of our creation we are pushing outward forever in crystal spheres that hold back floods and seek heavens. We push outward the ends of existence. We are forever breaking each concentric sphere, each sphere the precedent horizon. And the gemmed shards of dawn light pierce us, so God pours in rivers. And in this way we are greater than the limits of ourselves. We answer.

Atop the bridge tower, high above everything and staring into the empty box in its constellation of dry bones, I felt I was on the ancient hillock from which life sprang, the first land that parted the silent waters now resigned to rivers. This ancient life-source, and its ancient place, is claimed innumerable times by innumerable myths in every place under the sun. Even in the temples of this our timeless city. But the ancient hillock is a tomb. And buried in the tomb is a thief.

And that is why we hold dear the myth of the flood: the day the rivers will break their banks and burst their dams and tear asunder all bridges and their transmissions. Topple the towers and bring the Killer down from his forsakenness—plunge his bones into the swallowing waters. Raze all living tombs, and make the tallest monuments equal to the stones scattered upon the plains. The desolate becomes the creation place.

And it will sweep me away, too, the flood of this parousia. For there, on high, there in the swirling night—there, peering into the eyes of murder transmitted to us in the place of the great myth that trudged across the crown of the bridge burdened with beauty and fire and past and creation—there, high above the place where I lowered myself to dust to search for the speck of a man—there, high above Cat's beauty and Rabbit's clarity, aside Clement the love I had of my opposite—there I saw that I am this city.

I am swollen with its myths and history and wounds and unknown. Building outward and upward forever. I am full of its toppled towers and crumbling architecture, of its sieges and its labor, of its vogue sterility and its unconquerable fecundity. I am its architecture because I am its ancient temple and destiny. I am full of its newness that clamors in upon itself and unfolds a flower of endless petals, a sky of countless distant worlds. I am the city and I am the knife that pierces it. I am the silver lance of the river that opens it. I am the knife that goes into the heart of the Courier and spills his blood into the river of time. His life and his death are in me. Alone, I achieve nothing except what I raise from the well of regret. But in the city I am myriad life that is sufficient and together. I am its renewing, stratum upon stratum, transforming the generations of its never-vacant rooms. I am the city enraptured and ennobled with the treasures that do not come cleanly through time. I am the city clamoring for truth and teeming with life. Life and life alone is my story.

And each of our city's myths, stripped to the burning core of its center gem, is this religion of creation. We worship that which springs life in its myriad. And life is everywhere. That night it sprung thickly in phosphorescent light splashing over the hills and valleys beneath me, to the horizon; it teems abundant in those places that seem most barren and uninhabitable. It fools those who see only nakedness, who will not admit its abundance, its adaptability, its smallness; it's indefatigable. Life is the reason that all other things exist. To bask in it, to commune with it. And the world, the universe, is the ark of life that carries this precious content, whether raised up on flood waters or lifted on our blistered backs across scorching desert or burgeoning across tired bridges. We worship this creator life—the speaker in our stories that makes mystery in all things. We worship life in our own godlike creation, as before its final revelation.

And the flood, the unfulfilled myth that waits, is the fountain that wells up within us and outpours. The fountain where the Courier accepted his charge that was his death, that carried him to the river. The fountain that wells up for all to drink, to wash the dirty and the clean. Our fountain is the flood. We are the architecture it drowns. We are the dry stones struck and water flows. Opened with a knife and the fountain surges. And we out-stretch our arms in the perfect dance of bridges, enclosing within them all divides. Were we to open the mysteries of our own fountains thus, all the riverbanks and sea shores and ocean depths of all time would not be enough to contain our noble flood.

I looked out over the city one last time, the last time I would ever stand at this height, which recedes from me now like youth or like the brave faith of children. I looked out over the glittering expanse of the kingdom that is within me. I looked out over a city of flesh that is the mediated God, the Life itself that lives and moves in the heart of all the ancient shells of things that die. In my life that I must lay down. God who wears this city as a raiment more brilliant than jewels. All rivers and seas and hills and bridges and parades and buildings and their narrow skies and caves and expositions and forests and fortresses and all cities are as God's crown encircling the world so we have never been without. It is God's own authorship—I am that I should need this search. That we should search forever for the forgotten and unrevealed. That we should seek the source. Mystery authored for our identity and beauty that compels. Life the crown of all creation that peers inward enraptured. What else would its author wear that could express su-preme authorship. From the tower the illuminated city, the pumping heart of history, coursed radiant through valleys and washed in waves up glowing hillsides, and swarmed with vigor—it was the flood, a flood of light, God adorned in life.

It seemed only yesterday I came from my mother, drew my first breath, and unfurled my voice into endless existence.

From silence, Clement and I came slowly down from the tower arch, disturbing nothing. If someone had found the bones before us, it did not matter now. Clement lowered himself gently along the cable and lightly set his feet on the deck of the bridge. He was sobbing to himself. Rabbit had been struggling at the bottom to join us, and Cat held him tight in her grip. But, as we came down, even Rabbit was silent. It was as though the death had just occurred and we were fresh with mourning. As though death was new and we had just received the sentence of exile.

Clement leaned upon the railing and his head hung down over the river. He allowed himself to weep fully. He wept his life away. Wept so he was bathed in tears. He wept all his greed, and his art, and his anger, and his sex, and his pride, and his drink, and his pity. He looked to Rabbit and his tears redoubled. And I realized for the first time that Clement carried many things. And I watched the awe, the compassion, that spilled from Catherine's eyes, when she realized in his abandon that she could love him truly. I looked at the alluring idol of her, and it was the same as looking at the scattered bones atop the tower. I looked at the true love of her, and I accepted that she was not mine—only a moment after I first thought she could be. A heartbeat, a doubt, a speechlessness, and it was over. Clement had his answer, and she had her Clement, and I had my mystery. I say again, all things in our city are married.

Clement wept until he was just as an innocent baby, left with nothing but a hunger. The tender blue dusklight reflected in tear streaks soft on his long face that glittered with the city, as though cities and skies poured from his knowing gaze, tiny convex worlds that dangled from his eyelashes. They swirled with their own circuitous sweep of bridge and river bent round impossibly upon itself, until . . .

Clement's tears fell and mingled with the river's flow. I watched them surrender to the fall, twist and arc in the breeze, as I had imagined the drops of the Courier's own blood spilling into the river. So that in Clement's weeping, the two were one in a death. This is how Clement earned his name. And how he contributed himself to the river. The river swollen with stories.

†

AND AS IT TURNS out—this, too, is a story. This is how I earn my name and pour myself into the river, though it pales before the great myths, divine authorship. This is my transmission, like the Courier's, though you would rightly say it is less pure, tinged with my own bias and failures. You may want to know the Courier's name. I cannot tell you. The ancients asked gods for a name, to cry for help, but the pronunciation of a name can be lost to Time. And there are unformable letters. I cannot tell you his name. I cannot tell you my name either. I can tell you this story. The arc of the bridge is the ark of my story.

Any centennial that ever was has long since passed; the dates and places are forgotten. No living eye has seen them. The Wayfair Bridge, the Courier's bridge, my bridge, was destroyed long before I was born. Through empty air where it stood, I walk it with the Courier in the paradise of my dreams. When its cables severed, its majestic towers splintered into the river where they rotted in its breathless, ageless silence. That's why I never told you the width of the river, because now the length of the bridge is infinite and thus different for everyone who crosses. The lights of the Exposition that winked and twirled in the night at the Courier's back—they are demolished. Their rocketing towers and rollicking banners, aspirations of beauty and hope and humanity—all are leveled for a mute efficiency, invariable and inviolable and irreversible. The ornamented stone of the train station, its leaded glass and brass clocks are tumbled. Now the stop is a dirty wreck, subterranean; it smells. It has lost its human pulse. It has lost its honor that made it worthy of creation by our noble hands. The neighborhoods above the station rest now also, uninhabited, in piles of brick and rubble overturned in dirt for highways. For motion that has no home. No peace. No temple.

Out from this chaos rises a single stone wall. It once lifted the road that leapt to the bridge's first tower. Now the homeless take shelter near the stone. Their eyes watch me through the slits of their shacks, wide with desperation and fear when they do not know what is rustling through the weeds. I walk haunted with an overflow of memories too heavy for me to bear alone. I traipse over the entombed architecture, where trees have rooted, up to stand atop the stone wall. To look out through the air at the path my Courier strode, and see a city transformed. There are a few cobbles of the old road left exposed, pointing toward the precipice of stone. I stoop down, and I touch them. I walk where my Courier walked. Just off the riverbank, the lowest part of one pylon remains. I leap the fence and cross the rail tracks to climb it. To stand as close as I can to where my Courier died. And when the toil of life consumes me, and steals me from my story, the Courier waits patiently, offering freedom in his outstretched hands.

I carry his life. I cast it out into a forgetful and devouring world. A banner that, too, will tear asunder. I raise it above the meager stones and ruin, fluttering above the vacant deck and towers. Above the coursing high and rising river.